Masterpiece
Of Betrayal

Masterpiece Of Betrayal

Joy's Song

By

Sharon A. Long

ISBN:9781544898094 (paperback)

Contents

Acknowledgments   vii

Prologue   xi

Chapter 1: Quiet Location   1

Chapter 2: Gracious Interview   7

Chapter 3: Distinguished Gentleman   11

Chapter 4: As the Night Falls   17

Chapter 5: Friends to Lovers   23

Chapter 6: Church by the Roadside   33

Chapter 7: The Truth is the Light   39

Chapter 8: Beginning of Love   45

Chapter 9: Family Ties   51

Chapter 10: I Will Always Love You   63

Chapter 11: Autumn's Proposal   67

Chapter 12: Lay It at the Altar   73

Chapter 13: Thanksgiving   81

Chapter 14: Christmas in Chicago   89

Chapter 15: Arriving Home   103

Chapter 16: To Trust God or Man   109

Chapter 17: New Year's Eve   115

Chapter 18: Matters of the Heart   125

Chapter 19: Out of Sight, Out of Mind   131

Chapter 20: His Word is Bond   137

Chapter 21: Plans, Dreams, and Thoughts   143
Chapter 22: The Words that Sustained Her Heart   147
Chapter 23: Prayer and Deception   153
Chapter 24: Face to Face   163
Chapter 25: We Can Make It Work   173
Chapter 26: Love Again on an Island   179
Chapter 27: Meeting Olivia   183
Chapter 28: Hiding in the Shadow of Truth   189
Chapter 29: Family Reunion   195
Chapter 30: Wedding Bells with a Blow   197
Chapter 31: Love and Let Go   205
Chapter 32: Trying to Mend a Broken Heart   211
Chapter 33: When It's All Said and Done   219

Epilogue   227
Sharon Anita Long   229
Insight   233

Acknowledgments

First and foremost, I would like to thank my Lord and Savior, Jesus Christ, for making this book possible.

I want to dedicate this book to my son, Hennard (Shareef), my daughter, Alonna, and my three grandchildren, Amari and Tania and soon to be born granddaughter.

I would also like to give thanks to my Father, Pastor Larry Baker, First Lady Betty Jean Baker, and my church family of God in Christ Deliverance Church.

My dedication also extends to my four siblings: Demi, Larry Jr., Laura, and Chanda.

I would also like to give a special acknowledgment to Minister and Prophetess Gloria Jean Johnson for her constant prayers, support, and simple words of encouragement and my friends, Sister Annie Ruth Wiggins, and Barbara Jean Williams.

My sincere gratitude also extends to everyone purchasing my book!

Many blessings!

Enjoy!

"He healeth the broken in heart, and bindeth up their wounds."
—Psalms 147:3

Prologue

A Masterpiece of Unrequited Love

Her heart now aches for forgiveness,
from the one she kept at a distance.
While he relentlessly spoke her name,
another has altered her in deception,
and shame filling her with despair,
the love she kept close.
God and Man tore at her heart, but
the mortal trust she chose.
Those beautiful pearls fell lightly to
the ground as she ran for cover,
singing in her mind before it begins
it can't be over.
She was trying to hang on to
the whiteness of her glory,
But unforeseen, and the tale has been
compromised to this intriguing story.
She's awakened before the
bellows of "I do,"
and the faces have been fooled,
leaving their wondrous smiles in adieu.
The sun slowly departs from the stained-glass window
of angels seemingly in tears;
a masterpiece of unrequited love and betrayal
playing in shameful fears.
—*Sharon A. Long*

Chapter 1

QUIET LOCATION

Joyce, a strong and attractive forty-year-old single woman who was full of life and ambitions, had never married. She had been single for over a decade, having never settled for a relationship just to abate her loneliness and deciding instead to wait for the day that true love would pick her. Well, love did find Joyce, unbeknownst to her; it chose her as profoundly as her imagination could take her.

A year and a half earlier, Joyce had decided to move from the big city and settle in a small country town. Joyce wasn't looking for anything more than peace, tranquility, and the pleasures of stillness. She knew that her move to Georgia's countryside would be complicated; it was a big difference from Chicago, but she would make do with her transition. Joyce settled in a lovely little rented house with the money she had saved for her relocation and purchased an inexpensive sedan.

Having left Chicago and her quaint office job behind, Joyce was forced to quickly find work because her savings were dwindling fast. She had already learned a lesson about relocating without finding a job first.

For two weeks, Joyce spent the scorching hot days driving to every office building in Savannah to look for legal secretary jobs. Joyce had no positive leads on interviews, and she knew nobody that could refer her in this town; she had a few resources from Chicago but that didn't help either, not even in

1

the least. Nevertheless, she believed she would quickly land a job because of her immaculate resume and her beautiful smile.

Joyce sat in Starbucks, resting from a long day of job searching. She checked her emails on her laptop, sipping coffee that was as strong as her desire to find work, but she liked it that way—strong and black, among other things. While looking in her emails, she came across a promising lead on a job offer. The email read: "New law firm in Savannah's business bureau district. Solomon and Paltrow are looking for an experienced secretary, preferably a legal secretary with a degree and approximately five years of experience in secretarial sciences. We chose your resume online and would like to speak with you at your earliest convenience."

Joyce felt confident that the job was hers. She wasn't even worried about not having the four-year degree specified in the email. She had an ample amount of experience, even though she just had an associate degree in accounting. Since it was still early afternoon, Joyce called the phoned number to set up an appointment. Joyce's cell phone and a laptop were her only friends in this new town, and they both served their purposes.

"Yes!" Joyce exclaimed as the interview was confirmed for the following week on Wednesday at nine o'clock in the morning. There was one thing bothering her—the degree. Still, she hoped that wouldn't play a significant part in her interview, given that the entire company had already seen her resume and cover letter, which hadn't listed a four-year degree among her credentials.

On Saturday, she decided to make the thirty-five-minute drive from her house to find a good shopping center or mall. She didn't want to look like plain; she wanted a signature suit oozing with professionalism and sensuality.

Joyce had mounds of clothes, shoes, and accessories, but not the perfect outfit for her interview. As she finally reached the mall, her adrenaline started to pump, as it always did during her shopping sprees. As she left sweltering heat, Joyce reveled in the coolness of the air-conditioned mall. She admired the outfits displayed in the window of a posh-looking boutique. Her eyes fixated on the most beautiful pantsuit she had seen in a long time. She knew she couldn't really afford it, but she wanted to buy it, feeling that it would make a fine impression on her interviewers. It wasn't always like her to walk into a mall and set her heart on something but on that day, it happened.

Joyce continued to search the mall for shoes, but not accessories. She had plenty of those. She was trying not to spend much more than she had already done. Finally, her wardrobe for that day was complete. She spotted a little café and decided to have a sandwich and some hot tea with lemon. She sat down, opened her laptop, and checked her emails—one of them was a confirmation of her upcoming job interview. Suddenly, a solemn feeling seemed to overwhelm her. Joyce was always a free-spirited and independent woman, but a sense of reality that she was now alone began to sink in; she knew no one, not a soul.

She had been in Georgia for three months and she still felt like an illegal alien. Everyone spoke, dressed, and acted differently in Georgia—a major change from Chicago, indeed, and one might say a culture shock. Joyce had two brothers in Chicago who she kept in contact with. She never had close friends, but at least Savannah was nothing like Chicago. Joyce's parents had both passed away when she was in her twenties. Since then, she had conditioned her life around herself and seemed to be content with it being that way. She had no major problems, drama, betrayal, a man, or close friends—she was simply fine. She always kept close control of her life and her decisions.

Joyce tried to shrug off her loneliness by admiring a white-and-yellow house with a white picketed fence of her rented home. She dreamt of buying that house one day; she had simply fallen in love with it.

She enjoyed the drive on the highway back home. Joyce always appreciated the beautiful scenery, and she noticed there were churches everywhere—not that Chicago didn't have any, but it seemed that churches were everywhere in the south. Joyce grew up in church but stopped going when she was old enough to make her own decision about attending. Joyce could never totally forget her Christian upbringing and her parent's spiritual guide, though. It seemed she wasn't a part of that Christian life anymore; she figured God would always look out for her, even if she hadn't acknowledged it over the years.

Sometimes she wondered if God even looked out for her at all—and if he did, she had a feeling that it was only through her parents' prayers.

The sun, charged with an orange glow, was setting as she neared the entrance to her house. *Beautiful,* she thought. The tranquility of the scene sent waves of peace through her heart and gave her a sense of stillness—something she had wanted for a long time.

Joyce enjoyed the rest of the night as she sipped hot tea, listened to soft music, and typed in her journal on her laptop. The only voices she could hear were the chirps of crickets. Sunday morning was creeping in; back in Chicago, Joyce's Sunday was usually spent getting ready for work on Monday. Still, on that Sunday, she had to get ready for her interview with Solomon and Paltrow.

As old thoughts and memories of past struggles and disappointments swirled around in her mind, Joyce felt truly blessed and happy about her move to Savannah. She then closed her eyes and envisioned another accomplishment—hearing the interviewer say, "You're hired, welcome aboard!" or, in a more professional manner, "We are offering you the position of legal secretary, and Solomon and Paltrow would be much obliged if you were to accept our offer." Joyce spent the entire Sunday doing her hair, some personal grooming, and the laundry, which was usually how her Sundays went anyway.

Although she was usually a night owl, Joyce decided to get to bed early if she could. An interview always made her nervous, considering that she hadn't been on many; she usually held onto a job for a long period of time—six to ten years, to be exact. Now at forty-five years old, she hoped this would be a job she could retire from, as well as something that she could find comfort and a loyal atmosphere in. Joyce loved secretarial work and had been in that field almost for almost fifteen years; before that, she had been in the restaurant and hotel business for about ten and a half years. Though she loved that line of work, she was ready to move on to something different.

Joyce lay awake, staring into the ceiling, sipping on hot tea with lemon, and instead of counting sheep to fall asleep, she counted the blocks in her ceiling repeatedly. Finally, after setting the alarm for six o'clock in the morning, she entered a dream world—until the alarm snapped her awake. Joyce arose without hesitation, but with a little anxiety, though she knew it would surely pass after she had her first sip of morning coffee, which she usually drank no matter what time she awoke from her night's slumber.

Chapter 2

GRACIOUS INTERVIEW

As she waited for the coffee to brew, Joyce sat at her kitchen table for a little while after she showered. She considered reading some passages from her daily bread booklet, which her neighbor had given her. The coffee was ready, and she sipped it until her stomach was satisfied and she felt a little perked up.

Joyce sat up until about seven o'clock in the morning. It was now time to get dressed and start her journey, as she called it. As Joyce slipped into her new pantsuit, she smiled in the mirror at the perfect form and fit. She felt elated and confident. Joyce always toward black or blue colors, but today she would be going against that rule; besides, brown complimented her pecan skin tone. Her stilettos added poise and a tad bit of pride. The clock was ticking, and it was now eight o'clock in the morning.

Joyce always tried to arrive fifteen minutes early for interviews, which was precisely how long it would take to get to the law firm if there wasn't any traffic. Still sipping on her home-brewed coffee, she thought about all the questions she might be asked. Joyce's only concern was to answer each question with thought and precision and to ask intelligent questions so that the interviewer would have to answer each one with discretion. After all, Joyce would be conversing with lawyers, and they wanted to hire the perfect secretary.

Joyce arrived at the law firm twenty minutes ahead of schedule. As she approached the building, she studied the area and the business itself. She approached the desk with her resume and a small clutch in her hands. An older gentleman greeted her and introduced himself as Eric Solomon. Joyce then realized that the company did, in fact, need a new and friendly face. Since this was a new and rising firm, Joyce felt she had found her place and maybe some retribution finally. She had faced so many years of struggle, long hours, hard labor, and humiliation for less pay, but those lessons had made her stronger and more determined to live comfortably.

Mr. Solomon asked Joyce to be seated for a moment since he was with a client. The lawyer excused himself and told her he would be with her shortly. Joyce looked around the office; she admired the door, as well as the wall hangings of famous political leaders all over the world, who were all inspirational. Barack Obama had his own centered space in the sitting area of the office. The office furniture was priceless and posh. The carpeting was sleek. Joyce had to take her shoes off to feel the expensive and smooth fibers of the beautiful carpet. The walls were eggshell colored, tiled, and had the most beautiful nostalgic light fixtures. The aroma of peppermint wafted through the office.

Maybe a new Febreze fragrance? Joyce thought. Mr. Solomon finally finished his meeting with his prior client and began his meeting with Joyce.

"Miss Lomax, I will begin my interview with you now. Please have a seat in my office. How are you today?"

"Fine, thank you, Mr. Solomon," Joyce replied. She was a little nervous to be in the presence of a well-educated and well-kept attorney, who must have been in his late fifties to early sixties. Mr. Solomon asked many questions as he looked over Joyce's resume and studied her body language. He then went on to tell her about the company and his exact expectations of the role. Joyce had done her research; this was a successful law firm that had been in business for over thirty years. She was impressed by the company's history. She started compiling mental notes about stability and financial gain. Mr. Solomon seemed to be impressed with Joyce's resume and her job stability, in that she had no gaps in her work history. Joyce thought that Mr. Solomon seemed to be a mild-mannered gentleman with a firm yet meek demeanor. After their forty-five-minute discussion, Mr. Solomon asked Joyce if she would like to join their law firm.

Joyce immediately stood, shook Mr. Solomon's hand, and accepted the offer, feeling elated. *The meeting couldn't have gone any smoother*, Joyce thought to herself; her heart felt like it could burst out of her chest with happiness. Mr. Solomon instructed Joyce back to her seat to discuss the pay rate and work hours. Joyce hadn't considered this aspect of the job; she was already overwhelmed with the pleasure of being hired by this prestigious law firm. Mr. Solomon offered Joyce thirty thousand a year, with a full benefits package. She would be working forty-five hours a week, with two weeks of paid vacation a year. She would be starting her new job the following Monday from eight in the morning until six in the evening. Joyce had no problems at all with her days or hours; she was ecstatic.

He then told Joyce that of all the interviews that he'd had thus far, hers was the most promising, and he'd hoped that she would enjoy working for Solomon and Paltrow. Joyce was much obliged as she turned to leave the office. She thought about stopping somewhere for lunch but decided to go home, slip into some jeans and a tank top with some comfortable sandals, and let the tension of the interview melt away. She would treat herself to celebrate her new job. She put her head down in her car and said quietly to herself, "Maybe God is looking out for me after all."

Chapter 3

DISTINGUISHED GENTLEMAN

It was still a sweltering day in Savannah, and for Joyce, that was the only drawback of the city. Joyce wasn't a fan of hot weather; she was used to the cold, windy Chicago. After Joyce finished changing her clothes and touching up her hair, she decided to head out to Bella's Italian Cafe. She had an appetite for something Italian—maybe some pasta, some chicken alfredo, and a glass of wine to delight her taste buds. She was still on cloud nine from her interview but was famished after not eating anything all day.

She arrived at the restaurant with her book and tiny purse in her hands. Being single, Joyce often found comfort and solace in reading, even when she dined alone. Joyce was reading *Island Beneath the Sea* by the bestselling author Isabella Allende, which kept her engrossed. She then took a break to sip some wine and look around the room. That was when he caught her eye. It appears he had been waiting quite some time for Joyce to pull herself away from the pages. This distinguished gentleman was in a meeting with the store's general manager, and every now and then while conversing, he would peer at Joyce. Joyce just assumed this gentleman had a wandering eye, but she couldn't help but blush since she could he had sex appeal from her very first glance. Joyce lowered her head as she sipped her wine, trying not to look his way again if she could help it—but how could she not look at him when he was sitting straight in front of her about twenty feet away?

Joyce, who found the setting of the dining room relaxing, decided to continue reading her book. She was sitting at a booth table that offered her some seclusion. She was so engrossed in the book that she didn't even notice the sexy gentleman walking toward her table—but to her surprise, he headed straight for the men's room. *What an awkward way to go the men's room*, Joyce thought. Moments later, the distinguished gentleman walked out of the men's room and stopped at Joyce's table, acting as if he was trying to read the title of Joyce's book.

"That must a really good book you're reading," the gentleman said, "Joyce looked up, startled."

"Yes, it is," Joyce replied a little nervously.

"I didn't mean to startle you; I noticed the look on your face when I spoke. My name is Alim. I didn't mean to interrupt your intense reading."

"Hi, Alim. My name is Joyce," she said as he touched her hand gently. "Is that a Muslim name?"

"Maybe, but I am not Muslim," Alim replied with a sideways smirk. "It's just the name my momma gave me at birth."

"Oh, I see. It's a nice name," Joyce said, flashing a seductive smile. A few seconds of silence passed by before either spoke again.

"I hear that nice accent you have; I take it that you're not from the south," Alim said.

"No, I'm not. I'm originally from Chicago," Joyce replied.

"Oh, I've been in Georgia all my life. I was born and raised in Savannah, but I have done my share of traveling all over," Alim said.

He has the most beautiful smile, but it seems a little sneaky, Joyce thought as she sized the gentleman up.

"I've visited Chicago quite a bit, and it's a very good city; I grew kind of fond of it," Alim said.

"Oh, is that so?" Joyce replied.

"So, what brings you to Georgia, Joyce?" Alim asked.

"Well, I've visited Georgia many times, and I fell in love with Savannah, so I decided to move here. Besides, I've had enough of the big city and wanted a slower life, even though I've noticed things here are a little modernized, but not like Chicago. I chose the country because I like the quiet," Joyce said, shyly hunching her shoulders.

"Oh, I see, and I don't mean to keep prying, but are you married or in some kind of committed relationship?" Alim asked. He paused for a minute. "Let me know if I am being too forward; I am like that sometimes," he then said with a smile.

"No, I'm not committed at all to anyone, and I have never been married," Joyce said.

"Wow, never been married, huh? Joyce, that's kind of hard to believe, but I guess not everyone has been married," Alim said, looking a little surprised.

"Well, it's like that sometimes, Alim. Not everyone has been married and some not even once," Joyce snickered.

"I've been married before; I was twenty years old, and now I'm divorced," Alim said, bowing his head slightly. "It was good for a little while. Then somewhere down the road, we realized that we weren't compatible as husband and wife, so we decided to just be friends." Alim said with a frank expression."

"Oh, I see," Joyce said. "How long did your marriage last?"

"A year and a half," Alim replied. "But I did get something wonderful out of it—my baby daughter. Well, she's grown up now, but to me, she is still a baby."

Joyce smiled out of respect for his pleasant remarks about his daughter.

"I do have to say that I am not committed to anyone either, like yourself, so this must be my blessed day, as my momma would say. When there was a good day, she said, 'blessed day' instead of 'lucky day,' Alim said, looking bashful.

"So, where does your daughter live? Is she here with you?" Joyce asked after three seconds of silence.

"Oh, no. She is in school. She lives in Greenville, North Carolina. She attends Eastern Carolina University, and her mother also resides in Greenville," Alim replied.

Joyce attentively observed the gentleman before her, watching his body language while gazing into his wonderful eyes, and him the same.

A very well-kept man…He must be in his late forties to early fifties—a very distinguished persona, indeed, Joyce said to herself. His hair and beard were neatly trimmed, the richness in his dark skin was glowing, and his body was fit. Joyce could tell that this man took care of himself. She even noticed that his teeth were straight and even.

"Okay, Joyce! What's your story? You've heard a little bit of mine," Alim exclaimed.

"No story, Alim. I'm just single. I never gave marriage too much thought, and I didn't have a man when I left Chicago either, but I have not been asked about any of the major issues in my life," Joyce said to Alim abruptly.

"I see, but you don't have to be so feisty about it," Alim said with a laugh. Joyce laughed too.

"So, how long have you been in Savannah?"

"Six months," Joyce responded.

"You sure you haven't met a man or dated anyone since you've been here?" Alim asked, looking unsure.

"Well, I have met a few men, but no one that took my interest in dating," Joyce said in an assuring way.

"Good. So, I shouldn't have any trouble getting a date," Alim said with a wide grin.

"Excuse me?" Joyce asked, her head tilted in surprise.

"I'm usually kind of forward, so I didn't mean to offend you; just trying to make some headway," Alim said.

"You didn't offend me. You kind of made me blush a little," Joyce said.

"Yes, I noticed," Alim replied with a nice smile. Then, Joyce chuckled again, albeit softly.

"You have a beautiful smile and the most appealing brown bedroom eyes. Wow..." he commented. "Now, can you save my cell number? That's if you're interested in getting to know me a little better; maybe I can show you around Georgia. There are other towns besides Savannah, you know."

"Okay sure. I'll save your number in my cell phone," Joyce said as she giggled a little. Alim was making it easy for her to feel giggly on the inside. Joyce wasn't looking for a social life at that moment, but Alim was just a little too irresistible, and besides, she felt she wouldn't mind having a friend to show her around Georgia. Joyce then gave her cell phone number to Alim.

"Okay, now you have made it a little easier for me to say this," he responded. "I would like to see you again! But we will talk about that more when I call you."

"I will be looking forward to your call and our next meeting," Joyce said softly as she sipped her wine while looking straight into Alim's eyes.

"Let me get back to my table. I know that my colleague is wondering why I deserted him for so long, but obviously, he can see why, and he knows that it was worth it," Alim said smiling widely. "Have a good evening, Joyce. It was a pleasure to meet you." He gently took her hand.

"Likewise," Joyce blushed.

Alim then turned to walk away as Joyce eyed him intensely. He then sat back down in his seat. Joyce had to admit that she had been immediately attracted to the man when their eyes first met, though she had tried to deny it. She tried to absorb herself in the pages of her book, but Alim's meeting with her took all her attention away from her novel and appetite. Finally, Joyce just lost interest in everything she was doing for that moment, so she decided to ask for the check and get out of the restaurant. She gave Alim a little wave and smile as she headed out the door.

Chapter 4

As the Night Falls

Joyce arrived home, feeling blissful about her meeting with Alim. As the night set in, Joyce took a shower, brewed some black tea, and sat in front of her laptop. She couldn't stop thinking about the handsome man she met that afternoon, and for some reason, Joyce started to feel alone. Of the few men she had already met since she'd been in Georgia, she'd never felt alone or in need of their company. *Such a weird feeling,* she thought, or maybe it was her heavy attraction for Alim that set her apart from not caring to caring. Her want for Alim was very strong, and although she had not even been out with the man yet, the lust was there. Her feelings were always buried deep inside her heart and guarded beneath her soul, but there was just something about Alim that made her anxious and wanting to pry into every aspect of his life to see and hear what he was all about. Joyce knew she was acting out of character because she hadn't cared about getting to know anyone before that moment.

As night fell, Joyce's phone rang, but she hesitated to answer.

"Hello," she said after letting the phone ring about three times.

"Joyce, this is Alim."

"Hi, Alim. How have you been since the last time we spoke?"

"Well, well. Were you busy, Joyce?"

"No, not at all, just sitting here, surfing the net."

"Okay, so Joyce, I know it's a weeknight, but if it's not too late, would you like to come out for a little while? I sure would like to talk to you more face to face. I know a little café downtown, which is really laid back. Do you know of it? It's called Samsara's, and its cozy."

"I have never been there, Alim, but I have driven past there quite often."

"Do you get out much, Joyce?"

"No, not that often."

"Okay then, I will be your official tour guide."

Joyce chuckled a little to herself.

"Oh, that's humorous?" Alim asked.

"No, I'm just a little silly," Joyce said.

"Glad to hear it. I'm happy to know that you're not one of those stuck-up city women; I have dated them before, and it's not a good thing. Believe me when I tell you."

"What time do you want me to meet you at the café?" Joyce asked.

"I am going that way now. I just finished my work for today and need some relaxation and a decent meal," Alim said.

"Okay, I'm on my way," Joyce said before hanging up. She paced across the floor for a minute, trying to decide what casual wear to put on—dress or slacks? She came across a khaki dress in her closet and decided to put on a pair of four-inch sandals and put some makeup on her face.

When Joyce arrived at the café, she found Alim sitting in the waiting area to greet her. They both smiled when they saw each other, and Alim gave her a gentle hug.

I didn't think they greet people like that in Chicago… Joyce was feeling a little apprehensive as the waitress escorted them both to the booth Alim chose for them to sit.

"Would this particular table be suitable for you, Joyce?" Alim asked.

"Yes, this is fine, and it is cozy, I see," Joyce responded. She was feeling nervous about their date. She hadn't been in this predicament for such a long time.

Joyce observed this quaint little café, and her eyes and ears is filled with delight. The music was R&B, and the vintage painting on the wall depicted famous people from all walks of life. It was a remarkably interesting and ap-pealing restaurant. The lights were dimmed, and the air conditioning was on the perfect setting for comfort.

"So, what line of work are you in, Joyce?" Alim asked, looking over the menu after they ordered their drinks.

Joyce proceeded to tell Alim of her new job that she would be starting next Monday. Alim smiled widely as he congratulated her.

"I was blessed to come to Savannah and land that position, and I thought that I would be job hunting for a long time," she said.

"I hear you, Joyce, because jobs are so hard to find—especially with the economy being the way that it is now."

"I would think it would be harder in the south anyway," Joyce said.

"Well, legal secretary is a good position, and I am sure that you have good skills and longevity in that area of your work history. The firm had no good reason not to give you the position," Alim said in all sincerity.

"So, what do you do, Alim? Just as Joyce posed the question, the waitress came over, wanting to take their order.

"Yes, Mama. I would like to have the steak, cooked medium-well, a baked potato with butter and sour cream, a little shredded cheese, and add a side of collards. That will be all for me," Alim said.

"Yes, I would like a nice-sized bowl of your soup of the day and a piece of Italian bread with that," Joyce said.

"That's all you're having?" Alim asked.

"Yes, that's all I need. I ate too much pasta earlier this afternoon, and I'm still trying to digest that," Joyce replied, giggling a little.

"Okay, that's all for now, thank you. Helen, is it?" Alim asked the waitress.

He then turned to Joyce. "You were asking my line of work? I am a real estate broker, and I own some hefty property here in Savannah. Oh, and by the way, I also own the building that you will be working in," Alim said.

"Oh, how ironic is that!" Joyce said.

"No, not ironic; you're just a little surprised, that's all. But don't get cute on me or I will have to revoke Solomon and Paltrow's license," Alim with a laugh.

"I love this song!" Joyce said as she started to move to the beat of the music and hum the melody as she sipped her white wine. Alim gazed at her as she started to swag.

"I know this is The Temptations, and I know the song, but what's the name of it?" Alim asked curiously.

"You're My Everything," Joyce answered.

"Yes, that's right. I love these oldies," Alim replied.

"Thank you for inviting me to this spot!" Joyce said to Alim with a seductive smile.

"My pleasure. I am glad to see that you are having so much fun!" Alim said confidently.

They both sat a little while and talked about families and relationships while enjoying the music. Joyce discreetly drilled Alim on his past relationships, and Alim knowingly did the same. By then, it was about eleven o'clock at night—way past the usual time Joyce would stay out at night, but she was having such a good time and didn't want the night to end.

"The music is nice, and the company is even better," Joyce said as she gazed into Alim's eyes. Alim blushed.

"You are so free-spirited and not uptight," Alim said, rubbing Joyce's hand.

"No, I'm never like that. If I ever felt uncomfortable or bored, I would have left a long time ago," Joyce said with a murmur.

"Oh, you would have just left a brother hanging, huh," Alim said.

"Well, I would not have had a choice," Joyce said as she laughed.

"You are really pretty," Alim said, gazing at her.

"Thank you, and you are not bad yourself," Joyce said with a sly smile as she winked at him.

"Well, it's getting late, and I better see you home," Alim said.

"Yes, I'm getting kind of tired. I didn't get much sleep last night. I was thinking about my interview, and it was a long day," Joyce said.

"Well, no more anxieties about that," Alim said as he helped Joyce up from her seat.

"Would you mind if I followed you to your house just to make sure that you arrived safely?" Alim asked.

"Thank you, but I will be all right," Joyce said.

"I understand, but I will call and make sure that you arrived home okay," Alim said, looking a little disappointed.

"It takes me about fifteen to twenty minutes to get home. I live on the other side of town," Joyce said to Alim.

They exited the café together, and Alim walked Joyce to her car.

"You made me feel good tonight, Joy. Oh, can I call you Joy?" Alim asked.

"Huh, yes. I guess so. I don't mind; you just caught me off guard with that," Joyce said, smiling and shrugging her shoulders in awe.

"I know this may sound corny, but I know that you'll bring me lots of joy as we tour the city!" Alim exclaimed.

"So, you gathered all that from one night?" Joyce asked.

"Yes, I sure did, sweetheart!" Alim said as he reached out to hug her. Joyce felt that she could just melt in Alim's arms. She hadn't been held like that in a long time, and she sighed to herself as her heartbeat sped up. Alim kissed her forehead and cheeks and then moved his smooth lips down to her freshly glossed lips. Joyce's heart pounded as they shared that passionate kiss. Joyce could have stood there forever. She moaned a little when Alim slowly released his lips from hers, held her in his arms, and gently whispered in her ear, "It's getting late, and I don't want you driving home too late."

Joyce was lost for words and her facial expressions showed need—a need for sexual satisfaction but she managed to respond.

"Good night, Alim."

"Not yet, Joy. Remember, I'm going to call you to make sure you have gotten home okay."

"Okay," Joyce responded with a half-smile as she got into her car. Alim waited until she drove off, and then he went to his car. As she drove home, Joyce thought that she should have had Alim follow her, just for safety, or perhaps she was just kidding herself after that kiss—she wanted him tonight. Just as she was pulling into her driveway, Alim weighing heavily on her mind, the phone rang.

"Did you get home, sweetheart?"

"Yes, I just pulled in."

"Okay, I will stay on the phone with you until you get into the house."

"I'm in!" Joyce replied.

"Joy, I really did enjoy your company tonight."

"Same here," Joyce responded.

"Did you lock your doors?"

"Yes, everything is tight," Joyce said, giggling a little.

"Okay, baby. I must be up early with the chickens, I am exhausted, but I will call you tomorrow."

"Sweet dreams," Joyce said, preparing to hang up the phone.

"Most definitely, baby. And you are too. I am sure I will dream about you," Alim said. Joyce started to put down the phone.

"Good night, baby," Alim said once more before hanging up.

My new friend! Joyce thought excitedly. She could not wait until their next date. *This man makes me feel good!*

Joyce proceeded to take off her shoes. She lay on the sofa, her eyelids growing heavy as she gazed up at the moon through her blinds.

Chapter 5

FRIENDS TO LOVERS

That morning, Joyce slept in later than usual and almost missed the call she was eagerly hoping for.

"Hello?"

"Good morning, Joy!"

"Good morning, Alim."

"How are you this morning? Were you still asleep?" Alim asked.

"Yes, I was," Joyce said, tiredness evident in her voice.

"Oh, sorry for waking you up!" Alim said.

"Oh, that's okay. And I'm glad that you did; I needed to get an early start out into the mall anyway," Joyce replied. She took a breath and continued. "Your kiss exhausted me last night, but I would like to say, in a good way. It's been a long time since I have been kissed like that."

"That makes me very happy. I think that I saw fireworks—or was that in my dreams? Hmm…I don't remember!" Alim said with a big laugh. Then he said frankly, "Hey, we can see each other more and more, but don't let me push you away by being so forward now. I just don't believe in wasting time, and I like you a lot."

"I would like to have some fun before starting my new job on Monday," Joyce replied.

"What would you like to do tonight?" Alim asked.

"I really don't know."

"Okay, we will figure it out, but I really must go, even though I don't want to hang up. I will call you later, love!" Alim said.

"Okay, Alim. Have a good day!"

"You too, baby!" Alim responded. Joyce loved it when Alim called her baby. To Joyce, she felt it was an intimate thing, but she kept reminding herself that they were just friends, even though he made her feel different than any other man she had been with before. After Joyce got back from her shopping trip, she started rummaging through her closet to find something to wear for the evening. She came across a dress that she hadn't worn before—one she had almost forgotten about entirely. The evening would be hot, and that casual dress would be perfect for any occasion.

Just as she was getting ready for her bath, the phone rang.

"Hello."

"Hey, Joy!" Alim said.

"Hi, Alim!" Joyce replied.

"What Cha doing?"

"Oh, just getting ready for my bath," Joyce said sweetly.

"That sounds soothing. Well, it's about six o'clock now. Will you be ready by eight?" Alim asked.

"Sure!"

"Joyce, are you comfortable with me picking you up tonight?"

"Okay," Joyce replied.

Alim could tell there was a touch of hesitation in Joyce's voice. "You're sure you're okay with that? Because I feel better picking you up than us meeting in separate cars."

"Yes, Alim. I am sure, and I will give you my address. Do you know where you are taking me tonight?" Joyce asked.

"Yes, I was thinking about that jazz festival in the park," Alim responded.

"That sounds awesome! I love jazz!" Joyce exclaimed.

"I thought you would!" Alim said confidently. "Joy, this may sound a little boyish, but I also love those lemon snow cones with those little lemon bits in them. Now that's refreshing!" he laughed.

"Not boyish; cute—because I like the same thing, and you can have whatever ices your heart desires tonight," Joyce said with a little giggle, and Alim laughed back.

"Okay, see you when you get here," Joyce said. Suddenly, she felt a little apprehensive since no one had visited her since she'd moved to Savannah.

A little later, Alim pulled into Joyce's driveway. Alim exited his car and proceeded to walk toward her porch to ring the bell, while Joyce peered through her blinds, feeling a little jittery. She took a few sips of her caffeinated tea as he rang the bell, and then she opened the door with a pleasant smile.

"I see you've found my spot!" Joyce said to Alim.

"Yeah, like it was hard," Alim said sarcastically.

"Come on in!"

As Alim stepped over the threshold, he took Joyce by the hand and kissed her as if he had just lost and found her again. Joyce responded with shocked delight.

"You look so good!" Alim exclaimed as he gazed into her eyes. Joyce felt like she could have just melted all over him. As Alim slowly and gently let her go, he said, "Okay, it's time for us to go!"

"Okay, let me get my bag," Joyce said. Alim seemed kind of quiet as they proceeded on their way. Joyce wondered why.

"Alim…" she began.

"Yeah, baby?" Alim answered.

"Are you all, right?" Because you are a little quiet," Joyce said.

"Yeah, sweetheart. I'm sorry," Alim replied. "The night is beautiful, isn't it Joy?"

"Yeah, Alim. I love the night!"

"Is that right?"

"The night brings thoughts, romance…" Joyce replied.

"You're kind of deep, baby."

"No, no. I wasn't trying to be deep. That's just how I think at night.

Sometimes the daylight distorts my thoughts because there is so much going on."

"You know, Joy, I never thought of it like that before. The night does seem kind of soothing."

"You can hide in your mind during the night, so whatever might be in your mind, there is nobody there to disturb you," Joyce replied.

"I like the way you think, baby! I see that we're going to have a very good friendship and I am glad that we met. You seem so different from most of the women that I dated, which is why I just had to kiss you," Alim said with a seductive yet candid smile.

Joyce sat quietly and was at a loss for words because she felt the same way about Alim. But also wanted things to continue in slow motion—just talking, laughing together, and touching each other.

A short time later, they reached the jazz festival.

"Oh, wow! There are so many people here!" Joyce exclaimed.

"Yes, there are, like every time the festival is here. Now, let's go and get those ices. I'm thirsty!" Alim said as they maneuvered themselves through the crowd.

"Hey, Alim!" A few people that knew him greeted him simultaneously.

"Hey, all, what's up?" Alim introduced Joyce to quite a few neighbors, and friends. Joyce started to dance a little bit to the music, which sounded so good to her ears, and Alim swayed a little to the music himself. They were having a lot of fun and continued to dance with each other as the stars shone brightly in the night sky above them.

As the evening of jazz came to an end, Joyce thought about whether Alim would want to stay with her tonight. She wanted him just as much as she thought he wanted her, but she wasn't going to push it. Alim and Joyce held hands as they walked toward the car. When they reached the car, Joyce stopped for a second to slip off her sandals.

"You need some foot comfort, huh?" Alim commented.

"Yes, those shoes were very uncomfortable for those couple of hours," Joyce responded shyly.

"You get as comfortable as you want, baby. Always feel that way around me; friends with no conditions," Alim said with a concerned smile. Those comments kept playing in the back of Joyce's mind, leaving her confused about what she really wanted. One thing that she knew for sure was that she wanted Alim to meet her sexual needs, but it seemed best to keep that out of her mind for now. On the drive back to Joyce's house, Alim stopped by a pizzeria.

"Oh, I'm sorry, Joyce. I don't know whether you like pizza or not. I guess I just assumed that everyone did. Would you like something here?"

"I don't mind, Alim, and thank you for asking," Joyce replied.

"I didn't want to drive to the other side of town, but if you want something else, we can go," Alim said keenly.

"No, no, Alim. This is good!" Joyce said.

"Okay, baby. I hope that, you're sure."

"Instead of eating the pizza here, let's take it back to my place; I really don't feel like sitting in a restaurant tonight," Joyce said as she leaned a little on Alim's shoulder.

"Okay, baby. Whatever you want."

Joyce felt like Alim was the cool and easygoing type of guy, though she felt that Alim knew what she wanted for real—but maybe he didn't want to question it. Since it was only ten at night, they could sit and talk. Joyce was picturing the scene in her mind—some wine and soft music—as she smiled to herself, but once again, she wasn't going to push it. She wanted it all to fall in place naturally. *After all,* she thought, *there is nothing wrong with lovemaking between friends,* and if there was, she would find that out later. Joyce lived for the now and knew that whatever came later would be no detriment to her—she'd always been alone. She longed for Alim's friendly company, as well as his spontaneous compassion.

They finally arrived at Joyce's house. She fidgeted for her keys in a kind of nervous way, but she quickly got it together.

"You can put the food on the dining table," Joyce said as she sighed in relief to be home. "I do have some red wine, if you'd like some, Alim."

"Sure, I will have a glass," Alim replied. Joyce then put on some soft music and reached for the wineglasses.

"It's nice in here, baby. I like the way you have this place hooked up!" Alim said, looking impressed as he observed the lovely scenery.

"Thanks, I do try," Joyce said as she smiled in appreciation. They sat at the table and began talking. After eating a slice of pizza, Joyce went into the living room with her wineglass, expecting Alim to follow, which he did. Alim again asked Joyce why she was single; he just couldn't see a woman like Joyce being single and felt that she had a lot to offer. It wasn't the topic of the night that Joyce was hoping for, but she responded that even though she didn't like talking about her single life. However, she also explained that she liked being single and appreciated the time to herself.

"Maybe I just can't handle the relationship drama. It's not attractive and doesn't feel good at all," Joyce said honestly but looking a little confused. "I haven't been in a relationship in a long time, but sometimes I do miss the companionship—but I guess not that much!"

"I do understand, Joy, but someday you will see yourself letting someone into your heart. I have dated from time to time but haven't known anyone yet that I was interested in seriously or that captured my heart, but I wouldn't mind being committed again. It's been so long, but it's cool, I think," Alim said, smiling a little.

Joyce remained quiet for a moment, feeling a little confused about why Alim was talking about relationship stuff.

It's a little uncomfortable right now, she thought to herself, *but it's all right*.

As the evening drew nearer, Alim and Joyce just sat back on her big comfy sofa and talked about their lives, dreams, and hopes. Joyce was amazed that Alim liked to talk because she felt that most men didn't. It was kind of nice.

"Well, the hour has come, and I must be getting home now. It's an early day tomorrow for me," Alim blurted out.

"Okay. It was nice having you here with me tonight. Thank you for taking me to the jazz festival. I had so much fun," Joyce said.

"No problem, Joy. You are good company. I love that in a woman, and I see that we are going to be hanging a lot," Alim said. Joyce smiled and swayed a little at Alim's words of appreciation.

As she walked Alim to the door, he smoothly turned around to give Joyce a tight hug and kiss before heading to his car. Joyce shut the door and peered out her living room window to watch him drive off. She felt a little disappointed that he didn't hint around at staying the night, but then she felt that it was probably for the best. They were just friends anyhow, but he treated her with so much passion. Thirty minutes later, the phone rang. It was Alim.

"I just called to wish you a good night and sweet dreams, baby," Alim said in a low but sexy voice.

"Ah, the night is feeling even cozier now that you called. Sweet dreams, sweetheart. Good night," Joyce said sleepily before both receivers fell silent.

Joyce then got ready for bed and put on a movie on to help her fall asleep. She loved *Cold Mountain*, and she hadn't seen it in a long time. Just as she was dozing off halfway through the movie, her cell phone rang again.

"Hi, baby. Were you asleep?" Alim asked, his voice tinged with loneliness.

"I was dozing off. Is everything all right?" Joyce asked sleepily.

"Joyce, it's just one of those nights where it is hard to get to sleep, but I don't mean to interrupt your rest."

"No, it's all right. So, what's up, Alim? What's on your mind?" Joyce asked.

"I didn't go home, Joy. In fact, I stopped at this sports bar, and it doesn't close until two o'clock in the morning. I was thinking about you in many ways. I'm just being honest with you here—I need to be with you tonight."

"Oh," Joyce said, sitting up in bed.

"Can I stay with you tonight?" Alim asked longingly. Joyce was silent for almost a full minute.

"Okay," Joyce answered softly, albeit a little hesitantly.

"Are you sure?" Alim asked.

"Yes, I'm sure, Alim. You should not have left anyway. In fact, I was having the same feelings you are having right now, but you never asked about staying overnight," Joyce said.

"I'm on my way back, Joy," Alim said.

"I'll see you when you get here," Joyce replied.

Joyce waited on the sofa for Alim to return as all kinds of thoughts rushed through her head. She got up to peer through the shades as Alim pulled up on her driveway before going over to meet him as he walked up the front porch. She looked at him sensually. Inside the house, music played softly in the background—Maxwell's "'til the Cops Come Knockin'." Joy had a slew of CDs with soft, slow love songs and had made sure to put one in.

Alim kissed Joyce as soon as the door shut behind them. He ran his hands all over her body as Joyce breathed heavily, her heart beating rapidly. He then pressed his lips onto her neck and lifted her to the sofa. Once there, he lifted her nightie and tenderly tugged on her nipples with his teeth. Joyce moaned as he kissed her stomach, and then moved down to her inner thighs. Joyce continuously moaned with a kind of pleasure she had never experienced before. She almost forgot how a man's intimate touch felt.

She rose slowly from the sofa and led Alim to her bedroom, where she slowly undressed him, all the while kissing him on the lips and chest. She leaned back on her bed as he followed. She began panting heavily as Alim kissed her between the thighs again. She let out a soft scream. She then whispered in his ear that she wanted to taste him, so Alim leaned back on the bed as Joyce wrapped her plump lips around his manhood. Alim moaned intensely, but he dared himself not to come because he wanted to do that inside Joyce. Alim lifted Joyce's head, laid her on the bed, and entered her, his face twisting in pleasure as he enjoyed Joyce's warm body. Alim made sure that he could feel all of her. Joyce let out a loud moan just as she reached her peak, and Alim sighed as he burst inside her. They both lay still for a minute to catch their breaths. Wordlessly, they fell asleep holding one another.

The sun started to peek through the bedroom windows, and Alim's cell phone began to ring. He woke up, startled by the sound.

"I'm on my way." He gently woke Joyce up and told her he had to go home and get ready for work. He kissed her goodbye as they walked toward the door.

After Alim left, Joy laid back down in the damp spots in the sheets they had made love in the night before.

That afternoon, Alim called again to check in on her. Joyce had some shopping to do for her new job on Monday, so she decided to start her day. She felt like a different woman—happy and rejuvenated. Still, in the back of her mind, she kept thinking

wondering whether they were friends or lovers but decided that it didn't matter right now. She just wanted Alim more and more. She recalled the pleasure she felt with him—one that she didn't want to ever dissipate.

Soon, Joyce's shopping trip came to an end. Just as she headed back to her car, Alim called.

"Hi, Alim!"

"Hey, baby. Are you still out shopping?" Alim asked.

"No, I'm done. I'm on my way to the bookstore," Joyce said.

"Oh, okay. Can you pass by my office?" Alim asked.

"Sure, where is that?"

"It's on Seacrest Drive. There are a few office buildings there. The sign will read Seacrest Real Estate Brokers," Alim explained.

"Okay, I'm on my way. See you then," Joyce replied.

Chapter 6

CHURCH BY THE ROADSIDE

Joyce began her journey down the country road that she knew was a short-cut to Seacrest Drive. She noticed a beautiful church on the roadside, close to a little convenience store, a gas station, and a diner. The church's sign read "Shepherds of Christ Deliverance Church," and on the front door of the church were words mantled in its bricks of tile that read, "Jesus Christ is the Way." Joyce admired the beautiful lettering and decided to visit it later. She had been toying with the idea of joining a church.

She stopped at the gas station on the same roadside to get some Breath Savers mints and fountain Pepsi. As she peered out at the church across the street, she noticed that a small crowd had gathered outside its doors. She was curious about the service that was going on and checked the sign again. It had the list of daily services and their times. Today was Bible study.

She started the drive to Alim's office again, still thinking about visiting the church the coming Sunday. She hadn't been to one in such a long time.

A short while later, Joyce finally reached her destination.

"What took you so long, baby?" Alim asked.

"I took an alternate route from the mall because I didn't feel like dealing with all that traffic," Joyce replied.

"Oh, I see," Alim said.

"Interesting thing too. I just drove by a beautiful church. It was small and beautifully decorated," she said excitedly.

"What's the name of the church?" Alim asked, intrigued.

"Shepherds of Christ Deliverance Church." Joyce responded.

"You go to church?" He asked, looking a little concerned.

"I did a long time ago," Joyce replied, hanging her head as though she were a little embarrassed by Alim's question. "What about you?"

"Well, I do occasionally. I was raised in a church outside of town that my mother attended since I was a child, and I still attend sometimes," Alim responded with a small smile.

"Oh, and what church is that?" Joyce asked.

"Blessed Assurance Baptist Church."

"I have passed that church many a times. It's beautiful!"

"Okay, enough with the churches. How have you been since we last spoke, sweetheart?" Alim asked, pulling her in for a hug.

"I'm fine, honey," Joyce replied.

She looked around Alim's office. "Nice office you have here, Alim. I love the décor; very exquisite," she said.

"Thank you," Alim said, nodding appreciatively.

"I thought that we could go for a drive tonight. Let's head out in a few minutes after I finish up here. It won't take long," Alim said.

"Okay, Alim. I will run over to the bookstore next door if that's all right. You can come and get me when you are ready," Joyce said.

"Okay, baby." Alim nodded.

Joyce browsed through the bookstore and picked up a few fancy-looking journals. She liked to keep a daily record of her days and nights—well, you might as well say her entire life. She enjoyed the calming rituality of it.

She decided she would love to come back to this lovely bookstore again and asked the clerk for the store's business card and a membership. Joyce loved bookstores, libraries, and coffee shops. She loved to read and keep journals on her laptop, along with some of her fantasy writing. She glanced down at the card, which just read, "The Bookstore." She hadn't noticed a sign outside.

As she left the building, she noticed Alim conversing with an attractive woman outside. She saw Alim hand that woman his business card. Joyce felt a flash of jealousy, but she played it off in her mind and tried not to let her emotions show on her face. Instead of walking right over to Alim, she stood back, pretending to rummage through her bag for something. The woman left, and Alim began walking over to Joyce as though he had been on his way to meet her all along before being distracted by the woman he was just talking to.

"So, what did you get, Joy?" Alim asked, looking a tad bit guilty.

"Just some journals. I like that bookstore. It seems better than the one in the mall," Joyce replied. Alim just smiled and took Joyce's hand to lead her to her car.

"I will follow you to your house to park your car, and then we'll be on our way," he said. "Let's take that scenic route you took, Joy, so that we can see that beautiful church you were admiring."

"Okay, Alim. Just follow me," Joyce said, giggling a little.

As Joyce pulled out of the parking lot, she wondered why Alim hadn't mentioned the woman he was conversing with. She pushed away the thought; maybe that woman was just a business associate. Besides, it shouldn't be any of her concern. She wanted to forget about it altogether.

As Joyce approached the church, she slowed down and called Alim on his cell to point it out.

"That's it, Alim," Joyce said.

"It is a really pretty church," Alim replied.

"I may come for a visit on Sunday."

"That would be good," Alim said.

They proceeded to go to Joyce's house. As Joyce pulled into the driveway, she noticed a package on her porch. It was from one of her brothers. A housewarming gift. Joyce was delighted to see that he hadn't forgotten about her, and a smile broke out across her face. She knew that both her brothers loved her deeply. The package contained some China that her eldest brother had stored away after their parents had passed. He had moved into the family house after their parents passed away, and he had assured Joy that she always had a home there.

Joyce and Alim entered the house, and Joyce immediately called her brother to thank him for the precious gift. Joyce's brother was glad to hear from her. Even though he was married, he felt that Joyce was the one entitled to her mother's China.

After Joyce hung up the phone, she and Alim left for the drive he had promised her. Joyce found Alim's tour quite interesting; for the duration of the two-hour drive, he showed her some landmarks that would get her to different destinations throughout the city and surrounding towns. He showed her some of Savannah's most historical locations.

Darkness fell, bringing the tour to an end. They decided to stop at a little barbecue hut.

"I'm famished! I know you'll love the delicious ribs here," Alim said, rubbing his stomach. They dove into some ribs and coleslaw until they couldn't eat anymore. Joyce was having so much with Alim as always. She burst out laughing at the sight of all the barbecue sauce on Alim's cheeks. She picked up her napkin and wiped his face for him.

"So, Alim, would you like to go to church with me on Sunday?" Joyce asked, setting down the napkin.

"Yeah, I don't mind going. Besides, I haven't been to church in a while, but when I do go, I attend my Mama's church."

"Okay, Alim. It's a date for church on Sunday, and thank you for accepting," Joyce said excitedly.

"Since most folks down south go to church, it almost seems like a crime not to attend one," Alim said frankly.

"Oh, is that right?" Joyce asked.

"Yes, it is so, baby," Alim responded.

"I think everyone should go to church at some point in their life, and I sure do want to visit Shepherds of Christ to see if that's the church for me," Joyce said earnestly.

"Well, you ready to go, Joy?" Alim asked.

"Yes, I'm too full!" Joyce said.

Alim always left the waitresses good tips, and that impressed Joyce because she was a good tipper herself.

Chapter 7

THE TRUTH IS THE LIGHT

O n Sunday morning, Joyce woke up early to get ready to go to church. She called Alim to make sure he hadn't forgotten about their church date.

"Good morning!" Joyce said.

"Good morning, sweetheart!" Alim replied.

"So, are you getting ready for church?" Joyce asked excitedly.

"Yes, I am getting up as we speak right now," Alim answered, albeit without any excitement in his voice.

"Okay, we'll meet there at eleven o'clock!" Joyce replied.

"See you there, baby," Alim said and then hung up.

Joyce went over to her closet and picked out a long spaghetti strap dress, which was more than suitable for the hot weather that beautiful Sunday. She thought that a shawl and some heels would also go well with the dress. Joyce was excited about attending church services since she hadn't been to in a long time.

When Joyce arrived at the church, she heard the whimsical, soothing voices of the choir inside. *The choir sounds good!* Joyce thought.

She looked around for Alim's car, but he hadn't arrived yet. She waited in the sitting area of the church lobby for him. Fifteen minute later, he still hadn't shown up yet, so she decided to go inside and join the church service. *Beautiful church*, she thought as the usher led her in.

A nice crowd had gathered there, and the choir was still singing beautifully. When the choir stopped singing, the announcements were read, and the visitors acknowledged. Joyce stood along with a few others to be recognized as a visitor. The church clapped in appreciation, and someone greeted them verbally from the pulpit. Just then, she saw Alim being led by the usher toward her pew.

Joyce greeted Alim with a wide smile and a hug. As they were being seated, the offering plate came around. Alim apologized to Joyce for his tardiness, but she brushed it off; she was just grateful that he he'd kept his promise and showed up. As Joyce looked around, she saw that it was a Pentecostal church. The devotional leader finally introduced the speaker as Pastor Thomas L. Hinton. The pastor asked everyone to stand to praise and worship the Lord. Joyce and Alim stood together and knelt their heads down to pray. They held hands while the church praised the Lord. The pastor finally asked everyone to be seated as he proceeded with the sermon of the day. The theme of the sermon was salvation. Joyce's heart started to stir with conviction as the preacher spoke about love, repentance, prayer, and walking with God.

After the sermon, the preacher called for an altar call, inviting everyone up that wanted to accept Jesus Christ into their heart. Joyce wasn't unaware of this part of the church service. She could not bring herself to approach the alter this time. After the benediction, the churchgoers were asked to greet one another. As Joyce and Alim proceeded to leave, Alim was interrupted by a woman.

"Alim!" The woman blurted out.

"How are you doing, Lorraine?" Alim asked, looking a little surprised.

"I'm fine; can't complain," Lorraine said cheerfully. Alim proceeded to introduce Joyce and Lorraine to each other.

"I never thought that I would run into you here, Alim, but it's a good place to see you again," Lorraine, looking a little confused at the sight of Joyce and Alim's arms locked together.

"Yes, but I'm just visiting," Alim said with a hint of urgency on his face.

"Oh, this is a nice church. I've been coming here for about a month now, and you will love it here too!" Lorraine said excitedly. "Well, I must run now, but it was good seeing you again, Alim, and I hope that you will come back and visit the church soon, and it was also nice meeting you, Joyce."

"You too, Lorraine," Joyce replied, smiling. "Who was that Alim?" she asked after Lorraine left.

"It was just someone I used to know some time ago," Alim answered, not taking his eyes off Lorraine until she left his line of sight.

"Oh."

"Yes, but I'm glad I never dated her because she acted so needy all the time," Alim said, shaking his head in relief—but it seemed as though he didn't mind watching Lorraine walk away, and his eyes filled with hidden lust.

"Well, Alim, aren't all women needy at some point in their lives?" Joyce asked with a little smirk.

"Yes, I suppose so, Joyce, but Lorraine had a few issues that needed some medical attention—or so I thought anyway," Alim, chuckling.

"Well, maybe you drove her a little crazy," Joyce said, laughing back.

"Let's go and get something to eat because I see that hunger has you talking a little crazy now," Alim said, grabbing her hand.

"I do need some coffee," Joyce said.

"I know that you have an early day tomorrow, Joy, so I won't have you out late," Alim said anxiously.

"I guess I'll follow you, Alim."

"Yes, babe."

On the way to the car, Joyce thought about something the preacher had said. She had diligently written down some notes while at the church to read later. Some words lingered with her, and she knew that she would be attending that church going forward. *The salutation,* she thought. *Love and the ten commandments...*

Alim lead Joyce to a steakhouse just a little outside of town. She really didn't mind too much where they were eating because she was anxious for this day to be over, as she would be starting her new job tomorrow. After dinner, Alim offered to come over to Joyce's house for a little while, and she agreed.

Once at her house, Alim plopped her on the big cushy sofa. Joyce asked if he cared for anything to drink. Alim wanted coffee. Joyce brewed a fresh pot for him.

"So, Alim, you didn't say much about the service. Did you like it?" Joyce asked Alim, rubbing his back.

"Yes, it was good, but somewhat different from the Baptist Church," Alim responded, sighing with pleasure from the back rub Joyce was giving him. He loved the touch of her hands.

"Maybe I will visit your mother's church one Sunday; I have never been to a Baptist church," Joyce said.

"That will be good, baby," Alim responded in a soft and soothing voice.

The coffee finished brewing, but Alim wasn't craving that anymore; he wanted Joyce. They embraced intimately, the soft light of the TV casting a glow on them. Obviously Alim was in the mood for lovemaking, and Joyce felt the same. Something was different tonight with Alim in Joyce's bedroom. He had a look of concern or seriousness on his face. Joyce asked him if anything was wrong and if he was feeling all right.

"Joy, we have been spending a lot of time together, and I was feeling that we should call ourselves more than friends. I really care about you, and I don't want you to see anyone else. I feel that our relationship will grow into something special, but I won't try to pressure you," Alim said with a serious expression. "Joy, I feel like I can talk to you about anything. I really do appreciate you, and you make me feel good when I'm with you. I feel like we should take our friendship to another level."

Joyce felt happy at his words. She also felt like their relationship was growing deeper.

"I feel the same, Alim. I care for you a lot," Joyce said, gazing into Alim's eyes.

"This may sound a little weird, Joy, but I feel as though we belong to each other. Again, I am not trying to rush this thing, but I don't want to see you with anyone else, so that's why I am stepping up now," Alim said, stroking her hair softly.

Joyce was silent. Alim laid back on the bed to collect his thoughts. He didn't know what Joyce was thinking, but she had said she cared about it—that had to at least stand for something.

Joyce lay in bed, lost in thought too. Ever since Alim had walked into her life, he had made it better. She had nothing to lose now. She needed him as a soul mate and lover as well as a friend. They belonged to each other now. He hadn't given her any reasons to doubt him.

Chapter 8

BEGINNING OF LOVE

Monday morning arrived, and Joyce began to get ready for her first day at her new job. She felt happy with the turn her relationship with Alim was taking. The phone rang early.

"Hello."

"Good morning, baby! I was calling to wish you a good day at your new job!" Alim said excitedly.

"Thank you, honey," Joyce answered.

"I'm not going to hold you up. I called to let you know that I was thinking about you, and I'll give you a call this afternoon," Alim said.

"Thanks for your well wishes!" Joyce said.

"Anytime, baby!" Alim answered and hung up. Joyce finished getting dressed and then grabbed her coffee mug, purse, and business bag and headed out to her new job. She knew it would a long day at work with training, getting to know her bosses, and setting up her office.

"Hello, Mr. Solomon." Joyce greeted her new boss.

"Hello, Joyce. And how are you this morning?" Mr. Solomon asked.

"I'm fine thanks," Joyce replied.

"Well, let's get you familiar with the office," Mr. Solomon said. He introduced her to a woman named Mary Lynne, who was the office manager and would be training Joyce. Joyce was excited to get started.

She didn't call Alim until her two o'clock in the afternoon lunch. She didn't want to interrupt him during his busiest time. It had been a busy day for her too. She did notice two missed calls from Alim, one at eleven o'clock in the morning and another at twelve in the afternoon. Alim didn't pick up, so Joyce proceeded to a little deli in the same complex to get a sandwich and a juice. Her lunch break was an hour since she had ten-hour days. She sat in the deli and thought of Alim, and that made her smile to herself. As she walked back to the office building, Alim called her back, but the conversation had to be short because Joyce was finished with her lunch break and didn't want to be late getting back to her office.

Joyce's day was finally finished, and she couldn't wait to get home and talk to Alim. She thought about stopping by the grocer's so she could cook a nice dinner for the two of them. She thought about lamb chops, but she didn't know if Alim would like them, so she decided on something more traditional, like pork chops with gravy or macaroni and cheese but became indecisive on what type of green vegetable to make on the side. She called Alim while she was still at the grocers to alert him that she was cooking dinner.

Alim was excited about that and agreed to be there at seven o'clock. He knew that he could go to his mother's house for a hot meal, but it was a very special welcome coming from his Joyce.

Joyce rushed home from the grocer's, slipped a movie in the DVD player, and began to cook.

"Something smells good in here!" Alim said as he headed over to the sink to wash his hands. Joyce just smiled as she set the table.

"I told my momma today that I have finally found love," Alim said exuberantly.

"Oh, wow. Did you, Alim?" Joyce asked bashfully.

"Yeah, she was surprised, skeptical, and happy—all three of those rolled up in one," Alim said with a chuckle. "Momma always wanted me to settle down, but we will see if my Joy can make me settled for good!" Alim winked at Joyce. "Yeah, baby. You have to pin me down hard. Joyce smiled but paid him no mind at all.

"The food is good, baby. How was your first day at work?" Alim asked between bites.

"It went well. It's a lot of work, but I think I'll enjoy working for this company," Joyce said in sincerity. She took in her surroundings as she conversed with Alim. It was the perfect setting for a married couple, where the husband comes home, sits down for dinner, and asks his wife about her day, and vice versa. It seemed like the perfect way to do things.

"I have to let you meet my momma, and maybe you could visit her church one day," Alim said.

"Okay, I look forward to that, Alim," Joyce said earnestly. "Does your mother live near you?"

"Well, not too far. She lives on the outskirts of the town," Alim replied, "but I don't particularly care for the country too much. That's why I got an apartment in town."

"Oh, I see," Joyce replied.

"You can come and stay the night with me tonight or tomorrow night Joy, it is up to you—that is, if you feel up to going to work from my place," Alim offered he sipped his red wine.

"Well, I will probably stay with you tomorrow night, Alim. All this cooking has got me tired. I haven't cooked like this in a long time, sweetheart, but it was worth it, and it made me feel good to see you eat like that. It lets me know that you enjoyed yourself, but I'm not your momma. I know you enjoyed my meal tonight," Joyce said, giggling a little as she gave him a kiss and took his plate. Alim proceeded to the sofa with his glass of red wine. Joyce's huge, comfy sofa always looked very inviting.

"Don't worry, baby, I'm not going to hold you up. After I finish this wine, I'll be on my way," Alim said, looking a little too comfy and ready for bed.

"Take your time, Alim. I'm all right. I'm just going to wash these dishes," Joyce said.

"I'll help!" Alim insisted. "If not, I will fall asleep, and I don't need to be feeling sleepy on the way home."

"Okay, you can dry while I wash," Joyce said.

"Oh, come on lady. You think I can't wash?" Alim said as he rolled up his sleeves and grabbed the dishcloth from Joyce.

"No. All right, I'll let you handle the wash, and I'll dry," Joyce laughed.

There was an amiable silence as they did the dishes. Alim then broke the silence by suggesting they take a trip before the summer's end. He wanted to go across the water, maybe the Caribbeans. Joyce was delighted about the idea but reminded Alim that she just started and couldn't take a long vacation so soon. Alim understood; he hadn't thought about that. He suggested Miami or something of the sort, and Joyce agreed.

As they discussed their plans, Alim gazed into Joyce's eyes. He told her how beautiful and sexy she looked, especially while preparing his meal and doing the dishes. He said she reminded him of the song "Sunshine" by Alexander O'Neal. Joyce told him that she always adored that song because it was very pretty.

Alim told Joyce something astonishing—that he knew he loved her before their first phone called even ended. Joyce herself couldn't quite put her finger on it, but she had also felt a deep connection with him from that first phone call. She told him she felt the same way.

Alim finished dishes and picked up his car keys. He gave Joyce a deep, lingering kiss.

"I am leaving now, baby, but I'll call you before bed," Alim said as he continued to kiss her. "Please call me if you need anything, and keep your doors locked. Sometimes I worry about you being out here all by yourself,"

"Oh, Alim. Thank you for worrying, but I am all right. You just be safe driving home and let me know that you have made it home," Joyce said.

After Alim left, Joyce thought about her experience at church; the sermon weighed heavily on her mind. She picked up her purse to find the notes that she had taken from the sermon. She went over to her bookshelf to get the Bible and fumbled through the pages to find the scriptures she had written down so that she could read them.

Something kept coming to Joyce's mind—maybe just a little premature worry. She was concerned at the fact that Alim had been married before. But why wasn't he now? He had explained that sometimes men do not make good mates forever, meaning that not all men are cut out for marriage. Joyce knew that there were two sides to every story, and it wasn't like Alim had given her the lame blame the ex-wife story. Joyce knew that Alim and his ex-stayed in contact because they had a daughter together, even though she was an adult now. Joyce didn't know fully how marriage and divorce worked she hasn't experienced either; she just knew the basics, which, to her, were love and fidelity. She knew now that she was feeling love for Alim. He seemed to be the best man to come into her life since a long, long time.

Joyce began to read St. John, verse sixteen; Exodus chapter twenty; Matthew chapter six verses eight through thirteen; and First Corinthians chapter thirteen and fourteen. Joyce continued to read until her eyelids grew heavy. She glanced at the clock. It was a little after midnight, and she had to get up at six o'clock in the morning.

She rose to the sound of her alarm clock going off. Thoughts of Alim ruminated through her mind. As a ritual, she brewed her coffee and ran her bath. Then the phone rang.

"Good morning, sweetheart," Alim said, his soft, smooth voice filling Joyce's heart with delight.

"Good morning, Alim," Joyce said, her heart beating. She loved that Alim started her day with his voice.

"Hey Joy, I wanted to know if you'd like to go to North Carolina with me this weekend. I know that it is short notice, but I told my daughter that I would see her," Alim said.

"Yes, sure Alim. I wouldn't mind taking the trip!" Joyce said excitedly.

"Good, baby. I'm happy to know that you are coming with me. I'll pick you up at work, okay? I'm not going to hold you, baby. I know that you're trying to get ready for work. I think about you all the time. I love you, Joy. Have a good day," Alim said earnestly.

"Oh, Alim. Have a wonderful day. I love you too," Joyce said. "I will always love you."

Deep inside, Joyce felt that she was going to fall hard for Alim, but she didn't care; she was just happy that she loved a man who loved her back and cared for her well-being.

After she finished getting ready for work, she quickly threw some items in her duffle bag for her weekend trip with Alim, including some shoes, lingerie, and a pantsuit. She didn't want to make the trip back home after work, even though she felt a little uneasy about leaving her house alone overnight. After working and spending so much time with Alim, she had begun to neglect her journal a little. She didn't want to take her laptop to Alim's place, so she figured she would edit her journal during her lunch break at work.

Alim drove up to her workplace, just as she was finishing up. Mr. Solomon then gave her some assignments for the next week and bade her good evening. Joyce was the last to leave the office on many occasions, but this week had been kind of tedious and the attorneys were staying later than usual today. Joyce greeted Alim with a kiss and hug.

"Hey, baby. What do you want for dinner?" Alim asked.

"Well, I feel like Chinese tonight," Joyce replied.

"Huh," Alim said with a laugh.

"What's so funny, Alim?" Joyce asked as she looked at him sideways. He was overcome with laughter.

"Oh, I never cared for Chinese, but I'll eat it because you want it. Now, I didn't say I hated it, but I will tolerate it tonight, just for you. I'm sure that they will have something appetizing for me," Alim said as he caressed Joyce's hand.

"Okay!" Joyce said with a laugh, curious to know why Alim didn't like Chinese food. But she didn't ask him for fear that he'd tell her something silly that would spoil her appetite.

Chapter 9

FAMILY TIES

A lim and Joyce arrived at his place with the Chinese food and her duffle bags, among other things. As Joyce walked in, she admired his spacious apartment.

"This is a nice spot! I love the painting and the carpeting," Joyce said, looking impressed.

"Thank you, sweetheart!" Alim said.

Alim then went over to the bedroom to take off his shirt and tie and told Joyce to get comfortable too. When Joyce slipped on some boy shorts and a tank top, Alim's eyes almost popped out of his head. He watched Joyce's perfectly curved body as she proceeded back to the dinner table.

"Alim, will your daughter feel weird about me visiting with you?" Joyce asked.

"Well, we must see about that. I have told her about you," Alim said, smiling at Joy.

"You have? What a surprise! Because some people don't say anything beforehand, but I appreciate the heads up!" Joyce said.

"Well, we are one now, Joyce, as it seems—so why not let everyone know?" Alim said.

"I am still a little surprised," Joyce said.

"Hmm, my family means a lot to me, Joyce," Alim said earnestly.

"Oh, I know, Alim. I wouldn't have thought of it any differently, and I apologize if I made you feel uncomfortable with what I said," Joyce said bashfully.

"No need to apologize, Joy. I knew where you were coming from, babe. It was just me being a little sensitive," Alim explained, kissing her nose.

"My brothers mean a lot to me too, so maybe we could go and visit them one weekend as well," Joyce suggested.

"I would like to, Joyce. No problem with that. But enough with the family talk. Let's concentrate on us—this is our time. We can talk about us if you like. You make me feel so good when I'm with you," Alim said, wrapping his arms around her waist and pulling her in for a kiss.

"You do the same for me too, Alim. I always love hearing your voice, and I melt at your touch," Joyce said, moaning a little as Alim kissed her neck.

"Joy, please let me know if you decide to step away from me, seriously," Alim said earnestly.

"I'm not going anywhere, Alim—unless you decide that you don't want to be with me anymore," Joyce said, burying her head in Alim's firm chest.

"That won't happen, Joy," Alim said earnestly, and they both sat back down to finish their dinner.

"So, how did your daughter take the news that you're in a serious relationship now?"

"Oh, she didn't mind at all. She knows the situation between her momma and I, and she understood it. At first, she was not well with it, but she has matured," Alim explained.

"Oh," Joyce said.

"My daughter's name is Melanie. She's a daddy's girl for sure. Her momma and I were so young and still in school when she got pregnant with Melanie. We stayed together until we broke up when Melanie turned five, Alim said, looking reminiscent.

"Wow, what happened?" Joyce asked.

"Well, you know the obvious—or maybe you don't since you haven't been married or had any children. But anyway, I love my daughter, and I stayed in her life because I didn't want any other man raising my child; I will never understand how men can be comfortable with that. I just don't get it," Alim said.

"That's good, Alim. We both know that many men turn their backs on their children once they are separated from their significant others," Joyce said, listening attentively to Alim's story.

"Well, I loved her, and still cared for her momma, but after a couple of years of trying to make it work, we realized that we weren't compatible. I think we both knew from before, but we didn't want to accept that for the sake of the baby," Alim said, looking earnest.

"Oh, I see. So, what made you two realize that you weren't meant for one another?" Joyce asked curiously.

"We didn't agree on anything," Alim said.

"Oh, so don't tell me that you're not divorced yet because you told me you were," Joyce said a little sadly.

"You know, Joyce, we never discussed divorce at the time since neither one of us thought it was important, and the subject never came up," Alim said.

"Hmm," Joyce said as she dropped her head and looked down into her hands with a confused look on her face again.

"Joy, honey, what's wrong? I am divorced now. I just got a divorce a couple of months ago. It took a while, but we finally did it because she was thinking of getting married again. Honey, it was just something that we didn't think about because we were comfortable with the way things were, but I know that meeting someone would change things. So don't look like that. I am divorced now, and I can prove it to you. I have the papers," Alim said, looking panicked.

Joyce decided not to ask any more questions. She got up and started to clear the table before asking Alim if he enjoyed his chicken wings from the Chinese restaurant. Alim just nodded his head. Suddenly, while Joyce was standing at the sink, she burst out laughing.

"What's so funny, babe?" Alim asked.

"Oh, nothing much; just thinking about something that happened at work today," Joyce said.

"No, Joyce. Are you being a little sarcastic with me? or do you feel like I betrayed you by not telling you everything? Is that why you started to laugh?" Alim said, a quiet anger simmering in his tone.

"No, it's all right. I guess I just laughed out of a little hurt and shock. I didn't mean anything bad," Joyce said quietly. Deep down inside, she knew she wasn't all right, but she tried to put the whole thing out of her mind. "Man, I will never get any more wings from that place again because that's one thing they don't know how to make," she said lightly, trying to change the subject.

Alim rose to massage her shoulders, realizing he needed to ease the tension between them. Joyce sighed.

"You know all the right spots that need attention," Joyce said as she enjoyed the massage, her eyes closed.

"Just trying to relax you, baby. I didn't mean for our night together to be hectic," Alim said.

"No harm done," Joyce said.

They had a long drive the next day, so Alim suggested that he and Joyce get ready for bed. Their night consisted of lovemaking and late-night snacking, but they managed to get an early start in the morning to head to North Carolina. Joyce napped a little while Alim drove, but she didn't want to sleep too much, so she had Alim stop for coffee. They stopped at a nearby McDonald's off the highway for coffee and breakfast sandwiches. The road was terribly busy, but Alim seemed to enjoy driving and traveling with her. They held hands at times, and even kissed while Alim drove.

Upon driving to North Carolina, they drove past some hotels.

"Joy, this is Greenville, North Carolina," Alim said when he noticed her looking curiously out the car window.

"Oh, okay. It's a nice town, and some of the areas that we have been through remind me a little of Chicago," Joyce said.

"My daughter should be expecting me sometime this evening, but I will call her later to let her know that I'm in town. Let's get a little rest before we meet up with Melanie. She is full of energy," Alim laughed.

"Yeah, you're right, honey. I am kind of tired as well," Joyce said.

"I will also show you around Greenville later. I come here a lot to visit my daughter and to take her shopping. Sometimes we also go to Raleigh too. I don't know if we'll go there tonight, though, because I don't really feel like it. Maybe tomorrow morning, or at least before we go home. Melanie loves to drag me to the malls. Raleigh is a little better for shopping and nightlife. You'll like it," Alim said sleepily.

Joyce wanted to stay at the Holiday Inn, and Alim quickly obliged. After checking into their suite, they fell fast asleep. Alim had asked the desk clerk to give them a wake-up call; he didn't want to oversleep.

After being woken up by the call, Alim called his daughter, who was elated to hear that he had gotten into town and was anxious to meet Joyce. Joyce had mixed feelings about meeting Melanie because she had never dated a man with children before, and she didn't know what to expect. Alim promised his daughter dinner and maybe some shopping if time allowed all the traveling that evening. Alim and Melanie then said, "I love you" to each other before hanging up.

Joyce decided not to worry about impressions; she was going to let the weekend flow in the way that it chose to. She was not a pretender, and she always wore her heart and emotions on her sleeve.

Melanie arrived at the hotel and waited for her dad and Joyce in the lobby. She scurried toward her dad as soon as she saw him exit the elevator doors.

"Hi, Daddy!" Melanie said.

"Hi, baby!" Alim said as he hugged and kissed Melanie.

"This must be Joyce!" Melanie said, clutching onto her dad for dear life.

"Yes, it is. And Joyce, this is my pride and joy, Melanie," Alim said, reaching down to kiss Melanie's forehead.

"It's a pleasure to meet you, Melanie. What a pretty outfit. Love that skirt set!" Joyce said.

"It's nice to meet you too, Joyce, and thank you for the compliment!" Melanie replied. "Let's go and sit at the hotel bar for a little bit before dinner," she suggested.

"Okay, honey," Alim agreed.

"Do you mind, Joyce?" Melanie asked.

"No, not at all," Joyce said.

Joyce was noticing just how bubbly Melanie was. She seemed like a really sweet young lady. Joyce remembered Alim telling her that Melanie was a happy child, and he was right.

"So what time are you leaving tomorrow, Daddy?" Melanie asked.

"Perhaps around six o'clock in the evening," Alim answered.

"Oh, so we have some time for shopping. Are we going to Raleigh? Do you feel up to it, Daddy?" Melanie asked.

"Yeah, honey," Alim said.

Joyce stayed silent, listening to Alim and Melanie's conversation.

"No boyfriends, right Melanie?" Alim said with a serious look on his face.

"Oh, Daddy, come on with that now! And no, no boyfriends yet—did you hear that I said 'yet'?" Melanie asked teasingly. "Daddy, you know that it will happen one day; maybe tomorrow, you never know!"

"I know, Mel. Now don't get smart. I was just checking on you, like I always do." Alim said with a serious expression.

"Daddy, you know that I would tell you if I had a boyfriend or was talking to someone seriously," Melanie said.

"Okay, honey. Glad to clear that up," Alim said.

Joyce sipped her wine, astonished by the conversation between father and daughter but also deeply moved by their close relationship. She admired how pretty Melanie was. Melanie looked as if she had Black, Indian, and white heritage, but she looked just like Alim—a spitting image! Her facial expressions and features were all Alim and so was her long, silken hair. Alim had never mentioned what race Melanie's mother was; Joyce always assumed she was Black before even meeting Melanie, but she guessed it wasn't that important. Melanie was beautiful, and she reminded Joyce of a model. She was slender, with long legs and pecan brown skin.

"Joyce, how do you like Savannah? Daddy told me that you were new there. I love Savannah myself," Melanie said.

"I like it a lot, Melanie, but I am still trying to get used to it," Joyce replied.

"You'll like Raleigh too if you're a shopper, which I can tell you are. And if you enjoy the nightlife, there are so many stores and jazz clubs here!" Melanie said.

"Hey, I love jazz!" Joyce exclaimed.

"I do too, Joyce, and a lot of older people act as if they are surprised when I say that because I think they assume that the majority of young people are geared toward rap and R&B, which merges the rap thing, but I love all types of music, and I am very fond of jazz."

"I think that's good, Melanie," Joyce replied.

"Yes, you're right, Joyce, and now where do we want to go for dinner? Have you ever had Mexican food, Joyce?" Melanie asked.

"To tell you the truth, Melanie, I've never had Mexican food," Joyce replied.

"Oh, okay then. Well, what about Italian?" Melanie asked.

"Yes, I love Italian!" Joyce said.

"Daddy, you want Italian?"

"Sure, why not? I think that the decision was already made for me any-way," Alim said with mock sarcasm.

"Guess what, Daddy?"

"Okay, what Melanie?" Alim asked.

"I am treating us to dinner tonight," Melanie announced.

"What? What?!" Alim replied, laughing. "Thank you, baby. I am in total shock. You must be making big bucks now! But Mel, you don't have to pay for dinner, I got this."

"No, Daddy, I don't mind treating you and Joyce!"

"Thank you, Melanie, that's sweet of you," Joyce said.

"Daddy, we can go in my truck; you'll see that I am still taking care of it." Melanie turned to Joyce. "Daddy bought me this Tahoe, and he thought that I wasn't going to take care of it, but I love this vehicle, so I take good care of it," Melanie said proudly.

"Oh," Joyce said with a smile.

"I'm impressed!" Alim said.

"Daddy, you can sit up front with me," Melanie said proudly.

"Ok, you women can have your way today," Alim said, looking Melanie and Joyce proudly. Joyce and Melanie just smiled.

"Daddy, momma told me to say hello," Melanie said.

"How is she doing?" Alim asked.

"She's fine. She's still trying to publish her book of short stories while saving up for her trip to Hawaii next year," Melanie said. Joyce sat in the seat behind them and soaked in the conversation between her man and his spoiled but beautiful daughter.

"Oh, I see that she still stays busy with the writing," Alim said.

"Yes, Daddy. She writes every day," Melanie said.

"That's good that she still loves to write, I have read some of her stuff, and she's good; she has talent. I can say that much about her," Alim said. He turned around.

"Are you okay back there, Joyce? You're so quiet," he asked.

"Yes, I am fine. I'm just enjoying the view." Joyce said.

"I'll be glad when she can get her writing published. Working in the sales department in that hotel keeps her busy, but I am glad she is steady at her job because it seemed as though her writing was consuming her life," Melanie said.

"That's her passion, Mel. And writing can be a passion like anything else," Alim said.

"I know, Daddy. Oh, we're here now! This is one of my favorite restaurants in Raleigh. I don't come here often, just for special occasions like this one," Melanie said happily. Once they entered the restaurant, Joyce and Melanie headed for the ladies' room as Alim sat in the waiting area to be called for an available table.

"Yes, we would like a private booth or table," Alim said to the hostess.

"Sure, sir. Just follow me," the hostess said as she led him to a cozy booth in the corner. Your waitress will be with you momentarily," She replied.

"Thank you," Alim responded with a smile.

"Hey, Daddy. I see that you got a nice spot!" Melanie said.

"Yes, honey, kind of private, just the way I like it for my two ladies and I," Alim said with a candid smile. The atmosphere was warm, and they talked and laughed the evening away.

"So, Daddy, are we going to Raleigh tomorrow before you leave?" Melanie asked, her tone hopeful.

"Yes, honey, but it has to be early because Joy and I have to get back to Savannah so that we can rest up for work on Monday."

"Okay!" Melanie said as she signaled the waitress for the check. Melanie paid the waitress, and they proceeded to leave. As Melanie drove back to the hotel, she told Joyce how pleased she was to finally meet her, and that she hoped that they could get together again soon. Joyce also told her she was enjoying their time together. Alim kissed his daughter farewell and told her that he would see her tomorrow.

"I will be here bright and early tomorrow, Daddy!"

"I know that you will, sweetheart. Make sure that you call or text me to let me know that you have gotten home," Alim said, kissing Melanie again before she drove away.

Alim and Joyce went inside the hotel and sat at the bar for a nightcap before going up to their room. Joyce told Alim how much she enjoyed Melanie's company and how lovely and smart Melanie was. Alim beamed with pride as Joyce talked about Melanie.

"I'm glad you enjoyed meeting Mel, Joyce. She's an angel. I was kind of nervous at first because I didn't know how you were going to make of her. Some women do not respect or understand that part of me."

"I see that you are a proud father, and you deserve nothing but respect for that. Melanie is still young. She needs the father as well as the mother."

"Let's go and hit the sack, Joyce; an early day awaits us tomorrow," Alim said shyly, changing the subject.

He then smiled a little, letting Joyce know that he was hearing her. "Yes, I am a proud father."

Mel was waiting in the lobby the next morning. Alim and Joyce brought their baggage down for an early check out.

"Good morning!" Melanie called.

"Good morning!" Alim and Joyce said in unison as they greeted Melanie with a hug and kiss. They were off for their trip to Raleigh but drove in separate rides because Alim would be on his way back home to Savannah after the shopping spree.

Joyce was amazed by how many things Alim bought for her and Melanie. Joyce wasn't expecting anything from Alim; she was planning to spend her own money, but he had insisted the day was on him, and he treated both women well. After picking up shoes, bags, and outfits, Alim must have spent over fifteen hundred dollars on both women, but he didn't mind if they were having a good time.

"Daddy, aren't you going to get something for yourself?" Melanie asked.

"No, not this time, honey. I don't need anything for myself right now," Alim said, checking his phone for missed calls. Melanie and Joyce just smiled.

"Okay all, time is passing, and we have to get on the road," he insisted, and they headed toward the parking lot.

"All right, Daddy, but I am going to stay in Raleigh for a little while," Melanie said.

"Be careful, sweetheart. I love you. I'll call you tonight," Alim said as he hugged and kissed Melanie. Melanie turned to give Joyce a hug as well, which she graciously returned.

"I'll talk to you soon too Melanie!" Joyce said.

"Have a safe trip. Later!" Melanie said as everyone parted ways. Alim and Joyce's trip was tiresome, but they made it back in good time. After getting back to Savannah, Joyce gathered all her things from Alim's apartment to get on the road back home, where she hadn't been in a couple of days. Joyce thanked Alim again for all the nice things that he had bought her in Raleigh.

"This has been such a long day. I must hurry home and get ready for work tomorrow," Joyce sighed.

"I know, baby," Alim said sympathetically as he rubbed Joyce's hand. "You don't want to stop and get anything to eat before you go in?"

"No, I'm good. I'll find something to eat when I get home," Joyce responded. On the way home, Joyce thought about her trip to North Carolina and her meeting with the bubbly and pretty Melanie. Joyce thought about whether Alim was ready to settle down and maybe start thinking of marriage again. That made her think of church. She felt a little guilty for missing it this week but promised herself she would be there next Sunday.

He's just too good to be true, Joyce thought as Alim dropped her home. *I adore everything about this man.*

Chapter 10

I Will Always Love You

Joyce was having a great time at her new job. Everything was going according to plan, and she was grateful for the comfort and stability her new job provided. A new church in mind and a man. Life couldn't get any better for her.

Alim would often call her at work, which made her feel secure in their relationship, knowing that she was always on his mind. Sunday came and Joyce got ready for church, but Alim would be attending his home church that Sunday. Alim made plans for Joyce to meet his mother after work, and Joyce agreed. They would be going to his mother's house for dinner. His mother was eagerly anticipating meeting her. Joyce was extremely nervous about this but looking forward to it too. That day, the pastor gave a sermon on relationships and marriage, which made Joyce feel a little uneasy, but she planned to go home after dinner at Alim's mother's house and looked over the notes she took during the sermon.

Alim met Joyce at her house after church to take her to his mother's house.

"Are you ready, Joy?" Alim asked.

"Yes!" Joyce replied.

"Momma cooked a lot of good food and even made some desserts," Alim said.

"Wow, I can't wait," Joyce exclaimed nervously.

When they arrived at Momma Belle's house, Joyce could smell the aroma as they pulled into the driveway.

"Momma, you're not going to hug me first?" Alim asked playfully.

"Oh hush, boy, you know how I love you, and I know you!" Momma Belle said.

"It's a pleasure to meet you, Ms. Bell," Joyce said.

"Call me Momma Sweetie or Momma Belle. I've heard so many good things about you from Alim, and you are just as Melanie said," Momma Belle said, peering at Joyce's face.

"Thank you," Joyce replied.

Joyce and Alim held hands as they walked into his mother's house.

"I will always love you," Alim whispered in Joyce's ear. Joyce's heart melted; she blushed and whispered the same back to Alim.

"Momma Belle, it smells so good in here," Joyce said happily.

"Oh, sweetheart, I made a little of everything today," Momma Belle said.

"Hey, Momma. Where's the remote? I want to watch the game, football preseason just started," Alim said. Joyce and Momma Belle stayed in the kitchen and talked while Momma put the final touches on her meal. Joyce went into the parlor for a minute to have a look at the pictures of Alim that were placed on the mantle and hung on the wall. Joyce admired Alim's school pictures, even giggling a little.

"You have a handsome family, Alim," Joyce said with a smile.

"I know." Alim chuckled.

"Okay, you two. It's time to eat!" Momma Belle called.

When everybody sat down, they blessed the food. They enjoyed a good ole Southern meal with pies and cakes and some homemade iced tea.

After the dinner and once the game had finished, Joyce and Alim decided to head out. It was getting late, and they both had to get ready for work the next day.

"Momma Belle, thank you for your gracious hospitality. I enjoyed everything!" Joyce said appreciatively.

"My pleasure, Joyce, I hope you don't be a stranger now. Drop by anytime," Momma Belle said politely.

"She will be back for sure, and I will call you tomorrow, Momma," Alim vowed.

"Okay, baby, be careful now, and have a good night," Momma Belle said as she hugged Joyce.

"You have a good night too, and see you later," Joyce said as they gathered in the car. Alim leaned over and kissed Joyce.

"You want to come over for a little while before going home?" Alim asked.

"Come to my place," Joyce said. She didn't feel like packing clothes for an overnight visit.

"Okay, baby," Alim said. They made love for hours that night, and Joyce felt so close to Alim, more so than any other night, especially after he whispered in her ear again, "I will always love you."

Joyce's summer was divine, sweet, and very eventful. Savannah had brought her love and companionship. Her job was perfect, and it was a position she longed for and had come all the way from Chicago to take.

As the summer ended, as Joyce's spiritual life began to take another turn too. She began to attend church and Bible study regularly. She was enjoying life and its many adventurous. Alim didn't attend his home church much, but he did attend Joyce's church occasionally. Joyce didn't give herself to God totally, but she loved God for bringing her Alim. Something did stick in her mind from one of the sermons that her pastor preached on that Sunday. The "love from God" and the "love of God," the latter being much more important, as she was being taught. The alter calls at church would always make Joyce feel a little guilty she never attempted to attend one. Alim was the center of her life. She loved God, but she knew deep down that God wasn't first in her life, even though she tried to convince herself that He was. Alim had her hooked and totally in love with him. He treated her well and his words, "I will always love you" were ingrained in her mind and heart. Joyce knew that Alim meant it; she knew God loved her too, so that meant that she had it all, and she couldn't be moved by anything else.

Chapter 11

Autumn's Proposal

As fall approached and the days and nights grew cooler, Alim and Joyce spoke about family, marriage, and babies. This wasn't a topic Joyce dreamt of discussing before with any man, but Alim was different. He was her soul mate. She could see her future now, and Alim was in it forever. Momma often called Joyce, and they went shopping and to church functions together. Joyce also heard from Melanie occasionally and saw her when she visited Momma Belle and Alim.

Joyce loved autumn; it was her favorite time of the year. She loved the array of colors that the leaves would turn as they fell to the ground.

That Saturday morning, Joyce decided to rake her own leaves in her yard. She didn't mind the chore too much. Suddenly, her cell phone rang. It was Alim.

"Hey, baby! I would like you to come to Momma's house for dinner tonight. Is that okay with you? And by the way, what are you doing? You sound like you are out of breath."

"Nothing much, just raking the leaves in the yard," Joyce said proudly.

"Huh, you're doing what? Joyce, I could have paid someone to do that for you. You shouldn't be doing that. Now you have just made me feel bad that I didn't take notice. Woman!" Alim admonished.

"It's okay, Alim. I enjoyed it!" Joyce said as she laughed at Alim getting all bothered about the situation.

"No, baby, this is your last time doing this chore. You're not going to be doing that kind of strenuous work unless we do it together. Why didn't you call me?" he asked sternly.

"I just wanted to do it myself!" Joyce said.

"All right, but not again," Alim said.

"What time should I come to Momma's house?" Joyce asked.

"Around five o'clock," Alim said.

"Raking leaves. I can't believe it," Alim groaned to himself.

"Stop it, Alim! It's okay!" Joyce said, feeling a little frustrated now.

"Okay, baby, I will let it go for now," Alim said.

"I see you later," Joyce said.

"Okay, baby," Joyce said.

Joyce felt a little worn out from raking the leaves and handling those huge trash bags. She was just finishing up when Caroline, her friend from the church, called. Joyce loved talking to Caroline, who was positive, honest, and loved God. Caroline was married with three teenage children and had been a Christian for a long time, so she was good company for Joyce. She recounted to Caroline about how extreme Alim had gotten about her raking the leaves, and they both laughed about the situation. Caroline could tell that Alim was a little overprotective.

"Caroline, thank you for your help on the Bible question that I had; sometimes I do not completely understand all that I read, but there is something that I want to share with you. I do not talk to anyone but you about my concerns, and not even Alim because I don't think he would understand—or maybe he would, and I just haven't given him the chance to understand what I feel or think," Joyce said, feeling overwhelmed with confusion.

"Joyce, maybe you should discuss the things with Alim that concern the both of you. It can help if he is also aware of things that maybe bother you," Caroline advised.

"I have been going to church regularly, attending Sunday school and Bible study classes, yet there is something missing. I have a wonderful relationship, an awesome job, but why is it, just why, that as happy as I am, I don't feel as happy as I should be, Caroline? There is something missing. Why am I feeling this way?" Joyce asked frustratedly.

"Joyce, I am just going to give it to you point-blank. You must surrender yourself to God completely—no half stepping—and He will make you whole. You will feel that inner peace in your life. God will guide your footsteps."

Joy sat quietly on the phone, still confused, but she listened to all that Caroline had to say.

"A little is not enough, Joyce. It must be all or nothing—only then will you feel complete," Caroline said earnestly.

"Okay, Caroline. I hear you and thank you. I must get cleaned up. Momma Belle is expecting me for dinner," Joyce said.

"Remember the things that I have said, okay?" Caroline said.

"Okay, Caroline, and thank you," Joyce said as she hung up the phone. She knew that Caroline would not hold back anything and that she loved her like a sister and did not judge her.

Evening was approaching and Joyce began to get ready to meet Alim at Momma Belle's house for dinner. When she approached Momma Belle's driveway, she was surprised to see Melanie's vehicle there. Alim came out to greet Joyce as she parked.

"Hey, baby!" Alim said.

"Alim, why didn't you tell me that Melanie was going to be here? What a pleasant surprise!" Joyce exclaimed.

"Hi, Joyce!" Melanie said, running toward Joyce to hug her.

"Hi, Sweetie. It's good to see you. How are things going?" Joyce asked, hugging Melanie back.

"Well, come on in, Joyce. Grandma cooked a lot of good food today. She even made some of my favorite desserts," Melanie said excitedly, ushering them all in.

"Momma Belle, that cake looks so good. What kind is it?" Joyce asked.

"Oh, girl. This is my famous upside-down pineapple cake." Momma Belle said in her deep Southern drawl.

"Wow, I know that cake is going to be good," Joyce said.

"Everyone comes on into that dining area to sit and eat. I made all y'all favorites tonight; well, almost all your favorites," Momma said.

Chicken, mac and cheese, collards, fried fish, and cornbread were some of Joyce's favorite foods.

"Momma Belle, what's the occasion? Joyce asked.

"Momma. How well do I know my lady? Didn't I tell you she would ask you what the occasion is if you told her, you made all her favorite items?" Alim chuckled. He then turned to Joyce.

"Well, Joy. I have something to ask you," he said.

"What is going on, y'all?" Joyce asked nervously. Suddenly, she had an inkling of what was about to take place next. Alim walked to the living room, got the white satin ring box off the mantle, which was hidden behind the pictures, and walked back to Joyce.

"Joy, have a seat right here on this recliner because I want you to be comfortable as I asked this question. I will kneel here beside you—or no, I will change this entire thing up. I will sit in the recliner, and you sit on my lap. I want this to be very personal, baby," Alim said he looked seriously at Joyce.

Joyce was already crying a little. She couldn't hold in her tears, and she was already overwhelmed. Momma and Melanie stood standing next to Alim on each side of the chair as he knelt before Joyce.

"Joyce, you are my world and have made me so very happy. Your name is perfect suited to you because you bring me a lot of positivity and joy. Baby, will you marry me forever?" Alim asked as he looked into her eyes.

Joyce looked up at Alim as he extended a three-carat diamond ring toward her finger. "Yes," she whispered, and she began to laugh and cry at the same time.

They hugged and kissed, and Momma Belle and Melanie were also teary-eyed. Joyce said, "I love you," as Alim put the ring on her finger; it fit perfectly. The diamond was beyond beautiful.

"Let me see!" Melanie and Momma Belle yelled in unison. The excitement in the house was overwhelming. They started dinner and Momma Belle poured some white wine.

"Alim, this ring is so beautiful. I am sorry if I seem giddy, everyone, but I am still shocked at what just happened. I think it still hasn't hit me yet!" Joyce said.

"Joyce, can I be your maid of honor?" Melanie asked.

"Okay, Melanie. Momma Belle, can you help with catering!" Joyce asked.

"Of course. Sure!"

"Look at me, making wedding plans while this whole still seems like a big dream!" Joyce said, and everyone chuckled. "I am engaged in autumn, and how perfect—it's my favorite season! I don't even know what month to plan the wedding for; it will all come to me. Oh, and Alim, I see that you are quiet. You don't know the wedding date either?" Joyce said.

"Not yet, Joyce. We will discuss that later," Alim said.

"Okay. I must call my brothers, and Caroline, my new church friend," Joyce said.

"I am so glad that you've found a friend," Momma Belle said.

"Yes, she's a sweet lady and very helpful to me. I think that I will ask her to be in my wedding. Momma Belle, this cake is good. Everything is just perfect this evening! And this ring is just so gorgeous that I can't stop looking at it," Joyce said.

"Joy, are you going to church tomorrow?" Alim asked.

"Yes, why do you ask?" Joyce asked.

"Just asking, honey."

"Joyce, Alim tells me that you were raking and bagging leaves today. How come you didn't ask for help, honey?" Momma Belle asked.

"Oh no, Momma Belle. Don't tell me he told you that too. I wanted to do it all myself; it's my pleasure to be spending autumn here in the south. I am so grateful and happy to be here—not that I don't miss Chicago, because I still do, but I prefer to be here," Joyce said happily.

"I see how happy you are, Joyce, but raking those leaves is a hard job, and I think that Alim was just a little concerned," Momma Belle said.

"I know," Joyce said. He giggled and got up to hug Alim.

"Y'all have been so good to me. This was such a great evening, but I need to get home; I have Sunday school in the morning," Joyce said.

"We will be leaving soon enough," Alim said.

Chapter 12

Lay It at the Altar

The phone rang, and Joyce awoke to the ringtone.

"Good morning on this good Sunday!" Joyce's brother's voice was on the other end of the line.

"Hi Brian, I guess you got the message I left for you last night on your cell," Joyce said.

"Yeah, congratulations! And I must meet that southern dude that swept you off your feet, but I am happy that my little sis engaged now. Are you sure that this man is good to you and for you?" Brian said.

"Stop it, Brian!" Joyce said, giggling. "But yes, he's the one. Hey, Brian, tell Leon to call me. I left a message on his answering machine."

"He'll call, Misty. You know that he is always tied up with some woman, but he won't forget his baby sis," Brian said.

"Alim calls me Joy, and you and the family still call me Misty.

"Well, you are Joy, and that name, Alim. Isn't that a Muslim name?" Brian asked.

"Maybe, but Alim is not a Muslim," Joyce said.

"So, when will we get to see you, Misty? Leon and I were thinking of coming to visit you, or you can come to Chicago; however, it works out is fine with me, as long as we see you soon," Brian said.

"It would be great to see you both. I really do miss you both terribly. I'll be coming to visit you around the holidays, maybe Thanksgiving or Christmas," Joyce said.

"Okay, baby sis. I know that you must get ready for church now. I'm not going to hold you up. Say a prayer for me and Leon and do what you always do best and play Misty for us, you know what I mean—stay alert and cool, and remain smart as you always are, honey. I love you, baby sis," Brian said.

"Love you too!" Joyce said as she hung up the phone. Joyce felt that she was going to miss Sunday school today. She would look forward to the eleven o'clock service. The phone rang again, and she knew that it was Alim this time.

"Hello," Joyce answered.

"Hi, baby. How is your Sunday morning going so far?" Alim asked.

"Hi, Alim. I just got off the phone with my brother Brian," Joyce replied.

"How are they doing?" Alim asked.

"They're doing great. They just miss me a little, that's all. I told them about my engagement, and they were so happy for me," Joyce said excitedly.

"I'm glad to hear that, Joy. I know that you are getting ready for church, and I won't keep you. I just wanted to holla at my beautiful fiancée," Alim said.

"Are you going to church today, Alim?" Joyce asked.

"Maybe. I don't know yet, honey. Have a good day, and I will talk to you later," Alim said.

"I love you, Alim," Joyce said earnestly.

"Love you too, honey," Alim replied.

Joyce was feeling kind of tired, but she felt that she should still try to make it to church.

"Oh wow, I forgot communion was this Sunday!" Joyce said to herself. As she approached the church parking lot, it dawned on her that Alim didn't like going to church as much as she did, or at least he didn't find it too important. She decided to talk to him about that soon. Joyce was getting more involved with the church scene and learning again how to praise and worship the Lord.

Caroline approached Joyce to greet her with a hug as the usher lead them all to their seats. Caroline asked Joyce if she wanted to sit with her and her family, and Joyce accepted their offer, even though Joyce liked where she sat. She didn't mind sitting with Caroline and her family for just that one Sunday. Pastor Hinton would give another good sermon that Sunday. It was a sermon about conviction and the blood of Jesus Christ. Joyce listened attentively as she flipped though the scriptures. She noticed how Caroline nodded along with the pastor's words, and how she worshipped the Lord throughout the sermon. Joyce could that Caroline was always peace with herself, no matter what she was going through. She seemed to have it all. Pastor Hinton talked about not having peace without Jesus Christ, that he died for all our sins, that we should accept him as our Lord and Savior, and that there is no other way.

Pastor Hinton then spoke over the pulpit: "Our lives will never be complete, and the Lord shall always be the center of our lives. Our homes and our relationships should be centered around God. You can't say you love God if you don't follow him and worship him. You can't say you have Jesus if you never turn your life over to the Lord completely. The Lord will keep in perfect peace those who minds stay on him."

Joyce started to weep a little, and Caroline began to console her by holding her hand. Joyce's concerns were all being answered by the pastor's message this afternoon.

"You need to give up all your sins by acknowledging Jesus Christ and lay all your sins at the altar. God loves you and wants to keep you in the realm of his blessings by giving you the gift of the Holy Spirit. Jesus died that we may have life and have it more abundantly. He wants to take all your sins and wash them away, forever and forgotten. Your heart will be in contempt without Jesus Christ." Pastor Hinton was full of messages that hit Joyce directly in the heart.

Joyce knew what she had to do. All through the sermon, she was overwhelmed with conviction until her cell phone starting ringing in the small purse that she had strapped around her shoulders. She checked the phone to see who was calling her—Alim—but it was a text message instead, telling her to call him as soon as church was over.

Joyce was always overwhelmed with glee whenever Alim called her, but she knew that presently, she was being taken in by the conviction of Jesus wanting to be in her soul. After the sermon, Pastor Hinton called for all the unsaved who wanted to lay their sins at the altar. Joyce's heart and mind told her to go, but the pride in her feet wouldn't allow her to make the steps. Caroline just glanced at Joyce and smiled, but she didn't push. Joyce noticed numerous people going to lay all their sins at the altar, but she felt that it wasn't her time just yet. After the altar call and the call for healing, Joyce said goodbye to Caroline and proceeded to leave. On her way out, she called Alim.

"Is church over, Joy?" Alim asked.

"Almost; they are finishing up now," Joyce responded. She suddenly felt so uneasy in her heart and soul as she spoke to Alim.

"I want to take you out to eat," Alim said.

"Okay," Joyce responded.

"I'll meet you at your house within an hour, Joy."

"Okay," Joyce replied.

"Is everything okay, Joy? You sound kind of down." Alim asked.

"Sure, Alim. I'm fine. I will see you soon," Joyce said.

"Okay, baby. See you soon," Alim said. Joyce cried a little on the way home because she knew she should have made that altar call, but she told herself she had enough time to do that.

Once at home, Joyce changed her clothes and prepared to meet Alim for their dinner date. Just then, the phone rang. It was Caroline.

"Hi Joyce, I was checking in on you," Caroline said.

"Hi Caroline, I'm fine," Joyce replied.

"Call me if you need anything, Joyce."

"Okay, have a good evening," Joyce said. Joyce knew why Caroline called. Caroline saw that Joyce's face was despondent, and she could also feel that her heart was too. She wanted Joyce to accept Jesus as her personal savior so that she could have peace and an incredibly happy life, no matter what, but obviously Joyce wasn't ready.

Joyce's thoughts ran deep—if she accepted Jesus into her life, would Alim understand? She didn't want to lose Alim because life was going so great for her. She thought about talking to Alim about going to church with her, and maybe they could go down to the altar together. *Alim knows about church and what it entails,* Joyce thought, *so it may just be a matter of time—but how much time?*

A little later, Alim arrived at Joyce's house. Joyce was rushing around, getting dressed and putting the finishing touches on her makeup. Alim peered through the screen door and asked Joyce if she was ready to go.

"I'm ready, Alim! I'll be right there!" Joyce yelled as she continued to rush.

"Okay, Joy. I'll wait for you in the car," Alim said. Joyce finally came outside.

"So, how was church today?" Alim asked.

"It was a good and a well-preached sermon. You should have come and joined me today," Joyce said.

"I know, Joy, but I was so tired," Alim said, sounding a little irritated.

"I know, Alim. I was tired too, but I still went," Joyce said, also sounding a little irritated.

There was a pause for about two minutes until Joyce blurted out, "Alim, you really need to start coming to church with me more often than you do!"

"I will start, Joy. Please don't pressure me right now about that," Alim replied angrily.

"I just asked, and you don't have to be angry about the question. There's no harm in me asking, is there?" Joyce replied.

"So now, church. Are you having second thoughts about me, Joy?" Alim asked softly.

"No, Alim. You shouldn't go there. You know that I was just asking about us attending church together because it will be healthy for our relationship. And you know that you mean a lot to me, so don't question me about having second thoughts about our relationship. You know better than that. I love you so much that you know that you don't have to be doubtful, even if we do disagree on things," Joy said sincerely.

Joyce, she didn't feel good about this new turn her relationship was taking. It almost made her feel like she was violating him when she asked him certain things.

"Okay, Alim. I'm sorry for asking. Dang, you make me feel so bad," Joyce said, looking confused about what just transpired. Alim didn't respond for a few minutes.

"Momma wants you to call her so you two can talk about the wedding," he said, changing the subject altogether.

"Okay, tell her that I'll call her. She'll also want to know the date. We can set a date now. I don't see why we need to prolong it, Alim," Joyce said a little sarcastically, but she continued to smile.

"So what date is it, Joy? It's your call," Alim replied.

"This may sound strange, Alim, but can we set a date for next fall?" Joyce asked a little girlishly.

"The autumn, Joy? Most couples have their weddings in the summer. I don't know about the fall. I know that I proposed this fall, but that was only because I couldn't wait, and I know that you like the autumn season a great deal, but I didn't have any intentions to get married in the fall," Alim said.

"I know, Alim. I love the fall and the comfort of it, and I know that it seems kind of odd, but it will be a beautiful wedding. That will make me very happy!" Joyce said.

"Okay, Joy. I will have to get used to that idea," Alim said, chuckling a little. So did Joy. Joyce and Alim finally arrived at a famous steakhouse in Savannah that Joyce had never been to before.

"This is a nice restaurant," Joyce said.

"Yes, I love this place, but I haven't been here in a while. The food is excellent, and it is always crowded here, especially on Sundays," Alim said.

Joyce and Alim got settled at their table and started to look through the menu. Prior to dinner they ordered some red wine. As Joyce looked around the restaurant, she noticed some familiar faces from church, but she hardly knew those people well enough to converse with them. *They probably don't recognize me anyway,* she thought. When the waitress came over, they placed their orders. Afterward, Joyce asked Alim if he would like to join her on her visit to her brothers in Chicago during the holidays, and Alim seemed okay with the idea. Joyce was glad that he agreed.

Chapter 13

THANKSGIVING

J oyce got together with Momma Belle to discuss the basics of her wedding. They discussed hiring a wedding planner for the fall wedding. Momma Belle thought Joyce's idea was a little unusual, but she went along with it. The holidays were approaching fast, and Joyce was making early arrangements to fly to Chicago to visit her brothers at Christmas. Alim was pleased with the idea of Joyce spending Thanksgiving with him and his family.

Joyce would soon meet Alim's two sisters for the first time, even though it seemed like she knew them already because Alim talked about his sisters a lot. Alim talked of his childhood and his father's passing the previous year from a heart attack. Having lost both of her parents, Joyce could relate to his loss.

Both of Alim's his sisters would be arriving from Maryland with their families for Thanksgiving. Alim was excited because he did not see his sisters often, but they did keep in touch over the phone. Momma Belle and a close family friend would be preparing the Thanksgiving meal as always.

Joyce was also thinking deeply about the wedding. She bought all kinds of wedding magazines for inspiration, and she insisted that she wanted to wear white, even though it would be a fall wedding. She planned to have a small wedding, and maybe a big reception. Although she didn't know that many people yet, she was confident that she would get to know a lot of the church folk by the time the wedding came around. Savannah didn't have her interest as far as a friend, but she did have a maid of honor, and now she just had to gather up some bridesmaids.

Joyce thought she would ask Caroline's two teenage daughters, Pamela, and Suzanna, if they wanted to come to her wedding. She was sure that they would respond positively. Joyce knew that Alim had his best man— his cousin and best friend Mac, short for Mackenzie. Mac would be coming from Atlanta with his wife and children for the Thanksgiving festivities.

Joyce had been talking to Caroline about the wedding quite a bit. She always felt close to Caroline since the day they had met in Sunday school. Joyce was also friends with the other ladies, but she was closer to Caroline. Their chemistry was just perfect. Caroline told Joyce that most of her and her husband's family was right here in Savannah, so everyone would be congregating at her house for Thanksgiving, which was very convenient for Caroline since she never felt up to leaving her home for the holidays.

Caroline and her sisters would cook, and everyone else would bring covered dishes. Caroline's two teenage daughters would also help with the holiday festivities while her husband and teenage son watched football on television. Joyce admired Caroline's family life; it was a sure example of how she wanted her married life to be, but one thing was that Caroline was saved—she was a Christian woman, and so was her husband. Joyce knew that she needed to accept Jesus Christ in her life, but in due time.

On Thanksgiving morning, Joyce called Alim several times because he wasn't answering. She was sure he was just tired from running around for his Momma all week, well as being on the phone with her until late the previous night, so she thought she would catch up with him later in the afternoon. Joyce decided to brew some coffee and catch up on her journal. She called Momma Belle to wish her a happy Thanksgiving, and Momma Belle started to vent about the family getting to the house on time for dinner. She was worried since everyone had decided to stay in hotels. The families thought that it would be best instead of cramming themselves in Momma's three-bedroom house, with Melanie already occupying one of the bedrooms. Momma Belle wouldn't mind at all if they all camped out anywhere at her house. After the phone call with Momma was over, Joyce decided to pick something to wear to the big dinner and then decided to give Caroline a call to wish her a good holiday. Caroline was busy preparing her dinner, but she always had time for Joyce.

"Hi Caroline, and Happy Thanksgiving to you and your family!" Joyce said.

"Happy Thanksgiving, Joyce, and how are you doing today?" Caroline asked cheerfully.

"I'm fine, Caroline, all is well, except I was little concerned because I have been calling Alim all morning long and received no reply as of yet," Joyce said.

"Oh, maybe he is still asleep from all that running around he was doing last night," Caroline said.

"Yes, I figured that as well, but he always answers his phone. I guess there is a first time everything," Joyce said.

"Oh well, you know that he'll call you soon," Caroline said.

"I really do hope so because I wanted to know if we were going together to his Momma's house," Joyce said.

"Oh, I see. I'm sure he will call you back soon, honey," Caroline said.

"I know, Caroline, I'm just kind of worried," Joyce said.

"Don't be worried. He will call you soon, and did you call Momma Belle to ask if she had heard from him?" Caroline asked.

"No, Caroline. I didn't want to worry her because she has too much on her mind already," Joyce said.

"Okay, Joyce. My girls are calling but give me a call later. You know that I am always here for you," Caroline said.

"Thank you, Caroline, and I apologize for bothering you with my little woes, but have a good holiday, and I will talk to you soon," Joyce said and then hung up.

After Joyce hung up the phone, she felt a little uneasy about telling Caroline about Alim not picking up, even though she trusted Caroline wholeheartedly. She just didn't want Caroline to think that she didn't trust Alim.

Noon was approaching, and Joyce decided that she would call Alim once again and leave a message on his answering machine if he didn't pick up. She really didn't want to give Alim the impression that she was hunting him down; that might make him a little uneasy.

But right at noon, her phone rang. Joyce felt relieved to see that it was Alim.

"Hi, baby. Happy Thanksgiving!" Alim said.

"Hello, Alim. Happy Thanksgiving to you too," she said a little sharply.

"Hey, I got your missed calls, and I am so sorry that I couldn't respond right away. I left my phone in the car by accident. I was over at the hotel shooting the breeze with my cousin, catching up on old times," Alim explained.

"Oh, okay. Is everything all right, Alim?" Joyce asked, concerned.

"Sure, it is. Why do you ask, Joyce?"

"Oh, nothing. I was just wondering if I should drive to Momma Belle's or if you're picking me up later."

"I will pick you up, Joy. You know that that is not a problem for me. Now stop being like that. I just didn't have my phone on me; I will try not to make that mistake again," Alim pleaded.

"Okay, I was just wondering," Joyce said quietly.

"Anyway, what have you been doing today, baby?" Alim asked.

"Nothing much, just chilling here on the sofa all morning," Joyce said as she sipped her coffee.

"I wish that I could stop by now, Joyce, but I have family to tend to right now. They need to settle into their hotel rooms," Alim said.

"Yes, I understand, Alim. I'll see you around four," Joyce said.

"Yes, baby, and I hope that you have gotten plenty of rest because you'll need it! It's going to be a long night. My family do not know how to go to bed once they get together," Alim said.

Joyce just laughed. She was feeling a little better now that she had spoken to Alim, even though she was still kind of disappointed in him for the phone drama. She didn't want to have any doubts about Alim, so she put his feeble excuse out of her mind and decided to just let it all go.

Joyce then received several calls from her brothers to wish her a happy

Thanksgiving. She told them about her plans to visit for Christmas, which they were excited about.

"Joyce, we are glad to hear that you are still happy because Leon and I are always worried about you," Brian said.

"I know, Brian, but I told you two that I will be fine," Joyce said. Brian and Leon were at least ten to fifteen years older than Joyce, but they were very well polished men and very sharp in mind and spirit., Joyce loved them a lot. "I can't wait to see you two at Christmas, and I will bring presents," Joyce said, giggling.

"Deanna says hello to Joyce and that she misses you a lot. Yes, she misses her only sister-in-law," Brian said.

"Ahh, tell Deanna that I miss her too," Joyce said.

"She's waiting on Leon to find a nice woman and get married, but I told her that man will not settle. I don't think it'll happen in this life," Brian said as they both laughed.

"I know that's right, Brian," Joyce said as she continued to laugh.

"Hey, y'all, I'm back on the phone now; I know that you're talking about me," Leon said, cutting in. They all laughed again.

"Joyce, call us tomorrow. I must do some running around for Deanna," Brian said.

"Okay, I love you both," Joyce said.

"We love you too, sis," they said in unison before hanging up.

As time rolled by, Joyce got dressed and waited for Alim to pick her up to go to Momma Belle's. Joyce sat quietly, feeling kind of nervous because she knew that she would be meeting most of Alim's immediate family for the first time.

Alim finally arrived and greeted Joyce with a kiss and hug.

On the way to Momma Belle's house, Joyce sat quietly, thinking about how Alim's family was going to accept his new her. Alim talked excitedly about his family while he drove.

As they approached the house, Melanie ran out to meet them. Alim and Joyce went into the house with Melanie holding Alim's hand. Everyone was anxious to meet the new fiancé that they had heard so much about. Joyce got lots of hugs and greetings from the family members, which eased her anxiety a little.

Melanie asked to say grace as everyone stood and held hands around the table, which was different for Joyce; her family usually sat at the table and bowed their heads as her dad did the honors. After grace, everyone sat down for dinner, and Alim was asked to carve the turkey. Everyone started to talk among themselves. The aunts and uncles asked Melanie how school was going and Joyce how she was getting along in Savannah.

"Me and Alim must catch up on old times. We haven't seen each other in over a year," Mac said.

Joyce thought that Mac's comment was interesting since Alim had told her he had been in the hotel room with Mac, talking and catching up on old times, but she decided to let that go because maybe Mac meant something else—she didn't know what, but she didn't want to think about that right now.

Alim switched the conversation to sports. The family talked for hours, and after dinner, the women helped Momma clear the table and wash the dishes while the men sat around the television watching the game.

As the night ended, everyone got ready to leave for their hotel rooms. Momma was a little sad to see everyone leave, even though they were not officially leaving until the weekend. Alim drove Joyce home while promising to return later to spend the night with her.

Joyce decided to go online and book reservations for her Christmas vacation to Chicago. It was a blessing for her that Christmas would fall on a Saturday this year. She could leave Friday after work and return on Monday morning since the law firm would be closed on Monday, and she was confident that all would go well. She didn't wait up for Alim that night but decided she would answer the door when he arrived or called.

It was about two o'clock in the morning when Alim finally called. He said was too tired to drive back to her house, but he would come back if Joyce insisted. Joyce understood that he was too tired from all the festivities of the day and sitting up with his family the night before, so she told him that it was okay if he didn't come. He assured her that he would stay with her the follow-ing night.

On Sunday night, Joyce spent time at Momma Belle's to see the family off. Alim was in and out of the house, claiming that he had errands to run. Joyce felt a little weird about that, but she didn't think too much of it.

Joyce sat and admired the family as they said their last goodbyes. She also thought about her own family, especially her parents. *The holidays always bring wishes for our loved ones,* she thought. Well, she did have a beautiful experience with Alim's family, and she had enjoyed the festivities throughout. This was her first Thanksgiving in Savannah. Momma Belle had cooked so much, and there was so much food brought in by the family that Joyce helped herself to some of the food and desserts to take home.

The next day, Alim spent the rest of the day and night with Joyce. She was glad to spend that quality time with Alim; he'd been rushing here and there the past few days, and she hadn't seen him much since on Thanksgiving. Alim brought up the subject of Christmas and asked Joyce what she would like for him to get her.

"Alim, I have no ideas of what I want besides my birthstone in a ring and a tennis bracelet. These are stones that I couldn't afford to buy. Am I asking for anything too expensive?" Joyce asked bashfully. She knew Alim could afford it, and besides, he had asked.

"What! Huh? All that, Joyce? Alim asked abruptly, looking serious. Joyce didn't know what to say. How had he changed his colors so suddenly? She had a look of shock on her face.

"Just kidding, baby!" Alim said, laughing out loud. He had Joyce in a twisted way for a minute. He laughed at the look on Joyce's face, who was now a little hurt.

"Alim, stop playing. You scared me for a minute there," Joyce said sadly.

"Okay, Joyce. I'm sorry, but I just couldn't resist, baby!" Alim said as he continued to smile while kissing Joyce.

"Now, Alim, what would you like for me to get you for Christmas?" Joyce asked.

"Anything, Joy. I'm easy. I did miss hanging around you this Thanksgiving. There was just so much running around I had to do," Alim said as he continued to hold Joyce as he hugged and kissed her.

"That's nice to hear, Alim, and now back to Christmas. You're not easy to get for because you have so much, I'll figure it out" Joyce said as she hugged Alim back. "Alim, another thing, sweetheart. Can we exchange gifts when I get back from Chicago? I want it to be very special!"

"Huh?" Alim asked.

"Yes, I want it to be meaningful. Our first Christmas together!" Joyce said.

"Okay, Joy. Anything for you. I love so much that I will do anything for you, lady, just if you are happy," Alim said. After she thanked Alim with a long, passionate kiss, she pulled away slightly to gaze at that big, three-carat diamond on her finger, surrounded by baguettes on each side. It was beautiful and flawless.

Joyce was on cloud nine again. She loved Alim so much. He meant everything to her, and no one could take away her love for him.

Chapter 14

CHRISTMAS IN CHICAGO

The malls were crowded, and Joyce stayed there until closing time, which was late, considering that Christmas was fast approaching. Joyce was looking for the perfect gifts for her brothers, her sister-in-law, and the two babies. Her trip was the following day, and she also needed some last-minute items for herself. She had already bought gift cards for Momma Belle and Melanie, which was easy, and then she thought that instead of looking for special gifts for her family, she would get them gift cards, but she would handpick gifts for the babies.

After browsing some more, Joyce had to leave the mall because it was beginning to close. Her plane wasn't leaving until the following evening, which made it convenient for her to rest up before her trip. Joyce finally had all her gifts packed for her family in Chicago. She decided to go to Momma Belle's and give them their gifts and wish them a Merry Christmas early. Alim would be spending the night with Joyce so that they could have some time together before she left for Chicago. Alim made sure that she had all the extra money that she needed to travel and spend. He was good to Joyce as far as attending to her every need.

The next day, while Alim drove Joyce to the airport, she told him how much she was going to miss him. This would be their first time apart since they had gotten together. Alim waited with Joyce until her flight arrived, and fortunately, it was a nice, chilly evening, unlike Thanksgiving, which had been unseasonably warm. She knew that Chicago would be cold, so she brought her heavy coat along. Chicago did not spare itself in the wintertime.

When Joyce's flight arrived, she and Alim shared a long kiss and hug. Joyce enjoyed the plane ride, and of course, Alim had set her up in first class where she was comfortable. She pulled out her pocket Bible out to read a few passages from the book of Psalms. Joyce loved reading the Psalms because she found it refreshing and devotional. She finally arrived in Chicago and called her brother Brian. She waited patiently while he came to pick her up. She felt elated about seeing her family, but also a little anxious.

A short time later, Brian pulled into the airport. Joyce ran to greet him. She felt so excited, and the reunion was heavenly.

"Leon is going to meet us at my house, Joyce!" Brian said.

"I can't wait to see him!" She said as Brian put her luggage in the car.

"Joyce, do you want to go to the hotel first, or would you prefer to go straight to the house?" Brian asked.

"I will go to the hotel to check in first, Brian, and then we will go to the house. I am very anxious to see my nephews," Joyce said.

"Okay," Brian replied. "So, your Thanksgiving turned out well, huh?"

"Yes, it was beautiful. I missed you all, though, and Mommy and Daddy as well," Joyce said as she grabbed Brian's hand.

"Yeah, Joyce, I feel the same way. We will always feel that way, I guess." Brian said.

They arrived at the hotel so that Joyce could check in, and then they went to Brian's house. Leon was standing on the porch as they pulled into parking. He ran down the porch steps to meet Joyce as she exited the car. They all stood and hugged for a long time, so happy to be reunited at last. Joyce admired how healthy her brothers were looking.

"I'm so happy to be here at Christmas with you both," Joyce said, tears streaming down her face.

"We are so happy you are here too, Joyce," Brian said. Deanna came out to hug Joyce as well, with the babies all bundled up.

"Oh my! The babies are getting so big, and they are walking now. They are so handsome," Joyce said as they all walked to go into the house. Joyce excused herself so that she could call Alim and let him know that she had arrived safely.

"Hi, baby! How was your flight? Alim asked over the phone.

"It was good, and my brother came to pick me up from the airport," Joyce said.

"Of course, he did, Joy. I wouldn't have thought that he would let you ride a taxi to his house," Alim said as he laughed a little.

"Oh, be quiet, Alim. Do you miss me?"

"Of course, I do, baby. You shouldn't have to ask that question," Alim said earnestly. "Have you gotten settled in yet?"

"I did go to the hotel to check in, but I didn't go to my room just yet. I wanted to go back to Brian's house to hang out for a bit before I settled in for the night," Joyce said.

"Yeah, it's Christmas Eve, Joy, and I'm missing you terribly. I'll go hang out at Momma's, I guess," Alim said.

"I miss you too, Alim, more than you could ever imagine. I love you so much," Joyce said.

"I love you too, baby."

"I have to go now, Alim, and be with my family, but tell Momma Belle and Melanie that I said Merry Christmas and that I miss them," Joyce said.

"I will do that, Joy, and see you later," Alim said as he hung up.

Joyce and her family sat up half the night talking, drinking eggnog, and eating some snacks that Deanna had prepared. They decided to open their gifts early because it was late, the children were down for the night, and there wasn't anything else to do. They talked about old times and new times and Joyce's upcoming wedding. As ironic as it seemed for everyone to give gift cards, it was the best way because it saved trips to the store and standing in long lines trying to return unwanted gifts. The clothes that Joyce bought for her nephews were the talk of the early morning. Joyce always had a discerning taste for clothes, and she picked out only the best for her nephews for Christmas. Brian and Deanna loved everything. As the light of daybreak began to shine outside the windows, Joyce felt that it was time for her to go to the hotel and get some rest before rejoining her family in the early evening. Brian drove Joyce to the hotel and helped her get her luggage up to her room.

"What time do you want me to pick you later, Joyce? I know that you are tired," Brian said.

"Pick me up around five, but I'll still call you to confirm it," Joyce replied.

"Okay, honey. Get some rest. I'll be back later," Brian said.

Joyce called Alim before going to sleep to wish him a Merry Christmas, but she got no answer, so decided to leave a voice mail as her eyes grew heavy with sleep. She was too tired to worry about these missed calls that she was leaving on Alim's phone. She finally went to sleep and was awakened by her ringtone at two o'clock in the afternoon.

"Hey, Joyce, what time will you be ready for me to pick you up? Deanna is cooking dinner, and I don't want you to oversleep and miss all the good stuff she's making," Brian said, chuckling.

"Brian, you can pick me up at five," Joyce said.

"Okay," Brian said. He hung up.

Joyce slept until four-thirty and then jumped up to get in the shower while the coffee brewed. She decided to throw on some jeans and a heavy sweater before checking her phone. She noticed that she hadn't received any missed calls from Alim, so she called him again, wondering why he hadn't called or returned her calls and voice messages by now.

But just then Brian arrived, and Joyce scurried to meet him in the hotel lobby. He had Deanna and the babies with him, and Joyce and Deanna talked about doing some shopping and browsing stores the next day because she still had to get Alim's gift. While Joyce was in the car, Alim gave her a call back.

"Hey, baby. I'm sorry that I missed your call, but I was busy with Momma, and I did get your call this morning, but I was still asleep. I was so tired from Thanksgiving until now," Alim said.

"What are you doing?" Joyce asked.

"Nothing much. I'm just sitting here with Momma and Melanie," Alim responded.

"How is your Christmas so far? Mine is going well here with my family. I'm glad I came," Joyce said.

"It's boring without you, Joy, but Momma and Melanie are having a good time. I am missing you a lot. Tell everyone that I said hello and that I hope to meet them soon, and Merry Christmas and a Happy New Year to all," Alim said.

"I love you, Alim, and I will talk to you later."

After hanging up the phone, Joyce asked Brian where Leon was.

"He will be here later. You know, since Leon retired from the military last year, he's been bored and has been thinking about going into business for himself, but I think that it's just a thought," Brian said.

"Oh, I see. That would be great, but why do you say it's just a thought, Brian?" Joyce asked.

"I say that Joyce because he hasn't made any efforts to pursue his business."

"Oh," Joyce said, giggling. "How is everything going for you, Brian? I mean work, with you being the general manager of the most prestigious hotel in Chicago—which reminds me, thank you for my room. It is beautiful," Joyce said.

"You're welcome. Anything for my baby sis," Brian said.

"So, Joyce, you're really loving Savannah, huh?" Deanna asked.

"Yes, Deanna. It is beautiful, and you will have to come and visit soon," Joyce said.

"We sure will. I have never been to Georgia, and the furthest that I have been from Chicago is Virginia, and that was when I was a little younger. There was a beach there as well," Deanna said with a wide smile.

"Yes, she loves the beach, and I hope to get her to one summer comes in and before it ends," Brian said earnestly, smiling at Deanna.

Brian and Deanna had been together for twenty years but married for fifteen. Joyce always adored the way Brian treated Deanna; it was clear that she was the love of his life. All through their conversations, Joyce tried to say attentive, but she had Alim on her mind and wished that he were there with her.

It was dinner time, and Joyce enjoyed the meal that Deanna had prepared.

Deanna had always been such a good cook and she made everything from scratch. At dinner, Joyce and the family talked about the church that she was attending in Savannah. That was when Brian told Joyce that he and Deanna had also started attending church about three months ago, and they were loving it. Brian talked a lot about God and family. He told Joyce that God was the center of his and Deanna's lives, that he and Deanna had given their lives to Christ, and it had made them closer than ever. He then told her they were still new Christians and learning every day about God by praying and reading the Bible daily.

"So, what made you give your lives to Christ?" Deanna asked curiously.

"Well, we were having some problems, and I didn't want us to have to separate," Brian said.

"Wow, I didn't know that Brian."

"Yes. No one knew at that time what difficulties Deanna, and I were going through in our marriage."

Deanna sat in silence and listened to Brian as he explained to Joyce about their once-failing relationship and Christ being the center of their life now, nodding in agreement here and there.

"It seemed that we had been together so long that we were taking each other for granted and didn't even realize it, among other things. We weren't connecting, and something was missing, but I love Deanna, and I knew, and still know, that she loved me too, but it seemed like it wasn't a marriage anymore. If anyone was confused, it was me. I can't speak for Deanna on that; she is not usually confused, and she thinks things through while I just stay confused. Joyce, I know that is hard to understand because you haven't been married before, but hopefully you will be soon," Brian explained.

"So you got saved?" Joyce asked.

"Well, a guy at my job was saved and he's a bellboy. One day, while I was waiting for the valet to bring my car around the front entrance, he handed me a little daily bread booklet, and I thanked him. The next day, I told him that it was an interesting booklet and that my wife had read some of it too. He then invited me to come to his church, and I agreed. It was a good church. I came home and told Deanna that we were going to church and maybe even Sunday school, and she agreed. Heck, we didn't have nothing to lose, I thought, when I was first asked by that young man. The rest is history, and I know that I didn't get around to telling you, but I planned to—and well, now you know. I am trying to get Leon to go to church with me, and I know that he'll come very soon. I am praying that he will," Brian said with a look of pure happiness on his face.

"I am happy to know that you and Deanna are attending church now. It's such a good thing," Joyce said.

"Do you really like the church that you are attending now, Joyce?" Brian asked.

"I love my church, Brian!" Joyce exclaimed.

"Does Alim go with you to church, Joyce?" he asked.

"He goes once in a while; I am trying to get him to go with me on a regular basis," Joyce said, hanging her head a little.

"Yes, you two should really go together. As the Bible states, 'How can two walk together unless they agree.' You two must be on one accord for the relationship to work, and that is God being in the center of it. God comes first, and that is what me and Deanna had to learn and get used to," Brian explained.

Joyce just sat with her head slightly down because she knew that Brian wasn't telling her anything that she didn't know already. She had heard it all before.

"Joyce, Deanna, and I pray and read the Bible every day. It is not just going to church, honey, but we acknowledge Jesus Christ as our Lord and Savior, and we pray and follow his word every day," Brian said frankly.

Joyce listened attentively. She felt like she was talking to Caroline, who had spoken the same words on a few occasions. Joyce resolved to call Caroline when she had time the next day. Thoughts started weighing heavenly on Joyce's mind.

Joyce thought to herself for a moment. *So, Alim and I are not going to make it if we don't go to the altar and surrender our lives to Jesus Christ. We love each other too much to lose each other; our relationship is not old, and we haven't been together that long, so we can learn to grow together. Even if one of us is going to church, that should be sufficient to draw the other in. Our love is that strong. Neither one of us is going anywhere, and I can't believe that religion will destroy us. We know how to communicate, and we are going to make some mistakes—it's only human, and we are only human.*

Joyce also thought that Brian had always been a little selfish, because as much as she loved Brian, it was the truth. She felt that was probably why he was having problems in his relationship to the point that it sent him running to church to find Jesus. He'd always been a good man, but he never liked expressing his feelings at times or opening when he really needed to. Joyce had always told him that when they were coming up. But Alim, on the other hand, shared everything with her. She felt that she could ask Alim anything, and he would do anything for her.

Leon dropped by for a little while. He was on his way to a Christmas party and wanted Joyce to go with him, but she passed on that and wanted to go back to her hotel; it was getting a little late, and she and Deanna had to go for their shopping spree the next day.

Leon then offered to take Joyce back to the hotel to spend some time with her. Joyce knew that Leon was always on the go. He couldn't keep still, and he liked the nightlife. Leon had never settled down.

Once she was back in her hotel room, Joyce lay down in the bed. She was exhausted by the weight of Brian had told her, and she didn't feel like talking to anyone right about now. She was a little surprised that Deanna hadn't given any input when Brian was talking to her, but perhaps Deanna wanted to leave it all up to Brian to speak about their relationship and new life in Christ. Joyce could see that Brian and Deanna seemed so happy. With those thoughts ruminating in her mind, she fell into a deep sleep.

The next day, Deanna took the boys to her mother's house while Brian went to work for couple of hours. Then she drove by the hotel to pick up Joyce to go shopping.

"Deanna, I really do miss Chicago a lot, but I love it in Savannah," Joyce said.

"It's really nice, huh, Joyce," Deanna said.

"Yes, you would love it too," Joyce replied.

"Perhaps. I am a natural-born city girl, but I do love the beach," Deanna said.

"I was too, Deanna, but I needed the change," Joyce said.

"I understand, Joyce, and there is also something that you should know. Brian and I were on our way to divorce court," Deanna confessed.

"What!" Joyce exclaimed.

"Yes, it's true. He was working long hours, while I was home waiting, and this went on for some time. I felt that all those long hours weren't necessary, and that he didn't want to be home with me or didn't feel like being married anymore. I was tired of his routine, which had been going on for a year and a half, and I tried talking to him many times about it, but he wasn't open for discussion. He just didn't want to hear anything. I left him for a couple of months and stayed with my mother. I just didn't know what to do anymore. We separated for a little bit after you left town; he doesn't call it a separation to this day—call it space or whatever you want, but it was a separation," Deanna said.

Joyce listened in awe without saying a word. She wanted to know everything because Brian left a lot out of his side of the story. She knew that he wouldn't like Deanna telling her side. "We still called each other every night but I started to feel that he was getting used to me not being there at home with him. I cried every night because I loved him and needed him. I didn't want to lose my family, and I wanted all of us so desperately to be together. He would come and see the boys, but I felt in my heart that it just wasn't right. We had been together too long to be without each other. Then, as a few months went on, I started to feel like maybe this was the end, so I asked him if he wanted a divorce. I was hoping that he would say no, but he said that he didn't know what he wanted. My heart started to break again, and I began to suspect that he had another woman, but I was too afraid to ask him was he seeing someone else because he might have said yes or said nothing at all, which wouldn't have helped me. Through all my tears, I just came out and said that

I wanted a divorce and that I couldn't go through this anymore. And he said nothing, just silence on the other end of the phone. I was so hurt, I hung up on him," Deanna explained.

"Wow, Deanna, this is so much to absorb; I am still in shock at this story," Joyce said.

"No, not a story, Joyce—reality," Deanna pointed out. She continued to speak.

"You know, Joyce, before I asked him for a divorce, I did offer to see a marriage counselor, but he wouldn't hear of it. He felt like it was a waste of time, and his theory was, 'How can someone that doesn't know anything about us give us advice on our marriage?' I didn't know what else to do, and I was hurting, Joyce. You just don't know how much, and to this day, Brian doesn't know how much. I was thinking about all kinds of negative things to do to myself because, in some ways, I was also blaming myself. I was always saying, 'if only this,' or, 'if only that." Through it all, I didn't realize how much Brian was hurting too; he just couldn't express it; he didn't want to tell me, or didn't know how to tell me, so I left it alone as far as asking. I started praying to God, and Brian didn't know that I was praying. I felt that he didn't have to know that. My mother is a Christian, and she helped me a great deal. My mother told me that she was always praying for me and Brian, even before the separation, and sure enough, God worked it out. My mother had told me a long time ago that we had to give our lives to God when we were having some minor problems because we couldn't see that those minor things would turn into major things."

"That's something, Deanna, but that is good that you had your mother as your backbone," Joyce said.

"Yes, Joyce, it is, but I didn't want to listen to her at times," Deanna confessed.

"Momma and Daddy were together for forty years before he passed, and she knows what she is talking about. They both had Jesus in their lives, and although Momma told me about the rough times, she also and told me that they saw the light. Didn't see the light at the same time, but eventually, they got on one accord. I remember it was the weekend and Brian asked me to come to the house, and that we should go to church on Sunday, and we did just that. We went to church, and we honored the altar call, holding hands as we walked down the aisle to the altar. It had to be a decision that both of us desired, and we both did desire it—and it was good. It was like renewing our vows, but it was through Jesus Christ because he said in the scriptures, 'Therefore, if any man be in Christ, he is a new creature: old things are passed away; behold, all things are become new.' The Lord did make us once again, Joyce. And now Brian and I know how to settle things, and he has become more open and includes me in his life as his partner and wife," Deanna said.

Joyce was utterly amazed by what Deanna was telling her, and she was happy that Brian and Deanna were still together. Joyce thought about something that she had heard at church and realized it must really be true that "the family that prays together, stays together." Deanna and Brian were living examples according to their stories, Joyce thought. And although Joyce's parents talked about God a lot, she really didn't know if they were truly Christians or consistent church goers. As Deanna pulled into the parking lot of the huge mall, she continued speaking to Joyce.

"If it wasn't for that Sunday that Brian had in mind for the both of us to attend church, I don't know where we would be today, so I will always give the praise and glory to the Lord Jesus Christ for saving my marriage and family. I will always love the Lord—he comes first before everyone in my life or Brian's life. Okay, Joyce, now let's get in this mall and start doing some shopping. My adrenaline gets going when it's shopping time," Deanna said, giggling.

"I think all women's adrenaline gets going when it's shopping time," Joyce laughed. "I have to get Alim's gift."

"What did he get you, Joyce?" Deanna asked.

"Oh, I asked him for a ring and tennis bracelet with my birthstones in them," Joyce said.

"Wow, your man is paid, huh?" Deanna said with a witty chuckle.

"He does well. Can't complain," Joyce said.

"What does he do? I don't mean to pry, but yeah, I am being nosy," Deanna said as she and Joyce both laughed.

"He's into real estate and owns property. He even owns the building that I work in," Joyce said, feeling proud of her man.

"Wow, you never settled for less in a man. I have always known that about you, Joyce. You always said that you'd rather do bad all by yourself, and you stuck to that. I am blessed to have Brian too. Yes, the Lord sent me a good provider, among other things," Deanna said, with admiration on her face.

"Yes, I know. Brian has always been ambitious when it came to good jobs and making money. He doesn't settle for less either," Joyce said.

"I will be praying that everything will continue to go well for you, and I am so happy that you have someone to love, and he loves you back, but always remember that God comes first. And without him, we will fail because we can't do anything on our own," Deanna said earnestly.

"I know, Deanna."

"Okay, enough relationship talks. Back to shopping!" Deanna said, giggling a little.

"Now, what shall I get this man?" Joyce pondered out loud. "You know, Deanna, I have a new credit card, and I am anxious to break it in. I should get Alim a nice ring as well because I don't really see any rings on his finger, except his class ring. Let's go into Zale's, Deanna! I will get him a platinum watch, and I see one already as we are walking into this store. Oh my gosh!"

"That's beautiful, Joyce, and masculine," Deanna said as she ogled the watch.

"It is gorgeous, Deanna. I want his name inscribed on the inside with a little quote. It will say, 'I will always love you.' Let me see if they can have it done by tomorrow," Joyce said as she admired the watch.

"Excuse me, sir, but can I hold this?" Joyce asked the jeweler. He nodded.

"Wow, Deanna. Look at the diamonds at each quarter of it, with his birthstone centering it. Just fabulous!" Joyce said.

"I know, Joyce. It's lovely," Deanna said.

"Sir, I want an inscription on this watch. How long will it take? Because I need it as soon as possible," Joyce said.

"We can have it done by tomorrow afternoon," the jeweler said.

"Great. I will write the inscription down. Will you tell me the full price so that I can pay for it now Joyce asked gleefully the jeweler's face lit up like a light bulb and his eyes widened. He had a huge smile on his face; it must have been his first good sale that day.

"Okay, madam. This is the full price for everything, and the bracelet will be ready at about three o'clock tomorrow afternoon," he said.

"That sounds good. I really need that bracelet at that time because I will be on my way back to Savannah tomorrow evening."

"Deanna, I am so happy that Alim and I have agreed to exchange gifts when I get back home. It will be like our own special Christmas," Joyce exclaimed.

"Lady, I just can't stop looking at that rock on your finger. It is flawless!" Deanna said, shaking her head in admiration.

"Woman! Brian didn't do so bad himself with that rock on your finger. I remember the day he bought it and came to my job to show it to me. I was so impressed by his good taste," Joyce said. That made Diana blush and roll her eyes.

"Let me just pick up a few more things, and then let's get out of here, Joyce. I don't like leaving the boys with Momma for such a long period of time. I feel like they're too much for her to handle, even though she denies it. But she does love every moment of the boys staying with her," Deanna said.

Joyce and Deanna found a Starbucks and decided to stop for some coffee before making the forty-five-minute drive back.

"Joyce, spending this time with you has been wonderful. I am so glad that you came back to Chicago for Christmas. I have always loved you as a sister! I hope all the best for you. I have always admired your ambition and drive; you are such a strong and beautiful woman," Deanna said with sincerity.

"Ah, Deanna, thank you!" Joyce said, her heart melting at Breanna's kind words. "I have always admired you too. You treat Brian so well and you are a good mother to my nephews, so stop embarrassing me now. You know I love you like a sister too!"

"You go after what you want, Joyce, and that's good. God loves you and wants to really use you. You should ask him what is the calling on your life. You picked up and left Chicago. You did something daring like that. I never could have done that; I don't have the drive to do daring things. I love that persistence in you. Never let anyone take that away from you or your free spirit and joy. Never forget God," Deanna advised Joyce.

"I won't, and thanks for the uplifting talk. I am glad we can share things with each other, and this has been wonderful," Joyce said.

"It is time for us to go now," Deanna said.

Chapter 15

ARRIVING HOME

J oyce called Alim when she left the mall, but his answering machine picked up. She told Deanna to take her straight to the hotel so she could start getting her things ready for her departure tomorrow so she wouldn't have rush around to do everything. Then she would have the rest of the time to spend with the family and Deanna would pick her up late for dinner. She called her brother Brian because she knew he would be working. She wanted to spend some more quality time with her brothers. She suggested that they have dinner in the hotel restaurant. Brian gladly agreed and informed Leon of their change of plans.

While relaxing from her busy day, she called Alim again, but there was still no answer. She was trying to figure out if he had to do some things for Momma Belle or had some emergency at the office, but he could still have answered his phone, she thought. *The last time, he left it in his car by mistake,* she thought.

Joyce did get a little nervous when Alim didn't answer his phone. She really did not like to think the worst, but she still fretted. *He just started this routine recently,* she thought. She really didn't want to think that Alim was getting too comfortable not to answer when she called; she didn't want to be thought of like that.

Joyce pushed those thoughts out of her mind and started to get ready for her dinner date with Brian and Leon. She was elated to be sharing time with her brothers alone. Joyce and her brothers met at the hotel, ate dinner, and talked about old and new times. Even though Joyce was having a good time with her brothers, Alim was constantly on her mind—but then again, he was always on her mind.

After dinner, Brian and Leon walked Joyce to her room. After Joyce said goodbye to her brothers, she checked her phone again and realized that she had one missed call from Alim, which had come while she was at dinner with her brothers. She hurried to call Alim, and he answered.

"Hey, Joy. How are you doing, baby? I am sorry that I missed your calls earlier. I was doing some paperwork and didn't have my phone near me. I got a little tied up at the office," Alim said.

Joyce felt a little relieved to hear that.

"That's okay, Alim. You know my flight will be arriving tomorrow night," Joyce reminded him.

"Yes, Joy. I hope that you didn't think that I forgot, honey," Alim said.

"Well, this little vacation was so good, but I am so tired, Alim. I will have some hot tea with lemon and try to go to sleep," Joyce said.

"I will call you tomorrow morning, okay?" Alim said.

"Okay, good night."

"Sweet dreams, baby," Alim said before hanging up.

The next morning, Joyce got out of bed, washed up, and ordered some breakfast. She then started to prepare for her departure while waiting for Deanna and her brothers to pick her up after she checked out of the hotel. They all dropped by mall so that she could pick up Alim's bracelet from the jeweler. This was a sad day for everyone since the family did not want to say their goodbyes. Joyce was sad but she was ready to get back home—she was missing Alim and Savannah.

When they arrived at the airport, everyone sat and talked while waiting for Joyce's flight to arrive—and what an emotional time it was! It was finally time for Joyce to board her plane, and the family all hugged and kissed each other. They didn't finish speaking until Joyce had departed, and her place was in the air. Deanna had already been crying about Joyce's departure. She really did love her like a sister.

While on the plane, Joyce pulled out her little pocket Bible and began to read some passages from the Psalms. She thought about Deanna while she read, as well as Alim's late Christmas celebration that they would have when she got home.

Joyce was excited as the plane prepared for landing. She was anxious to see Alim, and she started to get goose bumps. The place landed in Georgia, and Alim was there, waiting, flowers in hand and looking extra good. Joyce could hardly contain herself. Alim watched as Joyce exited the plane and rushed over to greet her with hugs and kisses. He wanted to go straight to Joyce's house so he could give her the long-awaited Christmas gifts.

"This is nice, snowflakes! But it won't last. It never lasts too long," Alim said.

"The snow may last; I hope so. Then it will seem like Christmas. Chicago was beautiful with the snow at Christmas," Joyce said.

When they arrived at the house, Joyce hurried upstairs to change into something more comfortable while Alim brought her luggage inside. Alim then went into the kitchen to get a bottle of wine and some glasses. He waited patiently until Joyce came out of the bedroom in her little two-piece nightie. He pulled her close to him and poured her some wine. He had Joyce's gifts wrapped beautifully and sitting on her dining room table. Joyce also brought out Alim's gifts. Feeling a little bashful, Joyce then came back to the sofa and sat next to Alim with a wide smile. Alim had already turned the radio dial to the oldies station to set the mood just perfectly. He leaned over to kiss Joyce as he handed her Christmas gifts. Alim then told Joyce that he loved her, and Joyce did the same. The mood was so comfortable, and it seemed so much like Christmas again. The snow was falling continuously now and was settling on the windowpanes. Joyce could not stop blushing and smiling at her ring and tennis bracelet. They were both beautifully set, and the stones were flawless as they sparkled.

"Thank you so much, Alim. I love my gifts," Joyce said excitedly.

"Merry Christmas, baby. I handpicked these gifts especially, no Momma with me," Alim said.

"I will always love you, Alim."

"I've never seen such a masculine piece of jewelry before. I love it," Alim said, admiring his new watch. Joyce was glad to see how much he liked his gift. She always felt that men were hard to please when it came to gifts, and she was one to know because she had two brothers.

"Oh, I forgot. Read the inscription, Alim," Joyce said. As Alim read the inscription, Joyce blushed—not because she regretted the inscription, but she just didn't know how to handle all this love, happiness, sharing, caring, and giving in all earnest. This night was special, and Joyce was glad that she waited until she came back from her trip to exchange gifts.

Alim didn't say a word after he read the inscription; he just got up and led Joyce by the hand to her bedroom. Even though Alim was happy about receiving his gift, Joyce noticed that during their lovemaking, he seemed a little distant—not too much, but it was noticeable. She thought that he may just have been tired, so she asked him was he all right afterward.

"I'm fine, Joy. Why do you ask?"

"You don't seem yourself tonight. Now you brought me up here to the bedroom, and I'm not saying that I didn't mind, but you seem a little out of it," Joyce said.

"I am just a little tired, Joy."

"So, why are you so tired?"

"I don't know, Joy. Maybe all the holiday running and sitting up late with family and not getting any rest is catching up on me, and maybe I am winding down now," Alim said.

"I was looking forward to good night with you, Alim, and yes, maybe a longer one," Joyce said.

"I know, baby, and I will make it up to you. I know that you must get ready for work tomorrow, and so do I. I'm not going to hold you up late," Alim said as he started kissing Joyce again. As Alim arose from the bed to put on his clothes, Joyce just stared at him. She felt a little cheated out of a longer and more intense lovemaking night, but she tried to be understanding.

"What is it, baby?" Alim asked.

"Oh, nothing. I was just wondering if everything was all right," Joyce said.

"Come on, Joy, now quit that. I guess that I am only tired from all the running around that I have been doing for the past couple of weeks. Everything is fine, and I will be fine. I'll make it up to you, I promise," Alim said.

"If you say so, Alim. I will take you at your word. I am a little tired from the trip too. I know that we both are."

Joyce got out of bed and put on her robe so that she could walk Alim to the door. He kissed her deeply while saying good night. Joyce then went back to bed, thinking about Alim. She thought of Alim and her being together since the summer, so neither one of them would be the same as the day they met, but only much more in love, she thought. Alim called when he got home to say good night, and once again that he loved his Christmas gift.

"I love you too even more," Joyce responded as they hung up for the night.

Chapter 16

To Trust God or Man

A heavy workload awaited Joyce as she got back to work. She had to stay a little later that day, but she didn't mind it too much. She didn't have any plans after work, and Alim wouldn't be hanging out that night because they were both too tired. The days were longer at work, and the phone calls between her and Alim were getting fewer and fewer.

She finally arrived home from work, and even though Alim had called and made some suggestions for dinner, Joyce was just too tired. Alim said he understood. Joyce was thinking he just ought to understand because he could set his own hours or adjust his own schedule because he ran his own business. But she did speak to Alim over the phone after finishing up things at home. They talked until she fell asleep. She started on him again about going to church with her, as that was an important subject right now. Alim did not really resist the thought; he kept promising Joyce that he would start attending services with her, so Joyce was prepared to wait patiently for that to happen.

Although Joyce was totally committed to Alim, deep down inside, she felt like she was cheating God. *But this man is my fiancé*, she thought to herself. Alim was soon to be the husband that she loved and adored, and she felt that she had to give all her spare time to Alim. She was into pleasing her man for sure. Joyce trusted Alim with all her soul, body, and mind. When the time came, she wanted to be more than a good wife and wanted Alim to be a good husband to her. Joyce remembered the preacher saying, "Trust in the Lord and he will direct thy paths." She often thought of the scriptures, but she never understood the significance behind her occasional encounters with the passage.

Joyce started to write in her journal, which she had kept since elementary school. Her mother had bought the journals for her in the hope that it would develop Joyce's writing habits. Joyce did have some things rolling around in her mind, and she started the journal to keep her heart and mind in perspective, even as a young child. She never had any real close friends or sister, so she was motivated to start the journal, which soon became her best friend. The journal was something she could tell everything to—even her deepest secrets—without being judged.

But now Caroline was that friend she needed—someone physical and who could respond. She could trust Caroline and could talk about all her concerns. She still considered Alim the closest to her, and somewhat like a best friend, but she needed that female conversation as well. Joyce wondered what plans Alim had for the New Year. She wanted to ring in the New Year in at church. The next day, Alim called to explain to Joyce that he had been asleep when she called. She said she understood and then asked about the New Year. He said that he didn't have any plans yet but would rather sit at home and drink champagne with his lovely fiancé and watch the ball drop on the television. Even though Joyce wanted to bring up her New Year's idea, she went along with Alim's vision. She didn't want to welcome the New Year without Alim by her side.

They only had a couple of days until New Year's Eve, and Caroline wondered if Joyce would be attending church that night. Joyce waited until the last minute to tell Caroline that she would not be attending church on New Year's Eve. After work, Joyce called Alim and Caroline.

"Hey, Alim. Are you busy?" Joyce asked.

"No, Joy. I'm just finishing up some paperwork. What's going on?" Alim said.

"I just wanted you to come with me to the market and then the liquor store to get some snacks and drinks for New Year's Eve," Joyce said.

"Okay, Joy. As soon as I finish up here, I will be at your house," Alim said.

Alim was at Joyce's house within an hour, and they immediately headed out to the market and liquor store. Joyce loved the way Alim held her hand in public; it was Alim's way of letting everyone know that she was his lady. It was kind of chilly out, so Joyce snuggled up close to Alim, who didn't mind at all. As Alim and Joyce were walking up and down the aisles and placing the items in the shopping cart, she noticed that Alim's phone was on vibrate on his hip. Although she could hear it buzzing, he didn't answer.

"Aren't you going to answer that, Alim? I can hear it going off continuously," Joyce said.

"It's nothing, Joyce. It's just a client that I told I would call back later with some numbers on some property, but I haven't gotten the numbers prepared yet so they will just have to catch the answering service," Alim said.

"That's the same person that keeps calling you over and over and again, Alim. Must be desperate for some numbers," Joyce said shortly.

"No, I think it is Momma too, but I will have to call everyone back later when are done here," Alim said.

As they returned to Joyce's house, she found that he had turned his phone off completely, but she tried not to pay it any mind. Alim stayed long enough to help Joy put away the food and beverages that they bought, and they talk a little.

"I have to go to Momma's house, but I will call you later Joy, okay?" Alim said.

"Okay," Joyce responded, also thinking that he could have asked her to go Momma's house with him.

Joyce watched as Alim rushed to his car and drove off. She noticed that he called back whoever had been calling him when they were at the store. Joyce then gave Caroline a call because she hadn't talked to her this evening.

"Hi, Caroline. I just called to see how you were doing."

"Hello, Joyce. What's going on?" Caroline answered.

"Oh, nothing much. I'm just sitting here doing nothing at all. Alim and I just came from the market and the beverage store," Joyce said.

"I see, and how is Mr. Wonderful these days? And Joyce, you know I meant well when I said that" Caroline said.

"Oh, no problem, Caroline. I know, and Alim is doing fine these days. I wanted to say that I wish that I could attend the New Year's Eve service at church, but Alim suggested a cozy night at home to watch the ball drop on television, and that's why I was at the market getting a few items," Joyce said.

"Ahh, it would've been good if you two could have thought a little longer about ringing in the New Year in church, but okay," Caroline said. She then changed subjects. "How are your wedding plans coming along?"

"I am still looking through magazines and getting some ideas, and I did hire a wedding planner that I met through a client at the law firm," Joyce said.

"That's great, Joyce," Caroline said.

"Yes, and she comes well recommended too, Caroline," Joyce said.

"My wedding didn't require much, Joyce, because my husband and I couldn't afford a wedding. We went to the justice of peace to get married, and then we had the reception in my mother's big backyard, and it was nice," Caroline said.

"Oh, I see," Joyce said. "I hope the best for my wedding since it is my first."

"I understand, Joyce, and I agree to try to make it special and memorable since this is your first wedding, and I pray that it will turn out fabulous. You have your girls already, so that's a plus," Caroline said.

"Okay, Caroline. It is not going to be that big. I think that you are expecting a big turnout like Momma Belle," Joyce said, giggling a little.

"God willing, all will be perfect," Caroline said excitedly.

"Okay, Caroline, I am getting tired now, and I have to get off this phone, but I always love talking to you, you know that" Joyce said.

"I will call you tomorrow, Joyce. Love you."

Joyce went back to thinking about Alim and his phone. She figured he could have just answered that phone, no matter who it was. *He can answer anytime we are together if he's not hiding anything*, and then she thought she was making too much of the situation and tried to put it out of her mind. She truly trusted Alim, but she also had some insecurities because she hadn't been in a relationship for such a long time and didn't know how to handle little things like this.

Joyce heard it all the time from Caroline, Momma Belle, and the pastor: "Always put God and your entire trust in him, and he will guide you through all your doubts and concerns." She also heard it from her brother Brian when she was in Chicago. Joyce knew this to be true, deep down inside her soul, and sometimes she even reflected on her brother and his family life, but she also felt that she didn't have room for doubt in her relationship with Alim. It just wouldn't work if she had those issues. Joyce wanted the ideal relationship with her future husband.

Alim called as Joyce was just in the mood to sit and write in her journal. He wanted to wish her good night since it was getting late. They just so happened to talk for at least an hour before hanging up.

Joyce always loved to hear Alim's voice before she went to bed; it kept him on her mind, but for some reason, Joyce couldn't sleep, so she started planning her wedding some more. She went through some more magazines and wrote down some new ideas. *Having the wedding in the fall will be kind of odd,* she thought, *but I want just the perfect colors.* Joyce perused through magazines almost all night, until her eyes grew tired.

She did write down some things that she wanted to discuss with Alim, like where they were going to live, and if they were to buy a house or get one built from the ground, they needed to get started on those plans. She wanted them to share in that together. They were getting married next year, so there were a lot of things they needed to discuss. The honeymoon would be easy.

Chapter 17

New Year's Eve

It was New Year's Eve, and Joyce was finishing up at work to rush home and prepare the snacks for the night. It would be just her and Alim because everyone else would be at church. Joyce was elated about sharing the evening with Alim, albeit a little guilty about not attending church.

Joyce reached into her closet to find the perfect red lingerie to wear and a pair of earrings. No more accessories were needed; her Christmas gifts and wedding ring were sufficient. As she looked in the mirror, she said to herself, "Damn, this woman is loaded with diamonds." She smiled proudly at her reflection and then turned away. She prepared steak and baked potatoes, along with string beans for dinner, and for dessert, vanilla ice cream with whipped cream and strawberries. Alim loved ice cream, no matter what the flavor. She called Momma Belle to talk to her for a minute because she knew that she wouldn't be seeing her that night.

"Hi, Momma Belle!" Joyce said.

"Hello, Joyce. How is everything?" Momma replied.

"Just fine, Momma. Are you still going to church tonight?"

"Yes, Joyce, and you and Alim should be in church."

"I know, Momma, but Alim and I decided to stay in tonight," Joyce said. She did feel the pressure of Caroline and Momma wanting her to be in church.

"Oh, I see, but church is the best place to be, but I hope the best New Year for you, Joyce," Momma said.

"Okay, Momma. I just called to give you New Year's greetings. I will see you soon," Joyce said.

"Thank you, baby, and I wish you the same," Momma said as she hung up.

Joyce knew that Momma was hardly a Christian. She had just been a church goer for many years, but Joyce still respected her opinions, and she was right—she should be in church on New Year's Eve.

Alim was planning to arrive at Joyce's house at nine o'clock. He had some work to finish up at the office, which is why he arrived so late, but that gave Joyce plenty of time to prepare everything the way she wanted to. The night was chilly, and the moon seemed so happy to be shining so brightly.

Joyce went over to the window and gazed out into the moonlight to reminisce on how far she had come in her life and where she was going. She thought about Alim and their life together, both now and in the future. She wrapped her arms around herself and continued to look up the stars and moon, and thanked God for her life and the happiness it was bringing. She thanked God for her family, that they were still doing well, and for bringing Caroline into her life—the first good friend she ever had. Life couldn't be better, Joyce thought, but she still had a little emptiness in the inside of her being, but she knew that all would be well if she held on to this happiness she was experiencing. Suddenly, the phone rang, startling Joyce out of her daydreams.

"Hey, baby!" Alim said.

"Alim, where are you?" Joyce asked.

"I am on my way home. I must get showered and changed," Alim explained.

"You could have come here to do that, Alim," Joyce said pointedly.

"I know, Joy, but I decided to go home and wrestle with all that," Alim said.

"Okay then. Just hurry up."

"Okay, baby. I will see you in a little bit." He hung up.

Joyce finished getting the refreshments, laid the spread on the dining room table, and preceded to shower and get dressed. The phone rang just as Joyce stepped out of the shower. It was Caroline.

"Hi, Joyce. How are you?"

"Hi, Caroline."

"Joyce, I just wanted to speak with you before I headed out to church," Caroline said.

"Oh, how sweet of you to think about me, Caroline, because I know that you were busy with all the cooking and getting ready for this evening. Everything is good, and I hope that you have a good time at church and a Happy New Year," Joyce said.

"Happy New Year, Joyce. I love you," Caroline said as she hung up the phone.

After Joyce hung up the phone, she sat on her bed, thinking that Alim should have agreed to go to church with her that night. She felt it deep down inside her soul, but she also felt that God would understand. The bell rang. It was Alim. At the sound of the bell ringing, Joyce realized that it was time to give Alim his own key to her house since they were now engaged. They greeted each other with a kiss and hug when Joyce opened the door. She pointed to the stars and moon, and Alim agreed with her that they were beautiful.

"Everything smells good, Joy," Alim said.

"I have the glasses on the table, Alim, so you can pour the wine," Joyce said.

The music played softly, and the television was set to the news channel.

"Everyone is at church tonight, Alim," Joyce said quietly.

"Not everyone," Alim said with a smile.

"I know, Alim, but that is where we should be," Joyce said, hoping that would make Alim change his mind.

"Come on, Joy. Now don't start with that. I just don't feel like other people tonight; you understand, don't you?" Alim said.

"Of course," Joyce said, smiling. She really did feel flattered that Alim wanted her all to himself on New Year's Eve.

"So, how was your day today, Joy?" Alim asked as he held her hand.

"It was busy today, but good. No complaints. And yours?"

"It was all right. I just had a lot of paperwork waiting for me. The holidays set me back a little," Alim said.

Joyce noticed that Alim left his phone in the car, so she assumed he really didn't want any interruptions. *But what if his mother calls?* Joyce thought. Joyce put her phone on vibrate in case anyone called. While they ate dinner, they discussed their living arrangements after they were married. Alim had a surprise of his own for Joyce, and although Joyce couldn't wait to hear it, he promised to tell her after the clock struck twelve.

"What's for dessert?" Alim asked.

"Vanilla ice cream, strawberries, and whipped cream!" Joyce said excitedly.

"Wow, bring it on!" Alim exclaimed.

Alim dipped the strawberries in the whipped cream and fed them to Joyce, who fed him back. It was just half an hour away from twelve o'clock as they enjoyed dessert and watched the entertainment going on at Times Square on television, but Joyce was also thinking about church. She stared at the moon from time to time through the living room blinds, which she had left partially open. Joyce was once again filled with happiness; the night was of love, peace, and joy.

Five minutes before midnight, Alim poured the champagne, and they sipped from each other's glasses. Joyce didn't know why, but her heart started beating fast—maybe from the excitement of bringing in the New Year together. At the stroke of midnight, the ball dropped as they kissed and hugged. Joyce's phone also started to ring, and she instantly thought it was her family, but to her surprise, it was her bosses from the law firm, and what a pleasant surprise for her. When Joyce's family called, she and Alim talked to them and wished them a Happy New Year. They were glad to hear from Alim. It was a beautiful way to bring in the New Year. They could not stop hugging and kissing each other as they sipped the champagne. Alim finally decided to call his family, using her phone to do so.

Then they had a good time snacking, dancing to the music, and acting a little silly. Alim stopped for a moment and took some pictures of Joyce with her camera. He also told her how beautiful she was and that he was so happy that she was in her life. Those words made Joyce feel special and more secure than she had ever felt before.

Joyce was beautiful indeed, but Alim had had beautiful women in his life before. There was something different about her, though. Forty-five-year-old Joyce had a natural innocence about her. She stood five feet tall, with a medium build, pecan skin, a pure and flawless complexion, short brown her, straight white teeth, and deep black bedroom eyes accompanied by long eyelashes. Yes, she was gorgeous. The only makeup that she dared to wear was lip gloss, mascara, and a dab of eye shadow. She made Alim feel very blessed to have her in his life because she was a good-hearted and very meek woman. She had that shining personality that made him feel good when she was in his presence. He really loved her. Alim was all man, and Joyce was all woman—a beautiful combination, indeed.

After a perfect night, when morning came, Alim had a surprise for Joyce. He told Joyce to get dressed because he had somewhere to take her. He first took her to a little diner that was always open for breakfast. Joyce noticed Alim's phone vibrating as it sat in the cup holder in front of them, but she didn't mention it because she did not want to spoil the moment. The breakfast in the diner was excellent, and she loved hearing Taylor Dyane's "I Will Always Love You" playing in the background. She loved that song from back in the day; it was one of her favorites.

After breakfast, Alim took Joyce to the other side of Savannah to show her some vacant land with a beautiful house next to it.

"This is the surprise, Joy!" Alim said.

"What, Alim?" Joyce asked. Joyce did not realize that she had a domestic decision to make.

"Do you like this side of town?" Alim asked.

"You know, Alim, we drove through this side of town months ago, and I remember thinking it was beautiful," Joyce said.

"Yeah, Joy, so here is the surprise!" Alim said.

"What, Alim?" Joyce asked excitedly.

"Do you want to build a house on these two acres of land, or do you want to buy that beautiful house next to this land?" Alim asked.

"Alim, what a huge and wonderful surprise! I'm lost for words!" Joyce cried.

Alim finally brought the car to a complete halt, and Joyce stepped out to look over the land and the beautiful scenery. She then started to envision the house in her mind.

"Building a house would be awesome. I'll go with that idea because I can have it the way that I want it," Joyce said.

"I thought that you would go for the land, Joy. I will get started on that right away," Alim said.

"This is a perfect New Year so far; I am so happy, Alim!" Joyce said.

They then sat quietly for a few minutes as they drove to Momma Belle's house.

"Is everything all right, Alim?" Joyce asked.

"Sure, Joy. Why do you ask?" Alim answered.

"You're so quiet all of a sudden," Joyce said.

"Nothing wrong, baby. Everything is fine. I guess I was thinking about the property and what plans we are going to come up with," Alim explained.

"Oh, okay," Joyce said.

"I know something, and it's that Momma is waiting on her New Year's Eve hug from you. She has been asking if you are coming by the house tonight," Alim said.

"Oh, I did promise her that I would call her today, but going to her house is much more personal," Joyce said.

When Alim and Joyce arrived at Momma Belle's house, they greeted her with hugs and kisses, and Momma Belle was sure happy to see Joyce. While Joyce was inside talking to Momma, Alim went out onto the porch to chat on his cell phone, unaware that Joyce noticed his facial expression and body language, which didn't fit well. To Joyce, Alim seemed to be acting frustrated one minute and puzzled the next. Joyce couldn't understand his weird behavior, but she decided to ask him about it later. Joyce talked to Momma Belle about the land and the house they would be building there. Momma Belle was excited for Joyce. She then noticed Alim on the porch and insisted on calling him back into the house with a concerned look on her face.

"That boy is always talking business. He must learn how to let go work sometimes. It seems he lets that absorb him," Momma Belle said, looking frustrated with Alim.

"Momma, I have been meaning to ask you a question," Joyce said.

"Yeah, honey," Momma replied.

"Why did you give Alim that name?" Joyce asked. "It's kind of different, but I like it,"

"Well, Alim's Daddy suggested that we give him that name. Earl had a best friend that died in a gang fight when they were teenagers, and I mean they were like brothers. So, Earl wanted his name given to our first son. It's something that Alim never questioned before; well, maybe he liked the name so much that he never thought about questioning it, or maybe he didn't care," Momma explained.

"Oh, I see," Joyce said.

"You want something to eat, Joyce?" Momma asked.

"Oh no, Momma. I'm not hungry at all, but I am curious about what you have cooked," Joyce asked.

"I cooked some chicken pastry!"

"Oh, good. I will take some home. You know how much I love your chicken pastry," Joyce said happily before noticing Alim walk back into the house.

"Alim, why did you look so frustrated when you were on the phone? I worry when you look like that. It makes me uneasy," Joyce said.

"Don't worry, honey. It is always business, and this real estate stuff can be somewhat tedious at times. It's like that sometimes, honey," Alim said as he came over and kissed Joyce.

He then turned to his Momma Belle. "Hey, Momma, what's for dinner? And I know that you are not trying to feed Joy again because we ate at one of your favorite little diners."

"No, Alim, she is just taking home some of my good chicken pastry, and don't try to change the subject; you are all work, and too much work is no good!" Momma scolded.

"I know, Momma, but if I don't work hard, how can I support, oh, I mean spoil, this beautiful young lady of mine? And besides, I am fine, you two. Now stop fussing. Okay, Joy. Are you ready to go?" Alim asked, smiling at Joyce. "Joyce, guess where I am taking you for Valentine's Day?" Alim said.

"Huh, what a surprise, Alim! I don't know!" Joyce said.

"Ahh, come on, Joy. Where did you tell me you always wanted to go? And yes, I remembered you telling me this place, so I made reservations for Valentine's Day," Alim said.

"Oh, my goodness. Not Martha's Vineyard, Alim!" Joyce said excitedly, rushing over to hug him.

"Yes! Isn't that the place you said that you always wanted to go? I didn't know anything about it, so I went on the internet to find some information, and it does look interesting. So, tell your boss that you need that Friday off, and we can fly out to Massachusetts on Friday morning," Alim said.

"Thank you, baby. You are so good to me. This is going to be the best trip ever, and you'll enjoy it too, Alim," Joyce said as she continued to hold on to Alim.

"I'm not the one that I am trying to make happy; it is you, baby, and I want this to be the very best Valentine's Day ever for you," Joyce said.

"I am so happy to see my baby with a woman that he truly loves, and I hope y'all enjoy your Valentine's trip," Momma said.

"Yes, thank you, Momma, and I am not saying that I am ready to go, but I must go. I must work tomorrow, and so do you, Alim," Joyce said.

"I hate to see y'all go, but I know that this has been a tiresome couple of days," Momma Belle said.

"See you later, Momma, and I will talk to you soon," Alim said.

"Are you going to stay with me tonight, Alim?" Joyce asked.

"Not tonight, Joy. I have a lot of work to catch up with," Alim responded.

"Okay," Joyce said, feeling disappointed.

"I will call you later before you go to bed tonight," Alim said.

"Okay, good night," Joyce said as she got out of the car.

"Oh, Joy. Don't be like that. I just have a lot to do, sweetheart. Please understand," Alim said.

"I understand. I guess I just got my hopes up about your company to-night," Joyce said.

"I know, baby, but I will make it up to you, I promise. Just let me knock some things out and I will be free soon, okay?" Alim pleaded as he kissed Joyce good night while he walked her to her door.

"Love you, Alim," Joyce said as Alim walked away.

"Love you too, Joy."

Joyce watched through the blinds as Alim sat in the car, looking as though he was thinking about something before driving off. She noticed that Alim had been acting a little strange since before her trip to Chicago, but he still showed that he loved and cared for her deeply. Joyce just felt a little confused by his moods, but perhaps it was just that he had put aside all the work for the holidays, and now he had to play catch-up with work.

Chapter 18

Matters of the Heart

Joyce was feeling a little solemn as they arrived home on Monday evening from their Valentine's weekend. They had an awesome time at Martha's Vineyard, and Joyce seemed to be the happiest ever. Alim did not mind the trip at all either. It had been so romantic, and Joyce couldn't wait to tell Caroline all about it. Alim dropped Joyce off at home so that they could both get some rest for work the next day.

It was now midweek, and Joyce had not seen Alim since Monday, after he dropped her off from their trip, though they had spoken a little on the phone. *Work has been very tedious for Alim—or so he says*, Joyce thought. Although she was beginning to feel a little disrespected, she tried to understand his excuses for not being around as much. She hoped she could get him to attend church with her on Sunday and maybe go out to dinner on Saturday, since he probably wouldn't be busy then. Alim called her just as she contemplated calling him.

"Hey, baby, I'm sorry I haven't been attentive to you lately," Alim said.

"You should be, Alim. I miss you," Joyce said.

"I miss you too, baby, but there is something important I have to do this weekend," Alim said.

"What is that Alim?" Joyce asked.

"I have to go out this Friday on business out of town this weekend," Alim said.

"Oh, out of town? You didn't mention it before. Where are you going?" Joyce said.

"I have to go to DC to attend one of those real estate meetings again, and I didn't tell you because it slipped my mind from everything that has been going on," Alim said.

"Oh, do you want me to accompany you?" Joyce asked.

"No, not this time, Joy. I will be tied up all day Saturday and will be leaving Sunday morning," Alim said.

"You will see me before you leave, right?" Joyce asked.

"Come on, Joy. Why would you think that I would just leave like that?" Alim responded.

"I don't know, Alim. I haven't seen much of you this week. I really miss you," Joyce said.

"I know, Joy, and I do apologize. Anyway, let me finish up here, and I will be over tonight. I don't like you sounding like this, and these things will happen sometimes. You can't always act like that, Joy. I will not make any stops on my way over to your house unless you want me to pick up something on my way," Alim said.

Joyce, now in a frenzy, just stood there and stared out her window.

"No, Alim. Just get here as soon as you can," Joyce said. As Joyce let go of the phone, her heart grew heavy. She didn't want it to, but she and Alim had always been close, and now it seemed that they had grown somewhat distant, even though he didn't see it that way. Perhaps it was only going the mile distance and not heart distance, which was something that Joyce would have to get used to. She still felt that there was no reason to doubt Alim; he hadn't shown any signs of intentional disrespect or neglect, but her heart still felt heavy, despite all her love for Alim. *Women can be too clingy sometimes,* she thought, and she didn't want to seem that way. She wanted to make sure that her heart was in the right place and that she didn't appear selfish. She told Alim she understood, but deep down inside, she didn't.

Joyce called Caroline for a little womanly conversation. She didn't like talking about Alim that much to Caroline, nor did she want to bore Caroline, but she felt that Caroline didn't mind at all being her listening ear. She knew that Joyce needed some spiritual advice.

"Hello," Caroline said as she answered the phone.

"Hi, Caroline. How are you today?" Joyce asked.

"I am all right, Joyce, and how are you? I'm glad to hear from you!" Caroline said.

"I'm feeling a little despondent today," Joyce said sadly.

"Why is that sweetheart?" Caroline asked.

"My heart is feeling a little heavy. I haven't seen much of Alim lately. I guess it's work, or that's what he says," Joyce said.

"I see," Caroline said as she listened. Caroline was always a good listener.

"I did talk to him for a little bit today, just before I called you. I really do feel a little distance between me and Alim, though he denies it," Joyce said.

"Well, Joyce, I know you can always count on your women's intuition, but you must start leading on the word of God. As it is said in Proverbs, "Trust in the Lord with all thine heart and lean not unto thine own understanding. In all thy ways, acknowledge him, and He shall direct thy paths,'" Caroline said.

"Thank you, Caroline, but I really don't want to feel like that is where I need the help with security. There is nothing wrong; it's just my mind. Maybe I am just too spoiled by Alim," Joyce said as she laughed a little.

"Well, Joyce, the Lord always promised that he would keep our minds in perfect peace if it stayed on him. You can find that scripture in Isaiah, 'Thou will keep him in perfect peace, whose mind is stayed on thee: because he trusted in thee.' Joyce, you must really give your life totally to Jesus Christ so that he can show you things in your life that might be concerning. God always has our best interests in mind. The Lord said, plain as day, "Lean not unto your own understanding' and that he will direct our paths, so just lean on him, and go to him. We can really make a mess of things when we try to handle it ourselves," Caroline said.

"So, what does that have to do with anything, Caroline?" Joyce asked.

"It has everything to do with our lives, Joyce. We can't do anything, and I stress *anything*, without Christ in our lives. The Lord must be on our side;

if not, we will always be confused and have a heart that feels empty, even though it seems that we have it all. God said these things in his word. Trust him and obey. He is not a man that he should lie, and he can't lie,". Read it in Numbers," Caroline said.

"I see, Caroline. I think that the Lord deals with us on many different levels and many ways to get our attention. Man is not perfect; only God is perfect, and I know that he won't stray from the truth because he is not a man that would lie. Christ is the only one that can judge; and the same is true in life—because he is the only one that completely knows all," Joyce said.

"The Lord wants the best for all of us, and once you become his, he will let you know what is best for you. You have a good and trusting heart, Joyce, and you are a very intelligent woman. Your heart grows heavy for a reason that runs deep inside you," Caroline said.

"So, what are you saying, Caroline? That deep down inside my heart, I do not trust Alim?" Joyce asked.

"No, I wasn't saying that Joyce, but perhaps that's what's going on," Caroline replied.

"I don't, Caroline, and maybe I am being just a little apprehensive or used to things being the same all the time. No changes, please! I would like for our relationship to be the same all the time. And Caroline, I know what you will say what about growth, and I know that to be true," Joyce said.

"Well, Joyce. All I can say is that things do not stay the same, and that is something that you must get used to. I also know that you haven't been in a serious relationship in a long time, but that also takes some getting used to, and you can survive it."

Joyce listened attentively as Caroline continued. "Joyce, you also know that I must tell you from time to time about your salvation because I love and care for you a great deal. You are not saved well serving the Lord, and you are still of the world, even though you live in the world and the flesh is weak; only the Lord can keep you if the heart is given to him. You must get your heart right with the Lord, and you will see many changes if you are sincere," Caroline said.

"I know, Caroline, but what about Alim?" Joyce asked.

"Alim is not first, the Lord is, honey. Think about that now," Joyce said.

"Caroline, there is so much on my mind right now, and I don't know why I am putting myself through all these unnecessary changes," Joyce said.

"Well, like I said, Joyce, God will keep you in perfect peace if your mind is on him. It is all about God, and him only. God can only speak for your happiness and peace. I love you, Joyce," Caroline said.

"I love you too, Caroline," Joyce said as she hung up the phone.

Chapter 19

OUT OF SIGHT, OUT OF MIND

Alim and Joyce spent the entire night together the night before his trip to DC. Joyce was still not too happy about Alim going on this trip without her, but she knew that it was something that she had to accept. *I'm marrying a successful businessman, and it comes with the territory*, she thought.

"Do you need me to do anything for you before you leave?" Joyce asked.

"No, baby. Everything is good. I've already put everything together," Alim said.

"So, you will be back on Sunday morning?" Joyce asked.

"It will be more like Sunday afternoon or early evening, I hope. Trust me, I will try to make it back as soon as I can," Alim said earnestly.

"Okay."

"I will be gone before you get off work on Friday," Alim said.

"I know, Alim," Joyce said.

"Now, do you need anything before I depart, sweetheart?" Alim asked.

"I can't think of anything. Just call me and get back here as fast as you can," Joyce said as she kissed Alim.

"I will call, Joy, and don't you think otherwise. Let me go and get home now. I know you must get ready for work, and I must get ready for the road," Alim said.

"Okay," Joyce replied.

"I will call later, baby," Alim said. Joyce just looked away as he went on his way, but she did notice that Alim had left his phone in the car again when he came over to her house. *But whatever*, she said silently to herself.

Joyce thought she would just do some wedding planning while Alim was away. She had to meet with her wedding planner anyway to discuss a few things.

Alim surprised Joyce by dropping in with some lunch at her job. Joyce was elated to see Alim before he left for DC. He wanted to do this for Joyce because he would be leaving early on Friday morning and wouldn't see her before he left. How could Joyce have any distrust when it came to this man; he was so good to her, she thought, and she felt guilty for being so selfish and self-centered with her thoughts and her actions. She loved Alim even more, and every day.

Joyce decided not to go to church on Sunday because she wanted to be home when Alim got back home. Church would not have done her much good if the only thing she had on her mind was Alim, anyway. Alim called Joyce before he hit the road.

"Hey, baby, I'm getting ready to get on the road. I will call you again as soon as I get some miles on me, and maybe I will stop for some breakfast a diner or fast-food restaurant. I need some coffee," Alim said.

"Okay, baby. Be careful out there and have a safe trip. I miss you terribly already, and I love you," Joyce said.

"I love you too, Joy," Alim said before hanging up.

Joyce laid in the bed for a few minutes more, thinking about Alim. She then drifted off into a quick nap before getting out of bed and getting ready for work. She had a reoccurring dream of holding her hands out to Alim as he slowly drifted away, and she could never understand this dream. She thought it might just be her subconscious messing with her, or maybe it was just wedding jitters.

Her workday was absorbing, but she felt it was good for her since she had so much on her mind. Alim called Joyce as she was leaving work to let her know that he had made it to DC and was getting settled in his hotel room. She was relieved and happy to hear from him. They talked about twenty minutes before Alim had to leave to grab some dinner. Joyce still felt that she should have been there with them because they were inseparable. Joyce heard Alim greeting his colleagues in the hotel lobby, so they had to end their phone conversation. On the way home from work, Joyce decided to call Momma Belle to let her know that she would be stopping by to pick up a plate of food; she knew that Momma cooked almost every day.

"Hello, Joyce. I'm surprised you called because I thought that you would be going to DC with Alim," Momma Belle said.

"No, Momma. He wanted to make that trip alone," Joyce said.

"Oh, I see. Alim takes these trips a couple of times a year, you know. They have these real estate conventions, and I know that he misses not having you coming along with him."

"I hope he misses me, Momma," Joyce said.

"Now, don't you doubt that because he does. He even asked me to call you while I was gone, but you showed up here today to get some food, and I am glad," Momma told Joyce.

"Oh, that was sweet, Momma. I can't stay long because I am tired. I had a very heavy load at work today, and I didn't get much sleep last night. I need to get some sleep, but I thought some of your cooking would put me to sleep along with some hot tea," Joyce said.

"No problem, honey. I know that you are tired. You even look it, and it is always a pleasure to see you. You're always welcome," Momma said.

Joyce left Momma's house anticipating another phone call from Alim, but it didn't come this time, so she went to the liquor store to get a bottle of chardonnay, along with some candles. She thought that a long, hot bath with a glass of wine and some candles would soothe her for sure. She didn't know why Caroline's words interrupted her thoughts, but her words played in the back of her mind: "Put your trust in the Lord, and God is never second," and "God will keep you in perfect peace if your mind is on him," but the only man Joyce could think of was Alim. Joyce called Alim while pulling into her driveway, but she got his voicemail. She left a message to tell Alim that she was thinking of him. She then went inside and ran a lavender bubble bath. She then poured a glass of wine and set it beside the tub. Just as she started to get inside, the phone rang.

"Hi, baby! Hi, sweetheart! I just got your message, and I am thinking of you too. I just got through eating dinner, and now I am about to go up to my room to sleep. I am exhausted from all that driving," Alim said.

"I know you are tired, Alim, and I am glad that you called me back or I would have been worried," Joyce said.

"What are you doing, Joy?" Alim asked.

"Oh, nothing much. I was just about to get into my bubble bath before you called," Joyce said.

"I wish I were there for that bubble bath. You know I like to bathe with you, Joy," Alim said wistfully.

"I know, Alim. I wish you were here too," Joyce said.

"I am going to hit the sack soon because I have an early day tomorrow. I don't want to be tired at the convention. I must make a few calls, and I didn't even call Momma yet, but I will try to call you later, baby, if I don't fall asleep," Alim said.

"Love you, Alim," Joyce said.

"I love you too, Joy," Alim said as he hung up the phone. As Joyce tried to relax and enjoy her bubble bath, she felt herself drifting away to sleep in the tub as she listened to Brian McKnight's solemn song, "Is the Feeling Gone." Listening to that song always brought out a lot of emotions in Joyce, and it explained the ways in which she hoped that Alim was not losing the love that he had for her. She had several thoughts in the back of her mind as she got out of the bath and laid in bed. *If the other people attending these meetings that Alim has gone to bring their significant others...* and then she had another thought— *just let it go!* She knew that since Alim left on Friday, she couldn't have gone anyway, so she came to her senses and put that thought out of her mind. Still, she wished he had asked her...

She finally drifted off to sleep without another good night call from Alim, and in the late morning, she woke up hoping to see a message from Alim on her cell phone, but there was nothing. She decided to get some refreshments for the afternoon because her wedding planner was coming over, and that would keep her mind occupied for sure.

In the middle of the meeting with her wedding planner, Alim called. He was still in the convention but took a minute to call Joyce. The phone call was brief, but she was grateful that he did call. After the wedding planner left, Joyce decided to go to the mall and do a little shopping. As she pulled into the parking lot, she ran into Caroline and her children. She greeted them all with hugs.

"How is the planning for the wedding coming along?" Caroline asked. "I didn't forget that you told me you were going to meet with the wedding planner today."

"Well, Caroline, I'm making progress," Joyce said.

"That's great, Joyce. Is there anything that I can do?" Caroline asked.

"You've already lent me your beautiful daughters, but maybe you can go with me to pick up a wedding dress in a couple of weeks. I would love that, Caroline," Joyce said.

"Okay, I would be delighted, and I am glad to see you today, Joyce. I hope to see you in church Sunday," Caroline said.

"I will try to make it, Caroline," Joyce said.

"Okay, and I will talk to you later, Joyce. Love you," Caroline said as she left.

Joyce knew that she wouldn't be in church Sunday because she was going to wait for Alim to get in on Sunday. To Joyce, Caroline was a beautiful woman who loved her family dearly, and she admired Caroline for who she was and what she stood for, which was a steadfast, intelligent Christian woman. Caroline's husband Ray was one of the Sunday school teachers in the church, as well as a deacon. He often mentioned Caroline when he taught Sunday School and spoke highly of his wife. Joyce could tell he loved her dearly. She remembered reading a scripture in the Proverbs that said, "He who finds a wife finds a good thing," and it was a blessed thing indeed, as Ray would say in some of his teachings. Ray was a tall and handsome man. He could put you in the mind of a young Sean Connery, while Caroline was the spitting image of Priscilla Presley. Caroline and Ray were a beautiful couple.

Joyce finishing up her shopping as the evening set in. She hadn't heard from Alim yet that evening, and she thought that she would call him when she arrived home. Joyce started to feel a little neglected, and it had been a little like that when she went to Chicago. Alim wasn't always available to answer his phone. It seemed there was some distance between them, and she would get his voice mail more so than his voice when she called his phone. She was feeling like she was out of sight and out of mind for Alim. Joyce opened her laptop to keep her company for a bit. She wanted to order some books online, and just as she was pulling her credit card out of her wallet, her phone rang.

"Hi, baby!" Alim said.

"Hi, Alim. I've been waiting on you to call me back," Joyce exclaimed.

"I know, Joy. I've been tied up all day, and then I went out with my associate. But I am back now calling you," Alim said.

"Okay, I had a very busy and eventful day myself," Joyce said.

"So, what did you do all day, Joy?" Alim asked.

"I had a meeting with the wedding planner, and I did some shopping," Joyce said.

"Well, a day in the mall is always eventful," Alim said as he laughed a little. "I am so tired, Joy, and I have that long drive back tomorrow."

"I know, Alim. You must get your rest for that long trip back tomorrow," Joyce said a little sarcastically."

"I love you, Joy, and I will see you tomorrow. I'm not sure of the time, but I hope it will be early," Alim said before hanging up.

Chapter 20

HIS WORD IS BOND

When Sunday came around, Joyce had to stay home and wait for Alim's arrival, meaning that there would be no church for her. She woke up early in the hope that Alim would be home by the afternoon, and she was anxious. Alim didn't call early Sunday morning like Joyce was expecting him to. She was thinking to call him around noon to ask his estimated travel time so that she could surprise him at his apartment. Then, at about eleven o'clock in the morning, Alim called.

"Hey, baby," Alim said.

"Hi, Alim. Where are you?" Joyce asked.

"I am halfway home. And yes, left early to get back at a decent time. I didn't want to arrive late, but I do have to stop and get a bite to eat; the only food I had was coffee and a donut," Alim said.

"I am really missing you, Alim, and I didn't even go to church because that is not where my heart and mind is. I have you on my mind, and that is why I stayed home to wait for your return home. Yes, I'm anxious," Joyce said.

"Joy, you should have gone to church, sweetheart. I love you, and I will be home soon. I may try to call again," Alim said and then hung up.

Joyce still had the inkling to meet Alim at his apartment. She decided to go his apartment at around two in the afternoon. She knew that he should be home by then, giving the time he left DC. By that time, he still hadn't returned, so she decided to wait some more.

Half an hour later, she saw Alim's Lincoln Navigator pull into the apartment complex driveway. He was on his cell phone as usual but did not see Joyce. She got out of her car as he was parking and walked toward his vehicle. He looked over at her with a startled expression and quickly hung up his phone. She hadn't expected that look; she thought he would be smiling and happy to see her.

"Hi, baby! What a surprise, I didn't expect to see you here. I really didn't expect you to be waiting here for me," Alim said, getting out of his vehicle. By now, he was smiling.

"Oh, Alim. You're not happy to see me?" Joyce asked, sadness evident on her face.

"Yeah, baby. I'm elated to see you. You just surprised me, that's all," Alim said as he kissed and hugged Joyce.

"I missed you, honey, and I couldn't wait to see you!" Joyce said, smiling now. "You look tired, Alim. Here, let me help you with your bags."

"Okay," Alim said with weary smile.

As Joyce went to retrieve the rest of his belongings from the back seat and front passenger seat, she noticed a pink travel bag in the passenger door pocket. She picked it up and quickly looked around to see if Alim was there, but he had gone into the apartment by now. She opened the bag and began to rummage through it. It held some women's cosmetics and a small bottle of expensive perfume.

At that moment, Joyce felt a myriad of emotions—hurt, betrayal, and sadness. Her heard began to beat rapidly. She felt like someone had stabbed her. She put the cosmetics case back into the passenger door pocket and finished retrieving Alim's things. She took all the stuff into the apartment. Joyce was hoping that Alim had a good explanation for the questions that she was about to ask.

Alim met Joyce at the door as she walked into the apartment. He grabbed his things from her, and while doing so noticed shocked expression on her face.

"What's wrong, Joy? And why that sad and grim look on your face suddenly? If it's the bags, I could have finished unloading them. Honey, what's wrong?" Alim asked.

Joyce remained silent for a minute while she collected her thoughts. She then went over to the counter and poured herself some wine. Then she turned to Alim and told him what she had discovered. Who does the pink bag belong to?" Joyce asked in a curious tone simmering with hurt.

Alim just looked at her in surprise and confusion. Joyce held back her tears with all her might as she waited for him to respond.

"I must see what you are talking about. Let me see what you are talking about!" Alim demanded.

"Come on now, Alim. You know who was in your car. Now, why do you have to check behind me?" Joyce asked angrily. She felt like Alim was trying to make her look like a fool. Joyce waited in the apartment until Alim returned. He came back, but he didn't have the bag with him, just an explanation.

"Oh, Joyce. That belongs to the lady who rode with me to the convention center in Washington. Let me just tell you that not everyone who came brought their cars, so they needed rides to the convention center or took taxis from the hotels. I assumed that most of us gave people rides," Alim explained stiffly. "The young lady who I escorted to the convention must have left that bag in my truck, but I wasn't aware of it—or else it would not have been there, Joyce," Alim said, shaking his head.

"Well, it is weird that she didn't notice her bag was missing, whoever this woman is, Alim," Joyce said, still sipping her wine, her legs crossed.

"Well, it is obvious she didn't notice it missing, Joy, and I didn't either. Don't give me a hard time over this, Joy. It is not that serious," Alim said, shaking his head frustration while he rummaged through the bag, as though he were looking for some identification.

"Well, if you say so," Joyce said. She got up to turn on the television.

"What do you mean, 'if you say so,' Joy? That is the way it is, whether you want to believe it or not," Alim said angrily, tossing the bag in the trashcan.

"Why are you tossing it, Alim? Aren't you concerned that the woman may call for her bag?" Joyce asked.

"First of all, she doesn't have my direct cell number, but she does have my office number, so if she is concerned that she left the bag in my truck, she'll call and ask. But I doubt that she will remember where she left it because I didn't take her back to the hotel; she rode with someone else. And if she does call, well, the bag is history, and I haven't seen it," Alim said calmly.

"I am trying to understand why a woman would carry that bag to a meeting or a convention anyway," Joy asked as she back on the sofa, her feet shaking.

"I don't know, Joy. Your guess is just as good as mine." Alim said calmly as he went into the kitchen to pour himself a glass of apple juice.

Joyce didn't want to talk about it anymore, but she still feeling uneasy on the inside.

"So, where is my real homecoming hug and kiss? We got distracted by the mysterious bag, and it seems like my baby does not believe a word I say," Alim said mournfully as he sat down beside Joyce and pulled her closer.

"No, it's not that, Alim!" Joyce whimpered. "Seeing that case just threw me in a different way. And you would feel the same way if the situation was reversed, no matter how strange it seems." She kissed him back.

"Maybe not, baby, but I would have at least trusted your word because if I can't trust you, I can't be with you. You feel me, baby? My word is bond, baby. Please don't ever doubt it; I would not do anything to intentionally hurt you," Alim, his face holding an expression of sincerity.

Joy just looked down, feeling a little ashamed of herself. She didn't say anything else as Alim kissed her again. Joyce still didn't feel great with the situation, but she accepted what Alim was saying because maybe, just maybe, it was the entire truth.

Later that evening, Joyce and Alim went to Momma Belle's house for dinner because they both were too exhausted to go to a restaurant. She was happy to see Alim safely home and immediately fixed two plates of food for them. Now that she was eating some of Momma's chicken and dumplings, Joyce was in good spirits again.

"You look today, Joyce. Did you go to church today?" Momma Belle asked.

"No, Momma, I was waiting for Alim to come home. I guess I was so anxious about his arrival that I skipped church today, and I know that we both are glad that he is home." Joyce said, smiling. She knew that she should have gone to church that day, and she still felt a little guilty about that. She tried to push away those feelings while Momma asked Alim a bunch of questions about his convention and his trip. Alim wasn't shy about sopping down the chicken and dumplings while answering Momma's questions.

"Why are you so quiet, Joyce?" Momma asked. Joyce invited that question from Momma because she had remained quiet throughout the whole meal, with all manner of thoughts going through her head.

"I'm fine, Momma. Just a little tired, I guess," Joyce said. Time was passing by, and she wanted to get home so she could get ready for work the next day. As Momma was still talking to Alim, her mind went back to Alim's words of trusting him and that his word was bond, but then another thought ignited her mind: God said to put your whole trust in him. Now, this made her even more confused about Alim and God. She thought that if she had gone to church instead of waiting for Alim to come home, none of this mess would have happened. She would have been on the right track today and not sidetracked.

Joyce loved Alim so much that she was willing to believe anything he said, regardless of her doubts, even with the obvious things. She wanted to be as close to him as she could get. As she and Alim left Momma's house, he began to tell her about the construction on to build their new house, which made Joyce very happy. She and Alim would be meeting with the architect the following week. For some obscure reason, this made her feel secure again.

They pulled into the parking lot of Alim's apartment complex so Joyce could get her car.

"Joy, I will follow you home and sit with you a little while," Alim said.

"Okay," Joyce said.

As Alim followed her, she saw him on his phone again. She wanted to ask him about it but decided not to, considering they had just been through a whirlwind. She didn't want Alim to think that she was being insecure again. She wondered who he could be talking to so late on a Sunday night? Was it that woman asking about her bag? Did it really matter at all? She knew that Alim was hers and no one else could have him. He would never allow that to happen.

"I'll Always Love You" by Taylor Dayne began to play on her radio, and it struck a deep chord in her heart. Joyce thought about making love to him and being in their own world where no one else existed. She genuinely loved that man, and he was the only one for her.

Those were her thoughts as she finally pulled into her driveway. She had come too far to let anyone, or anything pull her and Alim apart. She would always love that man, and she wanted him to feel the same deep emotions that she felt. She tried to stop the tears that were welling up in her eyes, but to no avail—the tears flowed, full of love and compassion for Alim.

She quickly wiped her tears away so that he wouldn't notice them. As they walked up the porch steps, Joyce turned toward Alim and kissed him passionately. She whispered in his ear that she wanted to make love to him. Alim had no disagreements about that; he picked Joyce up and carried her to her bedroom.

Chapter 21

PLANS, DREAMS, AND THOUGHTS

Joyce couldn't wait to get off work on Wednesday to meet the architect, Mr. Clemmons, with Alim. As she drove, she thought about her and Alim's plans and dreams. She had never imagined in her wildest dreams that she would be marrying a man that had assets, ambitions, and who was well off and loved her dearly. Alim met all of Joyce's needs. Alim had told Joyce many times that she didn't have to work, especially if it was going to interfere with wedding planning, but Joyce loved her job and would never think of leaving it. She knew that Alim would understand why she would never leave the law firm; she loved the people there, and they loved her back. Alim completely understood that Joyce wanted to keep her job instead of being a stay-at-home wife.

They drove together downtown to Mr. Clemmons's office. Joyce was a little nervous at first because she had no experience designing a house. Mr. Clemmons laid out all the plans before them and specifically asked Joyce for her input. Alim just watched and agreed to whatever Joyce decided while Mr. Clemmons answered all her questions. Joyce began to feel more comfortable and spoke to Mr. Clemmons like they had known each other for a while. The meeting lasted about an hour, and Joyce was elated when she left the office.

"Dreams do come true!" Joyce said as they walked together to the car. Alim took Joyce to a steakhouse for dinner. They sat and talked about their plans and the wedding, and Joyce tried to bring up church again. She wanted Alim to attend church with her that coming Sunday. Alim said that he would think about it, and Joyce was fine with his answer. Just as Joyce was about to excuse herself to the ladies' room, a beautiful woman walked over to their table. Alim looked up with a look of pure shock on his face, which instantly made Joyce sit back down.

"Hi, Alim," the woman said.

"Hello, Carlotta," Alim replied.

"And your name?" the woman asked Joyce as if she was there for a specific reason.

"Hi, I am Joyce," Joyce responded with a confused half-smile.

"Well, as you know, my name is Carlotta," the woman said as she stood confidently in front of Alim and Joyce.

"Nice to meet you, Carlotta," Joyce said, still confused.

"I just wanted to come over and say hi to Alim. We used to work together at the real estate office," Carlotta said.

"Oh, I see!" Joyce said, feeling a little relieved now that the woman let on how she knew Alim.

"Do you live here in Savannah?" Joyce asked.

"Well, I live outside of Savannah, and I am here visiting relatives. I brought them to this quaint little restaurant. It is one of my favorites."

"Yes, the food is good here," Joyce said awkwardly.

"It was good seeing you again, Carlotta," Alim said, turning back to Joyce in the hope that Carlotta would get the hint to leave him and Joyce to their dinner.

"How are things going down at the real estate office?" Carlotta said.

"Good, just fine," Alim said curtly.

"Well, I must get back to my family now. It was good meeting you, Joyce, and good seeing you again, Alim," Carlotta said.

"You too, Carlotta," Joyce said.

Alim stood as Carlotta waved goodbye and returned to her table.

"She seemed kind of strange, Alim, didn't you think so? Well, you know her better than I do," Joyce said.

"Not really, Joy. Carlotta has always been modest and reserved," Alim said.

"Oh, so you do know her that well," Joyce said sarcastically as she left to go to the ladies' room. When Joyce returned to the table, she Carlotta glancing over at her.

"So, are you ready to go?" Alim asked Joyce.

"Alim! Don't be rushing me. As soon as I finish my wine and dessert, we can leave, okay?" Joyce said, exasperated. Joyce knew that Alim was feeling a little uncomfortable because he had never rushed her from a restaurant before.

"If you're feeling uncomfortable, Alim, then we can leave," Joyce said.

"No, I'm all right, baby," Alim replied.

"You're sure?"

"Yes, I'm all right, sweetie,"

"Well, I'm finished, so we can go now, honey," Joyce said.

After Alim paid the bill, he looked over to Carlotta to say goodbye. Joyce knew that something didn't sit well with this woman, but she didn't want to worry herself or bother Alim about it. Her night was going too well now to let anything or anyone to hinder it.

When they arrived at Alim's apartment, Joyce thought about sitting for a while, but Alim claimed he was tired, so he waited for Joyce to retrieve her car and followed her home. He didn't stay long before heading back home. Joyce understood because it had been a busy weekend, but Alim did seem kind of weird after he saw Carlotta.

While Joyce boiled some hot water for her tea, she sat and thought about why Alim would not be straight up with her about anything. There was no way he would have secrets or could hide them from her if he did have some because they were together all the time, and the only time that they were separated was Alim's Washington trip and Joyce's Chicago trip. Joyce sat at her kitchen table and allowed all kinds of thoughts to enter her mind as she stared hard at that big engagement on her finger.

The symbol of our love, she thought.

She knew that she would never love this way again. A song playing in the background—Dionne Warwick's "I Know I Never Love this Way Again."

Joyce really enjoyed the oldies when she was alone, reading, or just having those deep thoughts about her relationship. She took her teacup and went to lie down on her bed, where she stared into the moonlight that shone through her blinds. Joyce had more than a few pictures of Alim on her phone, and to some she attached a little message of poetry. She even had a video picture of Alim walking toward her with his arms stretched out. She also attached a message to that scene.

Forever in my dream.
I dreamed of you,
Walking into my distance.
You're my dream come.
True.

Finally, Joyce decided to rest for the night. Just before she fell asleep, Alim called to say good night. Joyce went to sleep with thoughts of Alim attending church with her on Sunday.

The rest of the week was a good week for Joyce. She was in good spirits because Alim called and agreed to go to church with her on Sunday. She called Caroline on Saturday to let her know that she would be attending church on Sunday with Alim, and Caroline was so happy to hear that. Joyce talked to Alim a little on Saturday because he had some overtime to do at the office. He was busy, but Joyce didn't mind because she was looking forward to Sunday anyhow.

Later, Joyce talked to Caroline about her situations that she encountered with Alim for the past couple of days. Hearing Joyce's situations didn't sit well with Caroline, but she listened, not wanting to give too much input right away. She knew that, right now, Joyce needed a friend, not a dictator.

Chapter 22

THE WORDS THAT SUSTAINED HER HEART

Early on Sunday morning, Caroline called Joyce to check in on her and confirm that she was coming to church today. Joyce assured Caroline that Alim was coming with her. It was a beautiful Sunday morning; even though it was a little brisk outside, the sun was shining happily, and the sky was clear. Alim arrived right on time to pick up Joyce.

'Hi, baby. Glad you're on time," Joyce said as she greeted Alim with a wide smile and a kiss.

"You look wonderful, Joy," Alim said as he helped her put on her jacket.

"Thank you for not backing out on me, sweetie."

"No, I wouldn't do that after I promised," he said candidly.

The choir was singing as they entered the church. The usher greeted Joyce and Alim and led them to the middle pews of the church. Joyce stood and clapped with the rest of the congregation in song and nudged Alim to do the same. She felt good about her man being at church with her. She thought this would be a good beginning for some spiritual comfort in both their lives.

After the singing and the collection, Pastor Hinton proceeded to give the sermon, which was all about faith in salvation. He appointed the church to know Christ and fill their hearts with faith in salvation. All his words were familiar to her, and she followed every scripture with Alim as the pastor read them.

"Salvation is the key to living and having trust and faith in God. Repenting from your sins can give you hope and peace in your life, and the wage of sin is death, but the gift of God is eternal life through Jesus Christ our Lord. Jesus came to give his life that we may have abundant life," Pastor Hinton preached.

Joyce listened intensely as she held Alim's hand throughout the entire sermon. Pastor Hinton said that having Jesus in your life was all you needed.

"You can do all things through Christ that strengthen you, and cannot have anything, or you cannot prosper without Christ." Pastor Hinton said to his congregation. "I've mentioned here the examples, love, relationships, and hope to name a few. Christ must be the center, or it won't avail. Christ is for all to be happy and rich in life and his glory, meaning faith in salvation."

Joyce let go of Alim's hand as she started to get convicted again, as she had done many Sundays ago.

"The Lord is calling every one of you that is not living in the faith of salvation. Jesus has the gift of salvation. Jesus loves you more than man can ever love you; we just have to surrender to the Lord Jesus Christ, and he will give you the desires of your heart, whatever is in his will. Jesus's grace is sufficient and wants to cleanse you from all your sins. People say, 'Pastor Hinton, you say to put your trust in no man,' and yes, that is what I say because if he or she is not walking with Christ, how can you trust that they are capable of anything? You must be totally committed to Christ, and I will preach that sermon repeatedly if I must for many to get it. How can you trust flesh? Again, Jesus must be at the center of your life because if one is walking with Christ, he will have a heart like Christ. Jesus will change your heart from the negative to the positive. He or she will think like Christ as well as being in the realm of his image. Sin will destroy homes, families, relationships, and friendships. I employ each one of you to try Christ, to experience his grace and goodness. The message is clear, people, Jesus is the way, and there is no other way. Confess your sins and take up the cross and follow Christ. The devil comes to steal, kill, and to destroy, and the Lord didn't make hell for us; he made it for the devil and his demons, but if you chose to follow Satan and keep sinning, that is where you will spend eternity. The Bible said when sin is finished, it bringeth forth death. Some of you may say that I am happy just the way I am, and everything is going fine. That is the way the devil tricks us, but I am here to tell you that without having a life of salvation in Christ, happiness can turn into misery, pain, and heartache—in some cases, without warning. Jesus can prevent these events from happening, or in many cases, can be there when they do happen and see you through it. Now, let's all stand." Pastor Hinton then proceeded to make the altar call.

Alim stood up and he excused himself, saying he needed go to the men's room and then step outside for some fresh air. Joyce wasn't pleased with his decision to step away in the middle of such a vital part of the service.

"If there is anyone here who would like to give their heart to Christ, please step down to the altar. Don't be ashamed, because Christ wasn't ashamed to give his life on that cross for our sins," the pastor beckoned.

The choir then started to sing "Try Christ" by the Hawkins Family. Joyce knew in her heart that she should make her way down to the altar, but she hesitated. Her heart was filled with so much conviction and was heavy. She knew that she needed to give her soul to Christ, and as the last call was being made, she joined the few that stood at the altar.

Caroline saw Joyce and immediately became overwhelmed with joy. She began to praise and worship the Lord while making her way down to the altar to support Joyce and take her hand. Joyce looked up and smiled at Caroline gratefully.

"Everyone repeat after me," Pastor Hinton said. "Oh, Lord, I am a sinner, and I ask you to come into my life and cleanse me. Wash me white as snow. I accept you on this day as my Lord and Savior Jesus Christ, and only you will I serve. Forgive me for all my sins, and save my soul right now, Lord, in the name of Jesus, and I thank you."

After Joyce said the sinner's prayer, Caroline hugged her and then escorted her back to her seat. Both women had tears in their eyes. Alim was back in his seat waiting for Joyce to come from the altar, and Caroline hugged Alim as she spoke to him before returning to her seat.

"Are you all right, baby?" Alim asked Joyce.

"Yes, Alim. I just gave my life to the Lord," Joyce said, smiling at Alim.

Alim didn't have to ask what that meant.

"You should have stayed and come with me down to the altar, Alim. I didn't like you leaving like that," Joyce said.

"I know, baby, but I needed some air. It was getting stuffy in here," Alim said.

Joyce just looked down at her hands and said nothing. She was very disappointed that Alim hadn't been there to make the altar call with her. And if she were being honest with herself, she wasn't even sure he would have come to the altar with her if he hadn't left.

After the service was over, Alim suggested they stop by a restaurant to eat, but Joyce wanted to go straight home. Alim knew that there was something different about Joyce's attitude today.

"What's wrong, Joy? You're not talking much," Alim asked.

"I didn't know that I would be so let down by your leaving when the altar call was about to happen. I was hoping that we both could have gone down together," Joyce, looking discouraged. said with discouragement on her face. "The Word really touched me, Alim and I had to go to the altar and get my life right with God."

"I know you did, Joy, and in due time, I will go to the altar too," Alim said.

"We both need God in our lives. You heard what the pastor said today, Alim," Joyce pleaded.

"I heard every word that the pastor said, and don't be that disappointed in me. Like I said, in due I am there," Alim said as he kissed Joyce.

"Okay, Alim, I will leave it alone for now, but I do still love you deeply, and you know that is right," Joyce said, grabbing Alim's hand.

"I hope you still love me, Joy!" Alim said, winking at her.

"I do, man!" Joyce said with sincerity. "I wanted to come straight home because I brought some work home from the office I needed to finish. I didn't want to be swamped with extra work on Monday," Joyce said.

"Okay, baby. I understand. No problem," Alim said, feeling a little relieved.

"You can come by a little later, Alim, if you are feeling up to it, or just call me and let me know what you are going to do," Joyce said. She leaned over and kissed Alim before going into the house. Joyce watched as Alim drove off and wondered how he really felt about her going down to the altar. Did he even care? She genuinely loved Alim, and she didn't want to lose him for anything.

Chapter 23

PRAYER AND DECEPTION

The months crept by, and spring was nearing its end. Caroline was always praying for Joyce to grow in Christ and faithfully continue her walk with him. Joyce faithfully attended church on Sunday and Bible classes on the weekdays. She had not fully given up all to follow Jesus and was still sexually connected to Alim. She wanted so desperately to get Alim to give his heart to Christ, which she often prayed for, and now she had to decide what she thought would honor God.

She brought to Alim's attention that they should go to the justice of peace to get married. There was no need to wait for the wedding, like they had originally planned. Joyce's motives were to have it both ways—Christ and Alim—but now she wanted to be into an honest woman as far as her sexual life was concerned. Alim didn't see fit with the idea to rush into marriage and told Joyce that everything would be fine between them until their wedding day. Although he clearly understood Joyce's motives, he wasn't ready to accept the altar of Christ or marriage right now. Joyce was sad about Alim's decision but didn't bring the subject up anymore. She just continued to pray about it, but in all of Joyce's praying, nothing less than totally surrendering all to Christ would help her aching heart. Soon, Joyce would be forced to put out of her mind an early marriage or elopement.

The weather is nice today, most enjoyable in Savannah. Things between her and Alim were basically the same, but Joyce still attended church faithfully, though Alim hardly attended with her.

Little did she know that she would soon discover she was sharing Alim with another woman.

Caroline introduced Joyce to a small café on the outskirts of Savannah—an elegant, quaint little place. She and Caroline had only been there once and decided to go that weekend to catch up on some girl talk. Joyce had spoken to Alim, but she didn't share the details with Caroline about the weekend. Alim was so happy to know that his Joy had a trustworthy friend and someone to hang out with when he was doing some overtime at work. The two women arrived at the café and got a window seat to watch the wonderful view. There was a park across the street from the café, with palm trees and pink flowers complementing the white benches. The children were happy to run, jump, and play with their pets while being chased by butterflies and bumblebees. Joyce enjoyed the scenery while sipping her cappuccino and eating a strawberry shortcake after a light meal. Caroline went on about the wedding with some paper and a pen in hand.

"Okay, Joyce, I have written down some songs for the wedding. Look them over and tell me what you think. I also have a couple of singers in mind. I have written them down, and I know that they are good, and if you can't take my word, then we can hear them personally," Caroline said. She looked up from the paper and saw that Joyce was staring out the window with a look of despondence on her face.

"Joyce, what's the matter?" Caroline asked as she turned her head to the window as well, following Joyce's line of sight.

"Oh, my God!" Caroline said in shock. She put her hand over her mouth, not believing what she was seeing. "Joyce, honey…" Caroline began, turning her head from the window to focus on Joyce. She watched the tears well up in Joyce's eyes.

Joyce became numb as she just sat and stared out the window. It appears she had lost her sense of existence. She couldn't even hear Caroline saying her name. It seemed like forever before Joyce broke her silence.

"Caroline, why is he coming out of that boutique with that woman? What's going on?" Joyce stuttered, clearly in shock.

"I don't know, Joyce, but do you want to call him now and find out why?" Caroline said as she reached for Joyce's hand to comfort her.

"No, Caroline. I really don't know what to do right now, and I don't want to jump to conclusions, but this is self-explanatory, isn't it?" Joyce said as she folded her hands under her chin with her head down as she watched Alim and the woman drive away in her car, with bags and all.

"Caroline, I have seen that woman before!" Joyce said.

"Where, Joyce? Who is she? Caroline asked.

"She is the woman from the restaurant that Alim and I went to the other night. She spoke to the both of us, but I felt like she was acting a little strange. She and Alim made it known that they knew each other; they used to work together at the real estate office. She introduced herself as Carlotta. She tried to be warm and cordial, and I guess all the staring that she was doing made me suspicious," Joyce said, holding a tissue to her eyes. She was completely devastated.

"You don't know exactly what is going on yet, but it is best that you find out right away. Don't sit on this thing! I will be praying for you and this situation, and I will be here for you. You know that Joyce," Caroline squeezed Joyce's hand again. Joyce just turned her head in silence and gazed out the window again. She was lost in thought as she watched children playing in the park.

"You know, Caroline, we have been sitting here for a while, and we didn't even see them drive up," Joyce said with wonderment on her face.

"Yes, Joyce. We weren't paying any attention, and we didn't notice the vehicle pull up. They could have been here in the mall before us; it really doesn't matter, anyway, Joyce," Caroline said, sounding hurt. She was really feeling the pain that Joyce was going through, and perhaps the Lord wanted Caroline to feel that pain so she would know how to deal with Joyce.

"Caroline, he told me told me that he would be working today, and I believed him, like I always do," Joyce said, trying to stop the tears, but her bottom lip would not stop quivering. Caroline just sat and quietly listened. The days were longer since the spring had come in, but Joyce didn't want to leave the café until the sun went down. She was embarrassed and ashamed and felt the daylight could not sustain her grief. At that moment, Joyce needed the darkness—because that's what she felt like. Caroline excused herself from the table to use the ladies' room, and to call her husband. When she returned, Joyce was still looking as if she had just lost everything.

"Caroline, I just called Alim, but he didn't answer the phone. I left a message to tell him that I needed to talk to him as soon as possible. I told him that I would talk to him in about an hour. It will be completely dark within an hour," Joyce said. She then saw the look on Caroline's face.

"Caroline, from the look on your face, I can tell you don't understand why I must wait until it gets dark to leave. I feel such a negative energy. I can't even hold my face up proudly like I used to. I feel like I have a big hole in my heart, Caroline," Joyce said, shaking her head from all the disappointment.

"Joyce, you gave your heart to Jesus Christ," Caroline said, tearing up at witnessing her friend's beautiful and happy disposition deteriorate before her eyes. "Joyce, the Lord will see you through this, and you must trust God, honey. I know that you are hurting, and God knows that. Just give it to the Lord, Joyce. God said in the Bible, and you can see for yourself in Psalms, where it says that the Lord is nigh unto them that is of a broken heart and contrite spirit. We can pray now, Joyce, even though I have already prayed for you in the inside."

Caroline knew that everything that Joyce was feeling was real. She also knew there was no way around this situation but to give it up. They took each other's hands at the table, and Caroline prayed she knew what Joyce was going to face with Alim once they departed ways.

When Joyce got back to the house, she was anticipating Alim's call, but she didn't have a clue about how it would turn out. Late in the night, Alim called Joyce back.

"Hey, baby. What's good? And how was your outing with Caroline?" Alim asked cheerfully.

"It was good, and what did you do today?" Joyce asked.

"I just finished up some work at the office and went for a bite to eat," Alim said.

"Oh, I see," Joyce said sarcastically.

"Why are you sounding so suspicious Joyce?" Alim asked.

"Why did I see you and Carlotta coming out of a boutique in that little mall early this evening? What were you doing there with her, Alim?" Joyce demanded as she started to tear up again. She couldn't be calm any longer.

"Calm down, Joy. What were you doing following me?" Alim asked in an angry tone.

"Following you? Be real, Alim! No, I had dinner with Caroline in a little café in the same mall as the boutique that you two were coming out of, so I had a window seat, just watching it all. And I'm not the one that is supposed to be doing the explaining now, am I?" Joyce said, her voice getting louder.

Alim just sat quietly on the phone and didn't say a word.

"Carlotta from the restaurant, Alim. Are you seeing her? What is going on! What, Alim?" Joyce asked in a frenzy. He was still silent.

"Alim!" Joyce nearly shrieked over the phone.

"Yeah, Joy. I'm still here," Alim said softly.

"Aren't you going to explain yourself? Joyce asked, resting her free hand on her forehead while she paced the floor.

"Joy, can I call you back tomorrow? I'm so sorry, but I can't talk about it right now," Alim said.

"What, Alim? There is no better time than now. I need answers now!" Joyce yelled.

"I'm sorry. Tomorrow, Joyce," Alim said as he hung up.

Joyce was even madder than earlier, but she gave him what he wanted. Joy ran to her bedroom and cried profusely. She yelled as she looked up into the ceiling. "I can't believe this is happening to me," She cried. "What am I going to do?" she sobbed into her pillow. "Is he betraying me? What is it?" Caroline kept calling, but Joyce not answer the phone. She didn't want to talk to anyone but Alim.

The next day was Sunday, but she would not be attending church because she had business with Alim—not with the Lord, but Alim. Alim had allegedly cheated, and he lied to Joyce. She had even seen evidence that he was with another woman, but deep down inside, she was hoping that he wasn't going to call back and say that it was over between them two.

Tomorrow arrived, and Joy was awakened by a phone call from Alim. She sat up in the bed with puffy eyes and a hoarse voice from crying all night.

"Good morning, Joy," Alim said softly. "Yes, I am calling to explain what I did not explain last night. You caught me by surprise."

"Well, what were you doing with her, Alim, and why were you two together?" Joyce asked, tearing up again.

"You were not supposed to find out this way, Joy. I was going to tell you about Carlotta," Alim said.

"What do you mean 'tell me about her'? I thought we were in the position that honesty and trust is the key, and that no one could get between us, so you should not be telling me about anyone!" Joyce snapped. "So, all that in the restaurant was a show, huh? Y'all are involved?" Joyce asked bluntly as she stared out at the birds chirping by her windowsill; she detested their cheerful chirping because this was not a happy day for her.

"Well, Joy, I have been trying to break it off, but believe me, I do not feel the same for her as I do you. My feelings for you are strong. You and I are going to get married. I didn't choose her to marry—I chose you. Now, that says something, don't it?" Alim said.

Joyce just burst out crying again. She was so confused and kept hoping this was just a bad dream.

"Oh, Joy. I didn't mean to hurt you, and I don't want to hurt you. I love you deeply, and I am not going anywhere. I just need to time to finish this thing," Alim said, sounding a little frustrated.

"This cannot be happening!" Joyce cried out in a disbelief. "How can you start a relationship with me knowing you are involved with someone else? How could you, Alim? I just don't get it!"

"Joyce, when I first saw you in that restaurant, I fell in love with you. I knew that you were the one for me. I didn't have any doubts in my mind about you, like I have for this woman," Alim said earnestly. "I know that I have made a mess of things, but I will fix it. I promise you that much. I swear on my mother that I will fix this situation. Please don't think about leaving me—please don't leave at all. I knew that I should have told you about this stuff from the beginning, but I thought that you would not give me the time."

"Who is this woman, Alim?" Joyce asked.

"Joyce, you must know that I have been with Carlotta a few years. I met her at my Momma's church, and she was married when I met her. She was being abused mentally and verbally by her husband, and I finally convinced her to leave him and then put her up in an apartment. Her son was just shy of being a teenager at that time. I took care of her; I am not going to lie about that. I wanted her and her son away from that man, and before you ask, she does pay her own rent, if that is what you were thinking," Alim said softly.

"Alim, you have no clue about what I am thinking, so don't even try to figure it out. If only you knew what was going through my head, and if you felt like you still needed her, then you should have never gotten with me. You should have handled all that business and been done with it, but I feel like you want to still hold onto that woman. And from the way she was acting in the restaurant, it seems that she goes along with anything that you say or do," Joyce said, sounding worn out. She had become exhausted by the situation.

"Joy, I know that you are...Well, I can't describe how you are feeling right now, or in the future, but I just want you to understand, even if you find it hard," Alim said.

"Alim, I really don't feel like talking anymore, but I have one more question to ask, among many others, before I hang up. Did you take her to Washington with you?" Joyce asked quietly, but she knew the answer to her question already. Alim was silent for a few minutes; he seemed stunned by the question.

"Alim, I asked a question!" Joyce raised her voice a little.

"Joyce, we have those conventions every year, and I did promise Carlotta that I would take her this year. It was already arranged, Joy, and if your next question is about that cosmetic bag, yes, it was her bag that I threw away," Alim said, sounding pitiful.

"I can't handle all this drama right now. I can't even fathoms the thought of you taking that woman out of town with you, and you are going to tell me that was a promise and that's why you did it. I asked you repeatedly if I could go, and you turned me down with a lame excuse. It really doesn't even matter what the reason was because that is who you wanted to be with, and you got it," Joyce said bluntly as tears streamed down her face. She held the phone to her side while she wiped away her tears, and she could hear Alim calling her name through the phone, but she didn't care; she was just trying to get herself together. After a little while, she put the phone back to her ear to speak to Alim.

"Does everyone know that you have made a fool out of me? Caroline surely knows because she was with me when I saw you and Carlotta," Joyce said, trying to choke back the tears.

"I didn't make a fool out of you. You are still the one I love and adore. I want our wedding plans to continue," Alim said desperately.

"Wedding? What in the hell are you talking about? You have someone that has been with you for years! What are you, player?" Joyce asked.

"Joy, come on with that. I am not. I just didn't know how to figure out my situation with Carlotta. And yes, I do love her as a friend, but it's not the way that I love you," Alim said.

"I can't believe I'm still on the phone listening to this," Joyce said.

"Joy, please try to understand," Alim said again.

"I must get off this phone and get my head together, plus my phone has been beeping the whole time we've been talking, and I know that it's Caroline checking in on me. I must go," Joyce said before hanging up.

She went into the kitchen to get a glass of wine, which she was reluctant to do earlier because she was a saved woman now. But right now, she trusted the wine rather than prayer to calm her. She picked up the phone.

"Hello," Joyce said as she sipped her wine.

"Hi, Joyce. You know that I was calling to check up on you. How are you doing today? I was getting a little nervous when you didn't answer the phone," Caroline said.

Joyce filled Caroline in.

"Yes, Caroline, I did talk to Alim, and it is what I suspected; he had this side piece—. I mean he had a woman before me, and I guessed he had no plans to give her up or tell me about her until he was seen with her but let him say he didn't know how to break it off, and he is still having trouble with it, as far as I can see," Joyce said calmly.

"Oh, Joyce. I am so sorry. Can we pray together right now?" Caroline asked.

"Caroline, I don't want prayer, I just want things back the way they were, before all this mess, and I don't want any advice. I just want to sit alone here," Joyce said softly.

"Okay, Joyce. I will respect that, and you know that I will be praying for you, sweetheart. God can fix this if you let him. Call me if you need me," Caroline said, sounding like she was about to cry.

"Thank you, Caroline," Joyce said as she hung up the phone.

Chapter 24

FACE TO FACE

Joyce went to work on Monday, but she could not function; she just could not pull herself together, and the partners noticed. They assumed that Joyce was just under the weather and sent her home for the day. Luckily, she had finished some backlogged work at home the previous days.

Joyce went home to have herself a sandwich and some hot tea with lemon. She turned on the television to watch anything; she just wanted to sit and stare at the television while she thought about her situation. She was confused about what to do about her situation, but she still felt that she and Alim could work this out. She thought that perhaps life was giving her a test to see how strong she was with relationship disappointment. *When you take marriage vows, it does say for better or worse*, she said. *So maybe she should take the good with the bad right now.*

"How naïve can I be?" Joyce asked herself out loud. She loved Alim and loathed thinking about losing or leaving him. "It just can't happen; I have too much at stake." She wrote these things in her journal.

It was now midday, so she figured she would drive to the farmer's market to get some fruit and vegetables. Joyce loved that market and felt that it could ease some of her despair. She called Momma Belle to ask her if wanted anything from the market while she was out there. She was reminded of Momma Belle because she was the one who had introduced Joyce to the market, and they would go together sometimes.

It was a good thing she called Momma, who said she needed a bell pepper for the meatloaf she was making for supper. Joyce was a lifesaver; Momma didn't feel like going out because her sinuses were acting up badly. Joyce put on her Jackie Onassis sunglasses because her eyes were red and swollen from all the crying.

At the market, Joyce tasted some grapes. The grocer didn't let everyone do that, but he always let Joyce. She then squeezed the oranges and the grocer helped her pick out the best bell pepper for Momma. He had known Momma well for many years. As Joyce got in line to pay for her groceries, she looked around, enjoying the weather, and observing the shopping complex when she noticed a familiar face—Carlotta—going into the deli. After Joyce finished paying for her food, she went to her car and thought about approaching Carlotta just to ask her a few questions. She was anxious to know if her and Alim's stories would match, but she didn't exactly know how to start the conversation.

Suddenly, her cell phone rang. It was Alim—what bad timing. She refused to answer the phone but listened to the message he left. He told her that he stopped by her office to take her to lunch, but her boss told him that she was sent home because she wasn't feeling well, so he had passed by her house and was getting worried. He wanted her to call him back.

Joyce then chose to leave the complex because she heard Alim's voice and lost her nerve to approach Carlotta. While she was driving to Momma Belle's house, she turned her radio up when she heard Brandy's "Angel in Disguise" playing.

When she arrived at Momma's house, she saw Alim's other car in the driveway—a beautiful black Buick Lacrosse that shone in the sun. She felt a little nervous as she is entering the house. Once inside, she found Alim sitting on the edge of the sofa, reading the newspaper. He looked up and watched Joyce as she came through the door. Joyce was still nervous, especially now that she was face to face with Alim, so she immediately she called for Momma. Joyce felt a deep longing when she saw Alim, but she didn't want to show it on her face. This man truly had her heart.

"I'm in the kitchen, Joyce!" Momma yelled. Joyce was already on her way back there, and she knew Alim was staring at her. It was a good thing she changed from her work clothes into some shorts with sandals and a tank top. Alim loved to see her like that.

Alim just sat and stared at her with those piercing, sensual eyes. He obviously didn't know how to greet Joyce, and he wasn't going to interrupt her meeting with Momma. It was clear that Momma didn't know what was going on. Alim finally broke his silence.

"Joy, can I talk with you when you finish with Momma in the kitchen?" Alim asked Joyce by way of greeting. She just ignored him.

"I'm bringing your beautiful pepper that the grocer helped me pick out, Momma," Joyce said.

"Okay, honey. Come on back," Momma yelled.

Joyce looked back at him as though she was going to say something, but she turned around and kept walking; deep down, though, she hoped that he would still be there when she returned after talking to Momma. She was wondering why he was even there when he was supposed to be at work.

"Are you going to stay for supper? I told Alim that you were coming by here because he called earlier trying to figure out where you were. I see that you two are having trouble, and I hope it can work out positively. You two must learn to talk things over if you want to have a successful marriage," Momma Belle advised. "I know, Alim, and I know that he has never loved anyone as he loves you." She gave Joyce a hug.

Joyce wondered whether Momma knew about what was going on—and if she did, would she still be speaking the same?

"Momma, I must pass on supper tonight. I am really exhausted today," Joyce said.

"Okay, honey. You go home and get some rest," Momma said.

"Good night, Momma," Joyce said as she left the kitchen. Alim met her as she entered the living room.

"Joy, can we go somewhere and talk?" Alim asked, grabbing her by the waist. He kissed her forehead, her cheeks, and began making his way to her lips.

"I don't feel like it, Alim," Joyce said softly as she gently pulled away from him.

"Can I hold you for a minute? I really need you and can't be without you," he said to Joyce, pulling her closer to him. He began to kiss her lips, but this time she didn't pull away. It appears she was giving in, but then she checked herself, pulled away from Alim, and ran out the door to her car. Alim just stood at the door and watched her pull out of the driveway. As Joyce drove down the highway, the tears started to flow again.

"Why did he have to touch me? Why did I let him touch me? I can't give him up! No, I can't!" Joyce sobbed as she drove home. She tried to get a grip of herself so that she could be well enough to go to work tomorrow. She had to find a way to hide her pain at work. Through all her tears riding home, she forgot that she had to stop by Rite Aid to get some personal items that she needed them. She got back into her car and headed down the road to the nearest Rite Aid. She walked through the aisles, picking up items. When she headed to the feminine hygiene aisle to get some tampons, she spotted Carlotta, who had just picked up a pregnancy test from the shelf.

How ironic to see her here, Joyce thought? *This is really a sad day, but at least I have a chance to talk to her.*

She walked over to Carlotta and tapped her on the shoulder. "Carlotta, isn't it? How are you doing? Remember me, Joyce?"

Carlotta looked stunned when she saw Joyce. She clearly remembered her.

"Oh, hello, Joyce!" Carlotta said as she quickly put the pregnancy test back on the shelf and picked up something else.

"Carlotta, can I talk to you outside when we are done in here?" Joyce asked.

"Ss…sure, Joyce, but what is this about?" Carlotta stuttered as though she already knew what Joyce was talking about.

"We'll talk when we are finished in here. I promise it will just be a civil woman-to-woman conversation," Joyce said with a little smirk.

"Okay," Carlotta said as she continued up the aisle.

Joyce finished first, so she went outside and leaned by the wall near the entrance to wait for Carlotta. Her phone started to ring; it was Alim, but she was not going to let him keep her from the conversation she was about to have with Carlotta. Joyce thought that it was kind of tacky to be having a conversation outside a store about a man, but she wanted to have this talk because she knew she might not see this woman again for a long time.

"Okay, Joyce, what is this about?" Carlotta asked, exiting the store.

"Would you like to sit in the car, or do you want to stay right here?" Joyce asked.

"It's okay right here. It's in a corner spot. Now, what is it?" Carlotta asked, looking nervous.

"All right, Carlotta. I saw you and Alim together on Saturday coming out of a boutique, so I asked him it." She filled Carlotta in about everything Alim had confessed to her, including everything about Carlotta's husband.

Carlotta stood there with a look of shock on her face.

"You know what, Joyce? I can't believe that Alim told you about my husband, but I guess he had to use that, and it is true. But I want to tell you something since you are digging for answers about Alim and my relationship. Yes, he did take me shopping at the boutique, and he does that and a lot more for me," Carlotta said. Joyce's face fell. She remained silent and just listened while the woman ranted on about Alim and their relationship.

"Yes, Alim has been here for me and my son through some hard times. He is still here for us, and he did convince me to leave my husband because he started to care a great deal for me after meeting me. He told me he didn't want me to stay with a man who treated me badly," Carlotta said. Joyce looked at her, but it seemed as though Joyce didn't want to believe the truth that was staring her in her face.

Carlotta was a beauty who was in her late forties. She was bout five-foot-nine and about one hundred and fifty pounds with milky, flawless skin. Her eyes were greenish-brown and adorned with long eyelashes, and she had long brown hair. She was wearing a tan spaghetti strap maxi dress with five-inch espadrilles.

"Okay, Carlotta, I want to know how deep you and Alim's relationship is. I need to know what kind of understanding you two have because he's still with me, and, of course, you know that we are still together. And I take it that you know that we are going to get married this fall," Joyce said as she held up her diamond ring.

"Well, Joyce, engagement ring or friendship ring, what's the difference?" Carlotta replied as she held up her own finger to show her ring to Joyce. Joyce's mouth fell open when she saw the sapphire ring on Carlotta's finger.

What an arrogant fool! Joyce said in her mind as she glared at Carlotta.

"Joyce, you must know that Alim is not going to leave you, and yes, we do have an understanding. And I know he was frantic when he told me that you had seen us together at the boutique. But you need to know it doesn't mean anything to me because he is not going leave me either, or yes, the understanding stands," Carlotta said. Joyce looked at her in disbelief.

"Joyce, I don't mean no disrespect, but you must grow up and face life. Men will be men, and yes, I am still married and trying to divorce a man that couldn't care less about how I felt or thought. Have you ever been married?" Carlotta asked.

"No," Joyce blurted with her arms folded across her chest. This woman really wasn't going anywhere.

"Then you may not know what I am talking about, but I'll break it down for you. You strike me as a little naïve," Carlotta said to Joyce, who rolled her eyes in reply. Carlotta continued to speak.

"My husband had someone else, and I was hurt, disappointed, and ashamed, and all the other feelings that came with that. I came to accept the extramarital relationship, but I didn't like the abuse that came with it, although many may say the extramarital affair was also abuse. But I wasn't going to struggle with my son, so I came to accept a lot of things from a cheating and abusive man. I didn't even look at it as a marriage anymore, but just as a couple raising their child. He was always good to his son, but I don't know what happened between us. I guess the other relationship got such a hold of him that he didn't have any respect for me anymore, and the guilt was probably eating at him, so he had to take it out on me. I didn't understand it. Then, about a year later, I met Alim and started an affair too. At least he treated me better than my husband and started to care about me. Alim then convinced me to leave my husband and told me would always be there for me and my son, no matter what. But he also made it clear that he wasn't trying to be committed at all. I understood that and accepted it because I didn't want anything more. I was perfectly fine with being a kept woman who didn't have to give up much to get a lot," Carlotta said as she squinted her eyes to make sure Joyce understood what she was saying.

Joyce just looked at her and shook her head. "Carlotta, don't you see that you are the one that is being stupid? Because if you call me naïve at the age that I am, then that is really calling me stupid. I don't what the new thing with relationships is these days; I still live the old-fashioned way. I don't share my man with any other woman. And you know deep down inside that you want Alim for yourself, but he is not willing to go there with you, so you accept things the way they are, just like you accepted things with your husband. Come on, woman. Give me a break. There is no one that hard on the inside when it comes to a man like Alim. So, all that you are talking is a bunch of garbage, and you know it. You may be a tad bit stronger now because you have been through a lot, but you're not happy with the way things are, and I am not here to tell you to leave Alim, so don't you think for one second that is why I called you out here I just needed to know some things, and now I know. And I did notice you with that pregnancy test, so I gather that wanting to just be a kept woman with no attachments involves tricking a man into getting you pregnant too, huh? You're a phony, but I do thank you for being somewhat candid with me about the relationship between you and Alim," Joyce said.

Carlotta was stunned into silence for a moment. She shook her head before putting it down. Joyce was feeling all messed up on the inside herself, but she tried not to show it on her face.

"Joyce, you called me out here because you didn't trust Alim's word when you confronted him. And maybe you do want me to leave him, but you're too woman to say that. Isn't that the truth? He is supposed to be the man you maybe marrying in a matter of months, but how are you looking right now?" Carlotta asked with a devious smile.

"Carlotta! Of course, I didn't trust his word after seeing what I did. Can't you even gather that, honey? But you know what? I have my answers now, and we don't need to go any further with this conversation."

Before Joyce could even finish, Carlotta threw her hands up in frustration and marched back to her car. She was not happy at all. Joyce just got into her car and drove away. As Joyce was driving home, she tried to come up with something to make herself feel less awful. Maybe Alim was having a hard time breaking up with this manipulative woman because he made her a promise, and he didn't want to go back on his word.

He has me now. He must break this thing off if he wants to be with me, Joyce thought frantically. *Does he really and truly want to break off this thing with Carlotta?*

As Joyce pulled into her driveway, she saw Alim sitting on her porch. He ran down the step and greeted Joyce with a kiss and hug.

"Joyce, I am starting to worry about you. Every time I call you, you don't answer your phone," he said. "I promise that I will make everything all right. I know this is a mess right now, but it will be better, you will see, sweetheart. I love you, Joyce, and I will never stop loving you." He held her tightly. Joyce just stood still and held her head down. She didn't know what to do or what to say aside from telling Alim about her conversation with Carlotta at the Rite Aid.

Alim's face just went blank. "Joyce why are you doing this?" he asked.

"Doing what, Alim? Huh, doing what? I needed some answers from Carlotta too, and it was just a coincidence that I ran into her at the store, and I took the chance that was there for me!" Joyce said, pushing him away.

"Joyce, please, baby. Can I stay with you tonight? I don't want anything. I just want to hold you and try to get the chemistry back between us," Alim implored.

"Alim, this is not about sex. Sex can't conquer what's going on between us. But for the record, I still love you. I don't lie when I say I love you, and it does turn on and off, but you hurt me deeply, and you are still involved with Carlotta. What do you expect from me? I know better than to enter a marriage like this. Please, I don't want to talk about it anymore," Joyce said, opening her front door and going inside.

She watched from her window as Alim got into his car and drove away.

Chapter 25

WE CAN MAKE IT WORK

The whole week passed by, and Joyce still hadn't heard from Alim, but she did speak to Momma Belle and Caroline a couple of times during the week. She only discussed Alim with Caroline.

Joyce had begun to miss Alim. She could tell that Alim was going to leave her alone for a while, but deep in her heart, she didn't want him to go anywhere, and she didn't want to lose him. She felt lonely and hoped that he felt the same about her.

She called Caroline just for some girl talk, but she knew that Caroline would tell her to look to God now that she was under distress. She wasn't trying to hear that right now. All she wanted right now was Alim and to never mind what anyone else said. Joyce felt like she could make this relationship work. She thought about some things that Carlotta said about being naïve and to just accept things the way they were. Joyce thought she could bring herself to share her man now that she had met that arrogant, stupid woman. How else was she going to keep Alim?

She called Alim, but he didn't answer. She immediately started to panic. Maybe he was with Carlotta, or maybe he was just ignoring her phone calls. She decided to leave a heartfelt message on his phone telling Alim how much she loved him and how she would like for him to come by her house that night, no matter the time. Joyce assured herself that she could make it work between her and Alim, even if she had to think of herself as being that woman who fights for her man.

I can make this work for us, Joyce thought as she lay on her bed drinking tea and writing in her journal. She couldn't bear the thought of being alone. She and Alim were usually out about on the weekends if there was no extra work going on for Alim. Just then, Alim called Joyce back, sounding a little confused.

"Hey, Joy. What's up? I got your message," Alim said.

"I know that things are not good between us right now, Alim, but did you have to go a whole week without talking to me?" Joyce asked.

"Well, Joy, after all that you told me and the way you felt the last time, I talked to you face to face, I didn't know what to do anymore. And I still don't understand why you had to approach Carlotta or even question her about me; after all, I thought that I had answered all your questions," Alim said bitterly.

"Alim, after all this, you just don't understand, do you? I don't know any more. I am so confused. I saw Carlotta in the store, so I had to get some answers from her as well. I don't know exactly what she told you, but I can tell you if you need to know from me," Joyce said, feeling a little nervous.

"No, I don't need any assurance. I just need you to try to take my word for what I tell you, and I know that I should have told you about Carlotta before, but it just wasn't the right time. I will come over if you still want me to, and we can talk more then," Alim said.

"Alim, were you with Carlotta when I called?" Joyce asked, sounding a little pitiful.

"No, baby, I was at the land we are getting our house built on. I am making a settlement soon, Joyce. Now, see, I am still going on with our plans, so what about you? But we will discuss all that when I see you soon, okay, baby?" Alim hung up.

Joyce felt good about the fact the Alim hadn't reneged on their plans for the house. She started to get ready for Alim's arrival that evening, and just as she was doing so, Caroline called to check up on her.

"Hey, Joyce, what are you doing?" Caroline asked, sounding chipper as always.

"Hi, Caroline. I am not doing nothing much except getting dressed because Alim will be stopping by tonight," Joyce said candidly.

"Oh, I see. So, you two have worked things out?" Caroline asked.

"Well, not exactly, Caroline, but we will be talking about it tonight, and I am going to prepare dinner as well," Joyce said.

"Oh, okay. I hope all works out for the good," Caroline said, sounding a little disappointed.

"Caroline, I know that you don't approves, and I am not saying that I need your approval, but Alim and I have a special bond. People make mistakes, none of us is perfect—not even Christians. We must learn how to forgive and move on, and that is what I am trying to do with Alim because I am saved and he is not, so what kind of example am I leading if I don't respect what we are trying to do? Maybe my light will lead him to Christ." Joyce said.

"You know, Joyce, I would never try to tell you whether I approve or not because you are a grown woman. I just can't get Carlotta of my head and the things that she and Alim told you. Don't you think that they have a bond too, and even more so given that they are still involved? That says a lot, Joyce. I don't want you to get hurt any more than you have already been hurt. The Lord said in Psalms that he heals the broken-hearted. I know that you don't see what I am saying right now because you are so in love with Alim, and I don't have any ill-will against him. I also know that you know him better than I do, but I do think that he likes having it all, including when it comes to women. He does not want to give up anything, and if he can get away with it, it will be his way and nobody else's. I can see that from what's going on here right now. I am not going to doubt that he loves you, but he likes to have his way too." Caroline said.

"Caroline! Come on, now. He is not like that! I know that it seems that way to you because you are not in this situation; you are just looking in and going by what I tell you, but you are not walking in my shoes right now," Joyce said, sounding a little annoyed.

"Joyce, are you taking your salvation seriously? That is what I want to know because you made vows to God a couple of Sundays ago, remember?" Caroline said.

"I know that, Caroline. Yes, I do take my salvation seriously. I know that you are not trying to judge me, right?" Joyce asked.

"No, honey, never. It's just that I just don't want you to forget about Christ, Joyce. I love you, and so does God, and I don't want to see you hurting for anything in this world. I love you as my sister in Christ and as a friend," Caroline said, sounding sad.

"Caroline, I know where you are coming from, and I am sorry for being abrupt with you, but I will be fine, sister. I know that you mean well and will always be here for me, but there are some things that I must figure out on my own, Listen, I must go now, but I will be calling you soon, okay?" Joyce said to Caroline.

"Okay, Joyce. Call me if you need me," Caroline said and then hung up.

Caroline left Joyce with a lot to think about. As Joyce prepared her meal for the evening, she thought not only about what Caroline had said, but also how she was going to handle the situation with Alim.

Joyce was almost finished with dinner when Alim pulled into her driveway. He greeted her at the door with a bouquet of tulips. They embraced with a kiss and hug. Alim was wet all over. The rain had started to pour as Alim stepped out of his car, and the lightning made its presence known, as though the thunder was not going to be reluctant with its voice.

"These flowers are beautiful, Alim, so you do deserve this meal that I have cooked for you, and I cooked everything that you like!" Joyce said as she put the flowers in a vase on the coffee table.

"Everything does smell good. Wow, I can't believe that you cooked smothered pork chops, woman! I am hungry too!" Alim said as he went over to the sink to wash his hands.

"Joyce, we do have to talk, baby, and it is about our situation. I don't know if that's why you wanted me to come over, but I wanted to talk about it anyway," Alim said.

"Okay, Alim. I know that we have some things to deal with right now, and I do want it resolved tonight," Joyce said as she sat down to the table. After serving the food, Joyce said grace.

"I did talk to Carlotta today," Alim said as he paused a little, watching Joyce's eyes closing in on him with all her attention. "I told her that I have to break things off between her and I, and that I am working things out with you."

"So, what was the outcome of that conversation?" Joyce asked.

"Of course, she didn't like that because I made her that promise that I would always be there for her and her son, so going back on my word made me feel a little bad inside," Alim said.

"Well, Alim, you have an obligation to me, and that does not include Carlotta. And yes, I will say that you made this mess when you met me. You didn't tell me that you were with someone else, so now here we stand," Joyce said, taking a bite of her dinner.

"Okay, Joyce, I hear you. It is a done deal; it's over between Carlotta and I, okay? Promises, words, or understandings, whatever it is, it's over. I don't want to lose you because of all this stuff. I realized that I love you more than I thought when I saw the hurt on your face. No matter what, I am not going to lose you, and if you can't trust my word anymore, I will understand, but try to trust me on this—I will make this up to you, I don't know how, but I will," Alim said. He pulled Joyce from the table and led her to the bedroom.

Joyce did not resist at all. The rain set up a romantic scene, tapering off the lightning and thunder, and it poured all night long.

The next morning, on his way out, Alim asked Joyce if she would like to take another trip somewhere, but this time out of the country. Joyce's eyes grew wide with elation.

"Where will we be going and when?" Joyce asked excitedly.

"I don't know, Joy. You pick the spot and get your vacation days ready. You can pick those too. You know I can abide by them because I don't have to answer to management," Alim said as he kissed her goodbye. "I will call you tonight,"

As always, Joyce watched as he pulled out of the driveway. She thought about the vacation and when she should take her days off.

"It is such a beautiful morning," Joyce said as she opened her blinds and began to get ready for work. Right now, everything seemed to be so right and perfect. She felt as though nothing, and no one could upset her on this glorious day.

Chapter 26

Love Again on an Island

The summer was fast approaching, and Joyce was getting excited about her Hawaiian trip, which was to take place in a couple of weeks. She went shopping almost every day until her trip, making sure that she had the perfect outfits and lingerie to take with her. She was almost finished with her wedding preparations, but not quite. She had been going to church without Alim in the attempt to live a Christian life. She took Alim for all that he said and tried not to doubt his word because she needed to go on with him in the hope that everything would be good between them both. Now, the only thing that was important to Joyce right now was the wedding and the completion of her house. She had been to the estate to help with the architectural details, and it was coming along beautifully. She was promised that the house would be finished at the end of the year, and she was fine with that. Alim was still being very attentive to Joyce and trying to assuage all her fears and doubts about him, and he was doing an exceptionally good job at it.

Momma Belle was excited about Joyce and Alim going to Hawaii, but Caroline was a little worried. As the day approached for Alim and Joyce to leave for their vacation, Joyce began to feel nervous. She had never flown over water before, but she was also excited about the thought of being with Alim and having him all to herself, without work or any other interruptions, for three whole days.

When Joyce hit the Hawaiian sand, she was elated. She loved the friendly greeting at the airport. She and Alim took a limo to the vacation home that Alim rented. Alim didn't tell Joyce that she was in for a breathtaking surprise upon their arrival.

When they got settled in the vacation house, they had the limo driver take them to the stores so that they could pick up a few items and some food. Alim really knew how to treat a woman, and he held nothing back. He promised that he would make up for his shortcomings, and he was surely making good on his promises.

Joyce felt like she was falling in love with Alim all over again in this gorgeous, whimsical atmosphere. She thought of nothing else. She even yearned to have his baby, so much so that it ached her heart. Alim was everything that she ever wanted in a man. He was wealthy, he was handsome, he was brilliant, and he knew how to take care of a woman—he was the complete package. Her heart began to melt as they walked on the beach.

To Joyce, love was the sweetest thing, and she didn't want too ever be free of it. *No matter what may come or what may happen,* Joyce thought, *I'll never leave this man or give him up for anybody else.* She would be lost and feel like a useless woman with nowhere to turn on this earth without her man by her side. She never wanted to be set free from this kind of love; it was beautiful and enchanting, and making love on the beach at night made it seem as though Alim had the sun in his eyes as he gazed upon her. She just closed her eyes and listened to the sounds of the waves. They soothed her mind, and the stars gave her hope as she looked up into the sky.

I belong to him, and he belongs to me. He looked up at me and kissed my face, Joyce thought.

"I love you," Alim whispered in Joyce's ear as he held her gently.

Joyce just smiled as she began to him without any intention of stopping. She felt different with Alim. She couldn't see past him; he was all that she needed. It seemed she was bewitched by his love, but she didn't care, and she clearly showed it.

Their vacation was coming to an end, so they woke up early the next morning to do some shopping. Joyce wanted to get some souvenirs for Caroline's family, as well as her own, and tour the island some more.

Since this was their last night in Hawaii, they decided to stay in and enjoy their cozy rented vacation home after the shopping and sightseeing. Joyce walked out on the upper deck with a glass of wine in her hand and admired the gorgeous Hawaiian sky. Just as she was becoming absorbed in its beauty, she felt Alim touch her shoulder and heard the music playing in the background. Of course, Alim wanted this dance. It just so happened he was playing Stevie Wonder's "Ribbon in the Sky," and she looked up into the sky once again as she danced with Alim, admiring the view as the sunset became an array of colored ribbons in the sky.

"I will never forget this Hawaiian sky," Joyce said breathlessly. Alim just smiled as Joyce lay her head on his shoulder as they continued dancing to a full Stevie Wonder playlist.

"I love you, Joy, and I promised you that I was going to make it all up to you," Alim whispered in Joyce's ear between kissing her earlobes. They were both having such a good time on this last Hawaiian night. Just before they were to retire for the night, Joyce looked up at the sky once again, admiring the cluster of the sparkling stars and the hope they gave her. Her heart was locked in love, and Alim was the only one that held the key. As genuine as the cool sand beneath her feet and her body that basked in the sun, her was being taken away each day and night that she was in Hawaii.

Chapter 27

MEETING OLIVIA

On the flight back home from Hawaii, Joyce was consumed by blissful thoughts. She couldn't wait to get home and phone Caroline and her family to tell them about her trip. Love was still in the air for Joy. She felt like she was just coming back from a luxurious honeymoon. She and Alim held hands while they were on the plane, and she just looked out the window, thinking that she would never feel this way again.

They finally arrived in Savannah, exhausted from the flight, and Alim dropped Joyce off at home so that she could get ready for work the next day. As soon as Joyce settled in, she called Caroline, who was ecstatic to hear that Hawaii had been wonderful. Joyce knew deep down inside that Caroline didn't trust Alim anymore for all the stuff that had taken place, but Caroline never mentioned it to Joyce, and instead simply accepted Joyce and Alim's relationship.

After she hung up with Caroline, she called her family, who were also happy for Joyce and appreciative for the souvenirs she had gotten them from Hawaii.

Well, it was the end of the week, and the days seemed to go by fast since Joyce went back to work on a Tuesday. She was slowly coming down from cloud nine, but she just couldn't get Hawaii out of her mind—at least for now. She wasn't going to miss church that Sunday, and again she found herself in attendance without Alim.

Momma had invited Joyce to dinner after church. She expected to see Alim's car there, but it wasn't there. Momma told Joyce that Melanie was also there, which was a great surprise for Joyce. She hadn't seen Melanie that year and had only talked to her a little over the phone about the wedding. Melanie ran outside to greet Joyce with hugs and kisses, and when Joyce got out of the car, she took her by the hand and led her into the house. Joyce noticed an unfamiliar face sitting on the sofa in the living room.

"Joyce, this is my Mommy," Melanie said as she introduced them both.

"Hi, Joyce. I'm Olivia, and as you know, I'm Melanie's mom," Olivia said, smiling and gazing at Joyce as if she was admiring her beauty.

"Hi, it is a pleasure to meet the mother of this stunning young woman here," Joyce said pleasantly, smiling back at Melanie. Olivia looked to be of mixed Indian and Asian descent, with long natural black braids and smooth bronze skin. She looked to be a little eccentric from the attire she was wearing, which was a loud, colorful draped dress. She was about five-foot-three and looked about a hundred and twenty-five pounds—a pretty woman.

"Oh, Joy, you made it?" Momma asked as she came out of the kitchen.

"Yes, Momma, and I was on my way to the kitchen to let you know that I was here, and what is that wonderful smell coming from?" Joyce asked as she hugged Momma.

"Oh, honey, I'm cooking some Salisbury steaks smothered in gravy with some mashed potatoes and veggies," Momma said.

"Well, it smells divine," Joyce said.

"Joyce, where is Alim?" Momma asked.

"I thought that he would be here when I drove in. I haven't talked to him since this morning," Joy said as she hunched her shoulders. Just as Momma was getting ready to speak again, Alim pulled into the driveway. Once again, Melanie ran out the door and was overjoyed overwhelmed to see her Daddy. She greeted him with a hug. He hugged her back tightly, and they entered through the door together.

"Hi, baby," Alim said as she walked over to greet Joyce with a kiss.

"Hello, Libby!" he then said as he walked over to hug Olivia.

"Hi Alim, you look good, I haven't seen you in a while," Olivia said.

"How is everything going, Libby?" Alim asked as he went over to sit next to Joyce.

"Everything is going well," Olivia said as she watched Alim intensely. She blushed. "You look very well, Alim. Joyce must be taking good care of you," Olivia said.

Alim did not say anything; he just smiled and nodded.

"Alim, where have you been?" Momma asked as she came over to hug him, putting down a pitcher of lemonade.

"I had some things to do today, and then I went to sleep, but I didn't mean to oversleep. I must have been more tired than I thought I was, Momma, can you put on some coffee for me please?" Alim said.

"Daddy, how was Hawaii?" Melanie asked.

"Aww, Melanie, it was amazing," Alim responded.

"Yes, it was, Melanie," Joyce said, agreeing with Alim as she sipped on the lemonade.

"So, Libby, how is your writing coming along?" Alim asked.

"Well, you know, I have a lot of stuff that I am trying to get published, but I do have some material that I am still working on, so hopefully I can become an official author very soon," Olivia said.

"You will, and besides, I think that Melanie and I are your biggest fans. I do remember you writing some interesting but brilliant stuff. Yeah, Joy, this gal can write," Alim said.

"I wouldn't mind reading sometime," Joyce said curiously.

"Oh, okay, I will give you the name of my website. I have some of my writing there, and I hope you enjoy it. And please do give some feedback; it is always appreciated, and it keeps me going too, no matter what opinions people may have about my work," Olivia said with an expression of seriousness.

"Excuse me, ladies, I have to go and see what's going on with my coffee and catch up with Momma for a minute," Alim said as he left the room.

Alim must have been in the kitchen for about fifteen minutes before Melanie decided she wanted to talk to her Daddy. Melanie left the other ladies sitting in the living room and proceeded to the kitchen. When she reached the end of the hall leading to the kitchen, she could hear her Nana scolding her Daddy. "How could you get yourself into this mess?"

She could see Daddy standing there, shaking his head as he responded to Nana. "I don't know, Momma, and I didn't mean for this to happen."

"Well, you should have been honest from the beginning, son." Before they could say anything else, Melanie walked in smiling because she didn't want them to think she was eavesdropping; she knew that that was something her Nana and Daddy didn't tolerate.

"Is dinner ready yet, Nana?" Melanie asked innocently.

"Almost, honey," Momma said as she scrambled around to get the food in the proper dishes.

"Is everything all right, Daddy? You look kind of flustered," Melanie asked.

"Yes, baby. I am just tired," he said to Melanie.

"The table is already set. I'm just going to put the food on the table. Melanie, tell Joyce and your mother that dinner is ready," Momma said. As the family sat down to dinner, Momma said grace, as she always did.

"So, I hear that you and Melanie are going to Cocoa Beach and then Orlando, huh, Libby?" Alim asked.

"Yes, we are. We are due for a vacation, and Melanie wanted to go to Florida. I don't knows exactly how long we'll be staying; I hope not a whole week like Melanie is hoping, but oh well," Olivia said.

"Mommy, it will be good," Melanie said.

"Melanie and I are due for a vacation too," Alim said.

"I know, Daddy. Will we be able to go before the summer is out? I would like to go while it is still hot to get a nice tan like Joyce."

"Sure, baby," Alim said.

"So, when are you two getting married?" Olivia asked.

"I want to have a fall wedding, so I am still working on that," Joyce said.

"Oh, I see. That is kind of different, so I take it that fall is your favorite season, Joyce?" Olivia said.

"Yes, it is," Joyce said.

"Congratulations!" Olivia said.

"Thank you," Joyce said, looking much obliged since it had come from one of Alim's exes, and even better, his daughter's mother.

"We can't stay long because we have to get started early," Melanie said.

"Oh, shucks. Before I forget!" Momma said.

"What, Momma?" Alim asked.

"Melanie, I bought some giant snow crab legs for you from the farmer's market yesterday, and I bought a cooler in which you can put some ice in for the crabs," Momma said.

"Thanks, Nana!" Melanie said.

"Joyce, I have been admiring your engagement ring, girl! That is fabulous, and is the other ring your birthstone or something like that?" Olivia asked.

"Thank you, Olivia. Yes, these are my birthstones," Joyce said bashfully.

After dinner, they all sat around in the living room and talked for a little while Momma served them coffee, lemonade, and dessert. They talked about old times and school days, things that Joyce had an interest in hearing. Then Momma pulled out the old photos, which was the winner of the night. Melanie began to yawn and asked her mother if it was time to get back to the hotel.

"You two could have stayed with me. I don't know why y'all would stay in a hotel," Momma said.

"Nana, we just wanted to stop at the nearest hotel because we did all the driving and were tired, and your house was about another twenty-five miles from the highway," she explained.

"Melanie, baby. You need anything?" Alim asked.

"No, Daddy. I'm all right," Melanie said; she started to gather her and her mother's things. Melanie and her Olivia then gave Momma a hug, and Melanie hugged Joyce while Olivia politely shook her hand.

Alim then walked them out to their car and carried Melanie's ice cooler with the giant snow crabs in it.

"You two have a safe trip and call me when you get to your destination. And Melanie, call me when you get back to the hotel room," Alim said as they drove away. Momma and Joyce stood out on the porch waving goodbye. Alim came back on the porch and took Joyce by the hand and led her into the house.

"Momma, I overheard Daddy and Nana in the kitchen just for a second discussing something, and Momma, I wasn't eavesdropping. I was in the hallway getting ready to enter the kitchen, and then I heard Nana say to Daddy, 'How could you get yourself into this situation?' And then Daddy said he didn't mean for this to happen, and that was when I walked in, I guess I didn't want to hear any more or get caught listening when, really, I accidentally overheard them," Melanie said.

"Well, honey, I don't know, and I hope your Daddy is not going to mess up this relationship because it seems like Joyce is a nice woman. I hope that it wasn't anything detrimental, but don't you worry about it. I think that God will only bless you with one genuine shot at real love, and if you mess up, that's it. Everyone has a lesson to learn," Olivia said as they drove away.

Chapter 28

HIDING IN THE
SHADOW OF TRUTH

The wedding arrangements were almost finished, but Joyce was getting very nervous as the time drew nearer. She hoped that her sister-in-law, Deanna, could be present at the wedding. Joyce hadn't told her family in Chicago about the problems she and Alim were having. She didn't want her brothers to try to make her break up with Alim, so as far as Brian and Leon were concerned, Alim was still the good guy in Joyce's life.

Joyce and Alim were planning a family reunion that would include Joyce's family and his family. The reunion would take place in the middle of the summer. It was a good idea for them to get the families together before their wedding day. They didn't want anyone to feel like strangers on the special day.

Joyce now wondered where they should spend her honeymoon; it had to be a place that would show up Hawaii, and she thought the perfect and most romantic spot would be Paris. Alim had been on his best behavior since the Hawaii trip, and Joyce had been incredibly happy. Everything was going according to plan, and everyone was being supportive. Momma Belle and a few of her church friends were out preparing her yard with flowers for the future family reunion that Joyce and Alim had planned. Joyce wanted the reunion to be cozy, with a family-oriented, personal feel, which is why they hadn't rented any meeting spots; besides, Momma's house had the biggest yard that she had ever seen at any house.

It was a hot day, and the reunion day was coming in fast. As Momma sat in her yard taking a break from work and sipping her famous iced tea, she looked up, and a familiar car drove up her driveway that she hadn't seen in while. She knew that it couldn't be that woman—why was she coming to her house, and what business did she have with Momma? This woman knew when to come—early, while everyone else was at work. The rest of her guests were curious as Momma got up to greet her intruder—or intruders, rather—but she told them to stay behind and finish the work because she knew that this conversation would have to be private. Momma walked over to the car that pulled into her driveway, looking confused and concerned. Out stepped Carlotta and her sister Lorraine.

"Hello, Momma Belle, I apologize for barging in on you like this, but I didn't have your phone number to alert you of my coming by. I know that we haven't spoken in a long time, so in all honestly, I do not mean to pop up on you like this," Carlotta said, wringing her hands nervously.

"Hello, Miss Belle," Lorraine said as she leaned against the car.

"What can I do for you ladies today?" Momma said as she took off her garden hat.

"Can we go inside, Momma Belle?" Carlotta asked.

"Please, call me Ms. Belle, Carlotta, and you are looking well," Momma Belle said in a friendly yet slightly caustic tone. "Okay, you ladies come on in." She led them to the kitchen through the back door.

"Momma, I don't know how to tell you this, and I have talked to Alim, but he doesn't seem to care, or maybe he is in shock and does not know what to do. He does not call like he used to. I know that he has tried to be faithful to Joyce. I am pregnant, Ms. Belle, and I have told Alim, and I don't know what else to do," Carlotta said.

Momma just sat for a second and looked at Carlotta and Lorraine before offering them some iced tea because she knew that this was not going to be good.

"Ms. Belle, my sister knew about Alim and Joyce because I told her the day, I saw them together at church. She's not trying to come between Alim and Joyce, but Alim was obligated to Carlotta, and now that she is pregnant, he is trying to act like he doesn't care, or he just don't want to be bothered. She told him that she has been to the doctor, and it has been confirmed, but he is still acting nonchalant about the entire situation. And he is still seeing Carlotta on the side, you know," Lorraine explained as Carlotta cried.

"Listen, you two. I do know about this situation, and Alim told me about it. And I know that he is to blame, as well as you are, Carlotta, but why would you even think that I would get into this; isn't it between you two? Carlotta, all this time, y'all have been seeing each other, and this is the first time you cry, so I wonder if it is because Joyce is in the picture that you trapped him now," Momma said angrily as a look of hurt came across Carlotta's face.

"Yes! I said trapped, dear, because I see it as that! I assumed the condom broke this time when it didn't any other time," Momma said angrily.

"Ms. Belle, how could you say those things? Why do you hurt me like that? I love Alim and would never try to trap him," Carlotta said as she began to pace across the kitchen floor.

"You have always been a money-hungry, grubby little tramp in my eyesight. I say that because you had a husband, and still you slept with Alim and made him believe that your husband was treating you badly. But the truth is, it was the other way around, am I right? And he was getting to you because you were treating him badly. Yes, Carlotta, I know the story. You and your husband were two of a kind. I know your Aunt Lena. We go to the same church, and I got all the details on you. She said that you have always been a tramp, but I can see it for myself too, so I am not going solely on hearsay. Alim wasn't trying to hear it because you were telling him all those lies, but somehow you made him care for you through all those pitiful stories you were feeding him. And now, you are pregnant. What a shame and pity," Momma said, shaking her head.

"Ms. Belle, Alim cared for me because he seen good in me," Carlotta said, crying.

"Huh, the good in you? My instincts told me that when Joyce and Alim seemed kind of distant for a minute that you probably had something to do with it," Momma said.

"Stop treating my sister like that. You are supposed to be a Christian woman! Why are you acting like this?" Lorraine said.

"I am, but the two of you have interrupted my good day by coming here with all this nonsense. No one asked you two here; you came here on your own, so you take it just like it is. I'm not for this drama today," Momma Belle said.

"It seems like no one wants to accept the truth but me. You are either protecting your son or trying not to see all that he has done. I have accepted the fact that Alim wants Joyce, no matter how bad it hurts."

"Oh, so it hurts, and is that what this drama is all about, Joyce and I?" came a mild but masculine voice from the dining room.

"Alim, what are you doing here, baby?" Momma Belle said as Carlotta and Lorraine looked up in shock.

"I was a shadow for a moment, and I heard most of what you all were saying. What the hell, Carlotta! Why are you and Lorraine in my Momma's house?" Alim asked angrily.

"Alim. These two women surprised me by stopping by here, but I got it under control.

"I thought that I recognized your car in my Momma's driveway when I drove by, so I turned around just to make sure that it was you. I can't believe that you would come to my Momma's house with this drama, Carlotta. She does not have anything to do with this!" Alim exclaimed.

"Well, Alim, it is a shame that it had to come to this. You just wouldn't talk to me about this situation. You were sleeping with me until I told you that I was pregnant just a couple of weeks ago. Now, does anyone know about that? And now you are trying to drop me suddenly. I brought the results from the doctor, and they are on the table. I pulled them out for your momma to witness," Carlotta said with tears in her eyes.

"I can't believe this is happening to me," Alim said, shaking his head. "Carlotta aren't you the same woman that told Joy that she needed to grow up?

But look who's making a spectacle out of herself. I told you to give me some time to absorb all this stuff, and now you are here talking to my momma. And yeah, these papers may be proof that you are pregnant, but is it mine?" Alim said.

"Don't go there, Alim. You know that this baby is yours. You are so afraid of the truth; you should have stayed a shadow and never shown your face because I don't know who I am talking to right now. You have never been this way before with me, Alim. We could talk about anything, no matter what it was, and now you are trying to be in denial about this and everything else," Carlotta said, hurt and anger evident on her face.

"You know what? It's time for you ladies to go now. I have heard enough," Momma said. Lorraine went out the backdoor to the car and Carlotta scurried behind Alim, who stepped out into the living room.

"Alim, can we talk privately?" Carlotta asked.

"I have nothing else to say," Alim replied.

"Well, when can we talk?" Carlotta yelled.

"I don't know, and since you didn't give me time, I can't give you an answer now. I don't appreciate you showing up at my Momma's house; please don't do that again," Alim said.

"When I try to call you, you don't answer. I've come by your apartment on several occasions, and you weren't there, so what did you expect me to do?" Carlotta asked helplessly.

"Right now, Carlotta, I don't expect anything. Please leave my Momma's house. I will talk to you soon," Alim said.

"If you don't want to be in my life while I am carrying this baby, I'll make you be there financially," Carlotta said as she walked away. Alim just sat on Momma's sofa and shook his head in disgust as he watched Carlotta go. Alim looked over at his momma and found her head in her hands sobbing silently from hurt and shame.

Momma. Alim says.

Alim please, I don't want to hear anything. You know I treated that Woman badly when she told me what was going on and you know why because I was shocked and hurt. I didn't know how to respond but to only go into defense mode and it wasn't even about me. I thought about her, you, and Joyce immediately. The lies, deceit, and betrayal. What about the pain and more pain that is going to come out of this, how could you have done do this? You need to tell Joyce and tell her now! Alim just apologized and walked out the door.

Chapter 29

FAMILY REUNION

It had been a little while since Alim last heard from Carlotta, and he hadn't bothered to tell Joyce about the surprise meeting he and Carlotta had at his Momma's house. He wasn't ready to tell Joyce of the news concerning the baby until he was sure, but he knew that he had to tell her soon because he couldn't get a DNA test until after the baby was born; if he tried now, it would be dangerous to Carlotta's pregnancy. Right now, he was feeling distraught, though he did well to hide it from Joyce.

That day, Momma Belle, Joyce, and Alim were all running around like crazy. It was Friday, and both their families were headed their way on the planes and roads for the family reunion that weekend. Everything was bought and ready for their big day. Joyce had gotten her lovely two-bedroom house ready for her family; she didn't want them staying in a hotel.

Joyce was anxious to see her family and Alim. Caroline helped Joyce with the welcome banners for both families and the rest of the table decorations. Joyce and Alim had been spending every waking moment together, and Joyce was still attending church without Alim, but he still promised to attend soon. Momma Belle had also been getting on Alim about not attending church with Joyce.

That evening, she and Alim picked up her family from the airport. Joyce introduced Alim to the family and they greeted him warmly. The family's hearts were now rested after having met the wonderful man in Joyce's life that they had heard so much about. They drove back to Joyce's house to get settled, and Momma called amid all the excitement because she was anxious to meet Joyce's family and had prepared a meal for their arrival that evening. The reunion would take place the following day, so Joyce did not want her family out late because she knew that they were tired. After they went to Joyce's house to freshen up, they drove over to Momma Belle's house; she was overjoyed to see Joyce's family and having them in her house did Momma's heart well.

The day of the family reunion finally arrived. Alim picked everyone up from Joyce's house in his Lincoln Navigator to take them to Momma's house for the reunion, and Caroline and her family were also there. The day was just beautiful, and the flowers seemed as though they were smiling as they swayed in the sunlight. The families smiled and laughed through the oldies of rhythm and blues and gospel that Momma and Alim were playing on the stereo as they greeted each other happily. The reunion lasted until midnight, but Caroline and her family left at about ten because they had to get ready for church the next day. Joyce even talked both families into visiting church on Sunday, including Alim. Melanie and Olivia seemed to love the all the singing and the energy of the church, being that they did not attend church often. Caroline looked over and was so happy to see both families out, so she walked over and greeted everyone.

It was truly a beautiful Sunday, and Joyce was overwhelmed with happiness. After the service, Alim took everyone out to dinner, and they all treasured in every moment with each other because they would not be meeting again until the wedding day. After dinner, Alim's family left to go to their respective homes, but Joyce's family wasn't leaving until Monday morning.

Joyce was going to miss her family terribly, especially her nephews. They sat up almost all night talking until they fell asleep. They told Joyce how much they enjoyed themselves and how impressed they were with her future family's hospitality, love, and respect.

Chapter 30

WEDDING BELLS WITH A BLOW

The months flew by, and there was now just a week to go before the wedding. Joyce scrambled around doing last-minute tasks and made sure that everyone knew their positions at the wedding. The law firm had given her two weeks off for the wedding and honeymoon to Paris. Her house would be going up for rent in the next few months, and she would be living with Alim in his apartment until their house was finished, which was only a couple of months away. Life was marvelous as far as she was concerned, and nothing could get between them this time.

When Joyce entered the nail shop to talk to the manicurist about getting her bridal party manicures, she saw that Lorraine was in the shop. She knew Lorraine because they had met at church. Their eyes met as soon as Joyce walked through the door. Joyce walked over to Lorraine to speak, but Lorraine replied in a cold manner. Joyce noticed Lorraine's demeanor, but she just walked off with a smile. She figured that she really didn't want to remember her anyway. She noticed Lorraine glancing over at her from time to time while getting her nails done and waited until Lorraine was finished because they had had the same manicurist, Mikala. Joyce just sat back and fumbled through a magazine until it was her turn. Alim called while she was waiting, and she informed Alim that Lorraine was in the salon, which made Alim kind of nervous. He hoped that Lorraine wouldn't start any trouble by venting to

Joyce about the situation that had taken place at his Momma's house. He really didn't think of Lorraine as a troublemaker, but that episode at his Momma's house had convinced him otherwise.

Joyce hadn't seen Carlotta since their last meeting, nor did she care to see her or know more about her and Alim's relationship, but little did she know that Carlotta's stomach was growing every month, allegedly with Alim's baby. Caroline made sure that she was there with Joyce every step of the way during the wedding season.

As Alim rented cars for the bride, the maid of honor, and the five brides-maids, he also made sure to rent a limo for the immediate families. This autumn wedding was going to be beautiful. Joyce would be wearing a fabulous white gown, and the bridal party would be wearing royal blue chiffon dresses that came just below the knee and matching blue pumps. The groomsmen would be wearing beige suits with boutonnières the same color as the ladies' dresses. Of course, Alim would be wearing all white.

It looked like wedding was going cost a fortune, but Alim could afford it given his work as a property manager, shareholder, real estate agent, and broker, as well as the numerous investments he had made. Joyce would not want for nothing. One thing that Joyce couldn't help feeling a little apprehensive about was her wedding day, and she didn't know why.

She decided to call Caroline and talk over her feelings. She had feelings for both Alim and God, and often thought about how the two were fitting into her life. She had begun to cry off and on, and didn't know why, but she kept telling herself that this was the right thing to do, and her life was coming together beautifully in the way that it was supposed to be—so why was she filled with so much anxiety? She knew that her prayer life with God wasn't as strong as it should be, and she hadn't been reading her Bible like she should have been. Caroline assured her that all would be all right if she started trusting in God because he would guide her through all her decisions.

Joyce's family arriving a week before the wedding. She and Alim were planning to take everyone out for a big family dinner the following night. Alim's family would also be arriving, and Melanie and Olivia would be staying with Momma Belle. After both families arrived in town and got settled for the evening, Joyce and Alim took a long drive to a nearby beach to spend some quality time together before their big day. The moon was beautiful, and the night was warm and cozy. Joyce wanted to be sure of the most important step that she was making by being alone with Alim that night, and she did feel she was making the right decision.

Today was the day, and everyone was scurrying around to get ready for the wedding. All the cars were waiting at the designated houses to carry everyone to the church. It was a beautiful autumn day. The sun shone brightly, the birds sang happily, the weather was mild, and the leaves were just beautiful on the trees and ground. When everyone was at the church, the girls and Joyce got their attire together. Joyce asked to be left alone in the dressing for a minute as she wanted some time to herself to get her head together and fully grasp what a big and a phenomenal day this was. Just as Joyce sat down at her makeup table, someone came in from the other entrance. Joyce was startled to see the silhouette of the woman behind her. Then she realized who it was.

"Carlotta! What are you doing here, and how did you get in here!" Joyce asked frantically as she attempted to put her veil down on the dressing table.

"Calm down, Joyce," Carlotta said as she locked both doors with a devious smile on her face.

"What do you want, Carlotta? I didn't invite you. Did Alim invite you?" Joyce asked as she got up from her chair and threw her hands up.

"No one invited me, Joyce. I knew of the wedding day already through some of Alim's family member. I thought I would come down here and let you in on a few things. You may think it is cruel of me, but I really don't care about too much at this point, and today was just the perfect day to talk to you. You do look beautiful, hmm…" Carlotta trailed off.

Joyce's face grew solemn. She could feel that this was the moment—these were the eerie feelings that she had been having for the last couple of weeks to a month. She wanted to tell Carlotta to leave, but she also wanted to hear what she had to say. Maybe this would be the end of Carlotta in her life;

however, judging by Carlotta's belly, she knew that the news would be ugly and devastating.

"I don't want any trouble, Joyce, so you can sit back down. This is going to be short because I know both families will be coming back to check on their precious Joyce," Carlotta said as her face, her face blotchy with hurt and anger.

"You see that I am pregnant, and you should have guessed it by now that it is Alim's. Here's is the evidence. Really, this shouldn't be a shock," Carlotta said as she handed Joyce the amniocentesis results naming Alim as the father. Joyce's eyes began to well up with tears. She stayed quiet while Carlotta went on.

"You see, Joyce, Alim has been lying to you from the very beginning. I thought that he would have told you by now, but judging by the look on your face, I see that he hasn't. Alim and I are expecting a baby, as you see, and I don't know how you are going to handle this, but I don't want to share him. I will admit, a relationship is not what I was after at first, and I was willing to keep his secret until I got pregnant, but now I want the family and all; I will not have it any other way. If you don't understand it now, you will later down the line," Carlotta said. She then turned on her heel and left as abruptly as she has entered, leaving Joyce bewildered.

Joyce just sat there. She didn't watch Carlotta leave. She was so overwhelmed with hurt, shame, and betrayal that she just put her head in her hands for a second or two. The only thought she had now was leaving this church because she knew that she could not marry a liar. She felt like she really didn't know Alim, and she didn't want to marry into a lie because she knew that her marriage would be built on that if she preceded with this so-called holy matrimony. She looked for some paper and a pen in the dressing room and wrote Alim a note and left it in an envelope on the desk. She knew that someone would find it, but she didn't care because she didn't want to face anyone after what she just encountered.

As she proceeded out to rush out front door of the church, one of the ushers stopped her and asked her if she needed anything. The rest of the family didn't notice her leaving.

"Miss Lomax, can I get something for you?" the usher asked, looking confused.

"No, thank you. I left something sentimental in the limo and I want to retrieve it myself," Joyce said. The usher was convinced and didn't follow her outside. Joyce disappeared into the sunset as quickly as she could.

It was almost time for the ceremony, and the women and men got into their designated places. Alim was at his stand. Brian and Leon went to the dressing room to get Joyce. The music began to play and was time for her to walk down the aisle. Just then, Brian and Leon saw Carlotta leaving the door of the dressing room. They both knew that it seemed kind of strange for anyone to be coming from the area, but they paid it no mind and just went in to get Joyce. When they knocked on the door, no one answered. They walked in. Joyce was nowhere to be found. Brian saw the envelope addressed to Alim and didn't hesitate to open it because he suspected it that something to do with his sister missing. They read the letter nervously.

"Leon, this can't be happening to us again. We almost lost Joyce before when she was going through a traumatic time in her life, and it seems as if we are going through this again. She came all the way to Savannah, and she's been hurt in the worst way. I just hope she is strong enough this time to take this big letdown, Leon. Where is she? This is a disaster!" Brian cried out as he raised his head toward the ceiling. Leon laid his head and hands against the wall, full of sadness and anger. Brian just stood there, reading the letter again in disbelief until voice interrupted his thoughts.

"Brian, what is going on! And where is Joyce?" Deanna asked as she and Caroline came running into the dressing room to see what was taking them so long.

"Deanna, Leon, and I just walked back here to get Joyce to walk her down the aisle. She wasn't here, but this note was sitting on the table. We searched all over this place back here, and no Misty! There was a woman coming from the room as I was approaching it."

"Oh my God, what is going on?" Deanna cried out as she read the letter that Joyce left before handing it to Caroline to read. Caroline bust out in tears, and the brothers were left to console both women. Brian and Leon were trying to hold back their anger as they watched Alim approach, looking confused.

"What is going on back here, and where is my bride?" Alim asked. Leon held Brian back from striking Alim in all his rage and anger.

"Hold on! What is going on?" Alim cried.

"Here, read this Alim!" Deanna said as she handed Alim the letter.

"I see that the envelope had my name on it, but y'all found it in yourselves to read it!" Alim said angrily.

"Listen, man, this is no time for secrets. My sister is missing because of you!" Leon yelled. The noise was so loud that the minister came out from the back to see what was going on. Caroline just pulled him to the side and tried to explain the situation and told him to tell the guests that the wedding would no longer be taking place, without giving them any details. The minister obliged. Caroline's family ran to see what the problem was, but with tears in her eyes, she just told them to go home, and she would explain it later. Caroline sat in the chair in the room and just prayed and cried out to God. Everyone else joined in.

Alim walked off into the church to read the letter Joyce had left behind, with Momma Belle, Melanie, and Olivia by his side. He told them that he just wanted to be alone while he read the letter. Momma Belle just kissed Alim on his forehead with tears in her eyes before leaving his side. Melanie grabbed on to her grandmother and mother and they slowly walked out of the sanctuary, crying softly. This was a sad day in the history of Alim and Joyce's relationship. Everyone could feel the spirit of sadness and confusion in the church's atmosphere.

"I don't know where to start, but I have to say that I have always loved you from the moment that I met you. I couldn't imagine life without you. I played by all of man's rules for love and relationships, and I thought that I had passed all the tests. I gave my life to God, but still I put you first because I may have loved you more than God. I let you master me by overtaking me with your false love, fake ideas, and distorted concepts of this whole relationship. I hung onto your every word, even in doubt, but I have always given you the benefit of doubt. I thought that you loved me more than life itself, as you said to me often. We all make mistakes, and then we account for them and move on, as what I thought that we

had done from your mistake. Carlotta came to me today while I sat at the makeup table in my beautiful wedding gown. I was perfect, or so I thought, as I sat and contemplated on you and our life after we would say "I do" today, but proof of your betrayal, fear, and clear deception looked me in the face through Carlotta's eyes. I saw you through her as she told me things that I would have never imagined coming from you, and especially on this day, our wedding day. You can't imagine how I feel because I don't even know what I feel. Carlotta was direct with the blow she dealt me, but I did see her pain. I think that she wanted me to feel the same, and she accomplished it. Her belly has grown from deception and a misconceived notion of you being that upstanding type of man. I have no ill feelings toward the child that you and Carlotta conceived while you and I were together, while you were supposed to be in love with me. It hurts so bad that I have no idea how to rid this hurt. I know that it is your child because she showed me the evidence. Yes, Alim, it only took her less than five minutes to tell me the story, and she came dressed for the occasion. When we went on vacation to Hawaii and danced on that balcony, I looked up to those beautiful clouds, which looked like ribbons in the sky, and I thought that they were a sign that we would last forever. But I was fooled, and I have to say that it is partly my fault for putting all my trust in man and not God. I should have known that you were never really in love with me because you didn't tell me about this situation from the beginning. It is sickening, and it makes me even sicker to think about it. I don't want to think about it anymore. I know that you can't feel what I feel because you're the heartbreaker that can't feel when he breaks the heart; he only wants to find a way to leave the scene without picking up the broken pieces because he doesn't want it on his conscience, and he doesn't want any of the broken pieces to cut him. You're a self-centered liar, and you will not be able to feel or accept any of the pain that you have caused me. I guessed those colorful ribbons in the sky were the colors of your deception. As you have gathered, it's over.

Joyce

After Alim read the letter, he just looked up and gazed deeply at the church's stained-glass window for a second and then dropped his head into his hands. At that moment, he realized how much Joyce meant to him. Alim sat in the church pew, trying to figure out where Joyce might have gone. He didn't want to believe this was happening, and his thoughts were to go see Carlotta as soon as possible, but first he wanted to find Joyce. No one in Joyce's family wanted to talk to Alim right at that moment, so they all just went back to Joyce's house. Caroline walked over to Alim as he was still sitting in the chapel.

"Alim, everyone has left the church, and I am getting ready to go home as well. I know that Joyce's family went back to her house," Caroline said sadly as she stood before Alim.

As she turned to walk away, she heard Alim's sad and shaky voice.

"I'm so sorry," Alim said with tears in his eyes. "I am such a fool, Caroline."

"You know, Alim, I love Joyce like she was my blood sister, even though she is my sister in Christ. I will be praying for the both of you," Caroline said as she turned to walk away again. Caroline didn't know how to take anything at that point, and her being a Christian, she wanted to do the right thing by having some sympathy for Alim; however, only God could let her feel that right now because she was hurting for Joyce and couldn't stand the sight of Alim at that moment. Even so, she was more compassionate than Joyce's family would be right now—they wanted to him to feel pain, including Brian, though he was a saved man. It was truly a sad day in paradise for everyone.

Chapter 31

LOVE AND LET GO

All of the limos were still in front of the church, so Joyce had to have gotten a taxi. Alim was the last to leave the church; he went on to search Joyce. It was already confirmed that she wasn't at her house because that was where her family was staying, but they did discover some of her clothes and a few other items missing, but this time, Joyce hadn't left a note, and her car was also gone.

Brian and Leon got a phone book and called every hospital in the area. They were informed told that quite a few people were looking for a woman named Joyce Lomax because they had been asked about that name over and over. Brian and the family weren't going back to Chicago until Joyce was found, or at least until they had heard from her. Caroline was just frantic with worry and constantly prayed for Joyce's safe return home. The lawyers from Joyce's office were also concerned and offered their services if the family needed any.

Momma Belle was hurting and so angered by the monstrosity that Carlotta pulled earlier, and she never stopped feeling anger towards Alim and the betrayal that he incurred. He should have told Joyce when she told him to tell her. Alim felt like going to Joyce's house to talk to her family about the situation, but he knew deep down inside that it was too early for explanations and forgiveness because Joyce was still missing, so he just settled on going home because it was getting late and all he wanted to know that Joyce was safe. He wanted to be rescued from the deep fear he had that Joyce may have done something unthinkable. He knew that she was a strong woman, but this day was the most important and celebrated day in any woman's life, and he wasn't sure how she would be handling all this chaos. He just laid on his bed with his clothes still on just in case Joyce call him. Nevertheless, something inside told him that she would not be calling him.

"Oh my God! Joyce, are you all, right?" Caroline asked as she picked up a call from an unknown number. It was by the grace of God that she immediately knew it was Joyce. She was so happy and relieved to hear Joyce's voice on the other line.

"I'm as fine as I am going to be right now, Caroline. How did you know that it was me? Joyce asked, her voice hoarse.

"It was no one but God, Joyce, because I have been praying all day and all night, and I said to God, no matter how late it will be, *let her call*, and I knew that this unknown number was you," Caroline said happily, thanking God.

"I felt like calling you before I called my family," Joyce said, sounding tired and sad.

"Honey, we have all been so worried, and we read the letter that was left for Alim and Joyce. I am so sorry. I think I'm still crying. I haven't stopped, and I have been praying," Caroline said.

"I know you have been praying, Caroline, I just don't know what to do right now, but I had to get away to clear my head and think about things. I didn't want to talk to anyone, and I still don't really want to. I am just calling to say that I will be all right. And before you ask, I do not want to tell anyone where I'm at. I did go home to get a change of clothes, my computer, and my journals, and I headed out to the road to nowhere, and I drove and drove until my mind told me it was time to stop, and that is just what I did. I am many miles away, and I just want to clear my head for a while. Nothing right now can console me. I just need to be alone."

"Oh, Joyce, I do understand, but I wish that you would come home so we could talk together. You know that you are my sister. I love you and miss you already. I need you home now. Jesus can fix this for you if you give it to him," Caroline said softly.

"I love you, Caroline, and I will talk to you again," Joyce said as she hung up and laid back on the bed in her hotel room in Cocoa Beach, Florida. She wanted to be near the ocean. She knew that she could at least find some comfort near the water. She purchased another cell phone but blocked her number before she made any calls. She didn't want them getting into her head right now. She sat up once again to take a few deep breaths as she called her family.

"Hello?" Brian asked as he awoke from his sleep.

"Brian, it's me," Joyce said in almost a whisper.

"Joyce, baby girl. Where are you? We have been worried sick about you," Brian said, waking up the family to let them know that Joyce was on the phone.

"I am fine, Brian, and please don't be mad at me," Joyce said tearfully.

"What Misty, mad? Never that, sweetheart. You are our heart—how can we be mad at you? But we would like for you to tell us where you are and if you need us to come and get you, so we can help you through this thing, Joyce," Brian pleaded. Before Joyce could respond, Leon took the phone from Brian and tried to coerce Joyce to come home as well, telling her how much they loved her.

"I do love you both, Leon, but I need to be alone right now. This really is a hard time for me, and all I want to see is nature right now. I am sorry, but I don't want to say where I am, but I am fine. The hurt and all that comes along with that is still there. I will not lie about that, but it is something that I must deal with myself. I made a mistake, and I must account for it. You may not understand, but this is something that I must go through for being disobedient to God and not listening to him," Joyce said tearfully. Leon just handed the phone to Brian with tears in his eyes. Her words almost made Leon want to pray to God.

"Joyce, please listen to us. We all love you, no matter what. Deanna wants you to desperately come home, as do Leon and me. Please come home to us. We will not invade your space. You know that our house is big enough for all of us. You will have all the privacy you need. I just need to be there for you physically. I need to know that you are safe going through this kind of hardship, and no matter how much you think that you don't need us, you really do, honey," Brian pleaded.

"Please, listen to me, Brian. I need this time alone. What I want you to do is go home back to Chicago, and I will promise to call again. Please stop worrying so much. It will work itself out. I just need this time, and there is no need for you all to waste your time in Savannah because I will not be there anytime time soon. I need to do what I have to do. Please go back home to Chicago. I love you all," Joyce said as she hung up.

Her last phone call was to Momma Belle, and she knew that if the other calls were tough, then this one would be the toughest because this was Alim's mother. But Momma Belle had not given Joyce anything but respect. She knew that it was late, but she wanted to be done with it all finally. Her hand shook as she began to dial the number.

"Yes," a sleepy voice said over the phone.

"I didn't mean to wake you, Momma Belle," Joyce said softly.

"Oh, my Lord, baby! Where are you?" Momma Belle asked.

"I don't want to discuss that, Momma Belle. I just called to let you know that I am fine, and I apologize for what happened at the church," Joyce said as she began to cry a little.

"You have nothing, and I mean nothing to apologize for, but I did wish that you could have come to us, or at least spoken to Alim about this situation, maybe in some way, we could have worked this out and proceeded with the ceremony. Joyce, I know that that awful woman caused this mess, and we will handle that accordingly, but please come home so we can work this out, honey. I do love you as my own daughter, and you have brought so much pleasure to our lives—both me and Alim. I know that Alim can't live without you, no matter what has happened," Momma Belle said through her tears.

"Momma, I have always appreciated you and loved you as my own mother, but I must do some things on my own. I don't know what is going to happen after this phone call, but I need to be alone right now. I need everyone to stop hovering over me like a little girl. I will admit that I am hurting a lot, and as the seconds and minutes go by, the pain gets stronger. I don't know what the hours and days will bring, but I know that I must deal with this on my own. I am not trying to blot you all out of my life, but I should have seen this coming. I guess that I did but just chose to ignore it. I don't know, Momma, but I will call you sooner or later," Joyce said and then hung up.

As soon as Joyce hung up, Momma Belle called Alim to let him know that she had heard from Joyce and that she sounded as if she was okay, albeit in pain. Alim was glad to hear that Joyce had contacted someone; he understood that she would not try to contact him at all. Alim did have some ideas for finding Joyce because he had friends in high places that he knew he could call on to help him. It would only be a matter of time.

Chapter 32

TRYING TO MEND A BROKEN HEART

Joyce wanted to go as far as she could drive, and she ended up in Pensacola, Florida. She awakened to a beautiful, warm day, even though it was autumn, and decided to go to go out for lunch. She took a table in a restaurant, and after eating, she wanted to take a walk on the beach. As she walked along the beach, she thought about all that had happened over the last few hours and felt that heart was growing heavier with every passing moment.

She knelt in the sand with her palms down. She wanted to feel the grittiness of the sand; its coolness felt good to her hands. She slowly sifted the sand with her hands as she thought about how she wanted every one of her woes to just sift away in the wind like the sand. She gazed out into the ocean, was wondering if this was where she would find tranquility. She started to jot down her thoughts in her journal, describing the horrific episode that had taken place several hours ago on the most important day of her life. The tears flowed as she jotted it all down, and her thoughts raced in love and hate every time she typed Alim's name.

When Joyce finished writing, she looked up at the sky. It was a beautiful evening, and the sky had a hint of deep orange, as if it were on fire. She asked God why this had to happen to her. Why couldn't things just go the way they were planned, without any interruptions? She looked down to the ground and shook her head in disappointment.

"Madam, are you all, right?" A passerby asked as he walked along the beach with his dog.

"Yes, sir. I'm fine. Thanks for asking," Joyce said with a little smile.

"Whatever it is, madam, God will make a way for the pain to go away, if you give it to him. All be will well after a while. You'll see," the stranger said before walking away. Joyce didn't respond and just watched as the stranger walked along slowly with his dog. She felt that it was time to leave the beach and go back to her hotel room.

Joyce thought about calling Caroline again, just for some conversation. When she finally got back to her hotel room, she made some hot tea and read her Bible for a little while. She got a notion that she should pray, and she did. God spoke to her in her mind, saying how he wanted to have her all to himself for her to talk to him in prayer and to read his word so that her heart, soul, and mind could be made whole.

Joyce was steady in praying to God, trying to put the thoughts behind her. She was trying to obey the spirit of God, as she continued to talk more to God about her situation. She cried and asked him, "Why this must happen? Will I make it through this big disappointment?" Lord this is the ultimate betrayal and didn't see this coming?

Joyce prayed so hard that she became exhausted. She fell into a deep sleep, and no one would ever know where her mind took her in that dream; it was as if she were in another world. In the middle of night, she woke up and immediately started to pray because fear and shame were entering her heart once again. She knew that only God could help her now and to get those negative thoughts out of her head. She remembered what the man on the beach said to her and what Caroline always said to her—to give it all to God. If she trusted in him, then he would fix it and be her friend through trying times. Joyce knew that even though she was being stubborn about it, God was the only one that could fix this thing, not man.

She woke up in the afternoon and decided to go out to lunch instead of ordering room service, even though she was exhausted. Her next thought was to walk on the beach, this time by herself, with no journals or tablet. Joyce just walked with her long shawl wrapped around her. Dressed in a T-strapped mini dress with some slip-on sandals, she just walked and talked to God. Just as she was heading back to the hotel, she noticed a tall, brown, and handsome man looked familiar to her. As the figure walked toward her, she realizes who it was. Her hands started to tremble, and her heart was beating faster than normal. She wasn't prepared for this; it was beyond her wildest expectations. Joyce came to a complete halt as she stared speechlessly at the tall figure walking toward her. She decided to walk toward the café. The gentlemen promptly followed her inside and ordered coffee.

"Misty?" The man asked, sounding a little confused.

"Yes, Cameron? I can't believe that is you," Joyce said softly.

"It's me, Misty. I thought that I would never see you again," the gentleman replied.

"This is a surprise, and I don't know what to say," Joyce murmured.

"Wow, Misty. It has really been a long time, and you are the last person that I thought I would run into on the beach, or even in Florida," Cameron said, acting a little shy, but Joyce knew he was far from that.

"I really don't know what to say, Cameron. I am really lost for words. It has been so long since we last spoke, and things were left undone. I was a total wreck when you left Chicago, but I don't want to dwell on that now because we both have moved on. I am just in shock after seeing you again," Joyce said.

"I know, Misty. I do feel the same, but I had to leave Chicago. I was caught between life and death, and you were in the middle of it all. I just didn't know how to tell you the important decisions that I had to make without you, so I just ran away to the military and later joined the Air Force. I had to get away, or I wouldn't be standing here now explaining it all to you," Cameron said as he reached in his pocket for money to pay for their coffees. Suddenly, he grabbed Joyce and kissed her passionately.

"What did you do that for?" Joyce asked as she caught her breath.

"I just needed to do that, Misty. Dang, you are still so soft and beautiful," Cameron said as she carried both their drinks to a table that in the corner.

"I must say though, you're still a good kisser," Joyce said as she tried to hold back the lust that she was suddenly feeling for Cameron in her vulnerable state.

"So, Misty, what are you doing in Florida? And as much as I have thought about you, I never thought in my wildest dreams that I would run into you like this. What are you doing here, Misty? Your eyes are telling a story right now. Your eyes always told your heart's tales," Cameron said as he stroked Joyce's hand.

"Well, I'm here, just walking on the beach, Cameron. Just getting away from it all for a little while," Joyce said.

"Oh, I see; so, are you still staying in Chicago?" Cameron asked.

"No, I moved to Savannah, and I have been there for almost two years," Joyce said.

"Wow, that's great. I visited Savannah a little way back, and I loved it. It's a real beautiful spot," Cameron said.

"So, what's your story, Cameron? Why are you here in Florida, and Cocoa beach at that?"

"Well, Misty, I have grown fond of Florida, and this is a great vacation spot for me. I have been all over the world and seen many places and things, and sometimes you just get tired. And since I have retired and settled in North Carolina, I like to vacation in Florida and come here for business too," Cameron said.

"Hmm…so where is your wife or significant other?" Joyce asked, smirking.

"No, Misty, there is no significant other, but I do have friends. You've crossed my mind from time to time, and I must tell you that I am so deeply sorry for what happened between us. I know that I hurt you when I left Chicago, but I had to go, honey. I was getting bigger in the game, and it was getting dangerous, and you knew it. I had to clean my life up, or else I wouldn't be talking to you here right now. I know you asked me why I didn't write you or try stay in contact with you. The truth is that I just couldn't, Misty. I did love you, and I couldn't stand the fact that I couldn't be with you," Cameron explained with a look of remorse on his face.

"Cameron, you have no idea how hurt and upset I was. I knew what was going on in your life, but one thing that I couldn't understand was if you loved me—and if you really loved me, how could you leave me? You should have taken me with you. We were not supposed to be separated, and we had planned so much together, but you just got up abruptly and left it all behind. I was torn and devastated," Joyce said, tearing up a little. Her current situation hadn't gone much better.

"Misty, what's the matter, honey? Come and tell me what is going on. I could see it in your face that something was the matter when recognized you on the beach," Cameron pleaded.

"I don't know, Cameron. I jilted my fiancé," Joyce said.

"Wow, you were engaged. Why did you leave him?" Cameron asked, surprised.

"Well, the other woman showed up at the church, just before I was to walk down the aisle, all big and pregnant. And the rest is history," Joyce said as she stared out into the ocean.

"I'm sorry, Misty," Cameron said, rubbing her hand. "Can I do anything for you? You shouldn't be left alone in this situation; you should have someone helping you through this."

"You know, Cameron, I will be honest with you. It is good to see you again, and I often thought about you until I met the love of my life. I am glad that you are well, and you do look good, but I will be all right, Cameron. I just need to spend some time to myself to think about what's next for me. I just need to get it to together," Joyce said shyly.

"Okay, Misty, I hear you, but can I at least take you to dinner tonight? Just for old time's sake," Cameron insisted.

"Cameron, give me your cell number and I will let you know what time to pick me up tonight," Joyce said as she stood up to go back to her hotel room.

"I will be patiently waiting for your call, Misty, and I promise you will have a wonderful evening, just to forget the negative moments even for a few hours," Cameron said as he stood up as well.

"I will call, Cameron," Joyce said. She gave Cameron a kiss on the cheek and walked away.

Joyce went back to her hotel room to rest a little before her big night with Cameron. She was beginning to feel a little nervous because she hadn't been with Cameron since he broke her heart into a million pieces several years ago, and now it had happened again. She decided to still go out with Cameron because she had promised to, and there was nothing wrong with catching up on old times with Cameron; he was full of passion, as she remembered, and she felt it when he kissed her.

As night fell, Joyce waited for Cameron in the hotel lobby, adorned in a red sleeveless chiffon dress that she purchased from the hotel's little boutique. She looked stunning. Cameron arrived and just stared at Joyce for a minute, admiring the glow of seduction in her eyes before telling her how lovely she looked.

"Misty, I was thinking that we could go for little drive to a restaurant that I admired. It sits on the water, and it is very romantic," Cameron said.

"That's fine," Joyce replied.

It took about forty-five minutes to get to the restaurant, and along the way, Joyce admired the beautiful evening sky.

What is she thinking? Cameron wondered as he walked Joyce to the restaurant. *I know she feels like she's not ready for this. She is still thinking about Alim and still loves him.*

"Misty, what do you want to drink?" Cameron asked.

"I would drink some bubbly cider," Joyce said.

"No wine, Misty?" Cameron asked.

"No, I don't drink anymore. I must tell you that I am a Christian now. I am trying to live by God's standards and not my own," Joyce said.

"Oh wow, Misty. That's wonderful," Cameron said as he sipped his wine.

"You might be wondering why I ran to Florida with all my troubles. Well, Cameron, I wasn't listening to God; I just did what I wanted and was loving man more than God, and the devil really tricked me up. Now I am here trying to mend a broken heart, but I know God is going to get me back on track," Joyce said.

"Misty, I know that you are a strong woman. You will conquer this; I know you will," Cameron said.

"I know, but to tell you the truth, Cameron, when you left me, I was devastated. I had my brothers to console me because you were my first love, and I didn't know how I was going to get over the hurt and pain that you left me with. I put everything I had into you and our relationship, and I knew nothing else but you," Joyce said.

"Joyce—" Cameron began.

"No, Cameron, let me finish," Joyce said as she put her finger over Cameron's mouth. "I must get this out of my system, and I think that our meeting was meant for us. I want to make things right between us since we are together tonight," Joyce said. When I saw you on that beach, I got kind of nervous about seeing you again because we hadn't spoken since you left, and I didn't know how to receive you. The past came back strong, and I believe it was because there was no closure to our situation, as well as my current situation now. Cameron, I must tell you that this should be a real mess right now, but while sitting here, I just realized that God is in control of this situation. He's going to rid me of the old emotional baggage so that I can move on. You know, Cameron, I am now realizing how good God is, and that he is healing me as we speak. I am not saying that I am all there, but greater things are coming," Joyce said, sounding hopeful.

"Wow, Misty. You have really changed from that innocent little girl I once knew. Even though you were a grown woman, you were so delicate and innocent, and that is why I loved you and admired you so much, and it hurt me so badly to leave you. Misty, you meant the world to me, whether you believe it or not, but I was from the streets and I didn't know how to express my feelings, but you know that I never mistreated you. I loved you so much, and I couldn't live with my conscious knowing something happened to you because of me. Of all the women that I have met, I never met anyone like you, with all the physical and spiritual attributes that you have. You are a beautiful woman inside and out," Cameron said.

"Thank you, Cameron," Joyce said.

"Misty, know this. Alim, is it? He knows what he has lost. A woman like you can make a man timid, especially if he's not honest. You are the real deal, and when it comes to you, there should be no indecisiveness in a man. Your magnetic personality is what keeps you on our minds. Perfection is not what I am talking about, but rather your meekness and attentiveness to a man's needs. Yes, Misty, I remember, and sometimes a man can take that for granted. We are stupid when it comes to women like you. Your beauty is as much on the inside as it is on the outside," Cameron said.

"Oh, Cameron," Joyce sighed.

"Misty, I am being honest. I saw the glow as soon as I saw you on that beach, but I also saw in your eyes that something wasn't right. I am so happy and fortunate that I have come to know you once again, and I am overwhelmed to be sitting here with you tonight," Cameron said.

Joyce just stayed silent and finished her dinner with a small smile on her face. As the two headed back to the hotel, Joyce thought about when she would go back to Savannah. She drew no conclusion on the day, but she knew that it would be soon. As they read Joyce's hotel lobby, she kissed Cameron goodbye and thanked him for the evening. Cameron was leaving the next morning to head back to North Carolina, and he implored Joyce to call him if she needed anything or just wanted to talk.

Chapter 33

WHEN IT'S ALL SAID AND DONE

Joyce went back to her hotel room, thinking about what Cameron said to her as she got ready for some hot tea and some bedtime journal writing. While she settled down, she noticed that there was a note left under her door that she didn't notice before. She picked up the note and slowly opened it. She really didn't know what to expect, but it was a note from Cameron sent to her by the hotel lobby staff. She read as she smiled of Cameron thanking her for a wonderful evening and asking if she wanted some company that night. He had asked in this manner so she could think about it instead of her hesitating in the phone. Cameron was staying just a few miles away from her. Joyce called Cameron and thanked him for the invitation but declined his offer. Cameron understood because of what they talked about earlier, but he thought he would give it a try anyway. All through the night, she talked to God and asked him questions about her fate. She wanted to know about the position she would soon be in, and where she would be. She asked the Lord in her prayers for a closer walk with him, and to guide her through her struggles with this current situation. She thanked God for letting her meet with Cameron because she needed closure on that past situation. Until she saw Cameron again after many years, she didn't realize that she was still carrying around the shame and confusion of their lost relationship, even though she thought that she had put it out of her mind. She read many scriptures for comfort and some clarity until she fell asleep.

The next afternoon, she decided that since the week was almost out and the weekend was heading in, she should head home Monday morning. She knew that she was not completely over Alim, but she also knew that she had to handle seeing him again and be strong for the talk they would have to endure when she got back home. As she headed out the little café on the beach for lunch, she saw Cameron walking on the beach but dared not let him see her. Even so, Cameron noticed her and started to walk toward the direction of the café.

"Hi, Misty," Cameron said.

"Hello, Cameron." Replied Joyce.

"Misty, I took a chance on seeing you out here this afternoon and was hoping that you were here. I see that I was right, but I did come this morning, and you weren't here. You must have been tired and slept in this morning."

"Yes, Cameron. I was a little tired. I was up praying and reading my Bible half the night," Joyce said as she smiled at Cameron and sipped her coffee.

"Oh, I see. It is a wonderful thing to be a woman of God. It makes you more beautiful," Cameron said, gazing at Joyce from across the table.

"So, when are you going to give your heart to the Lord, Cameron?" Joyce asked, laying her hand over his.

"Well, Joyce, I never really gave it much thought, but God has come across my mind more than once, and I guess it was only when I was in trouble," Cameron said.

"I understand that, but you know, we have all sinned and come short of the Glory of God, but we have an advocate with the Father, and we can go to him and confess our sins, which is how Jesus is able to forgive us our sins and cleanse us from all unrighteousness," Joyce said earnestly. "So, besides coming here and listening to me tell you about Christ, what can I do for you?"

"Well, Misty, I am getting ready to head back home. My business is done here for now, so I must be on my way out. I just wanted you to know that you can call me for anything, like I said last night, even if you just need to talk. I really do hope that everything will turn out well for you; not only well, but perfect. I wish nothing but the best because you deserve every good thing that comes your way," Cameron said.

"Bless your heart, Cameron, for those kind words. I will remember your offer of friendship, and I am so happy to see you again because it cleared up so many things for the both of us. This was truly meant to be, and especially for my closure. God works in mysterious ways is all I can say, and I love God for it," Joyce said and started to tear up a little bit. She didn't wants to get mushy in Cameron's presence, but she couldn't help it. Cameron got up from his chair and came around to her side of the table to give Joyce a hug.

"I hope to hear from you, Misty, but I do have to leave now. I love you always, Misty," Cameron said as he turned to leave the café.

"So long," Joyce said as she watched Cameron leaving the café. *Why could I not have run into Cameron earlier?* she thought to herself, *Maybe I wouldn't be going through this now.*

The evening was setting in as Joyce finished up her journal writing, so she decided to take a walk on the beach. The air was brisk, and the sun was setting. The water felt wonderful to her feet as she dipped in it. She just looked up into the sky and asked God what was next in her life, because right now she didn't have a clue. She was looking forward to going home, but she didn't want to face anyone and explain her disappearance. She wanted everyone to forget what had happened and just move on with their lives, and she wanted to move on with hers, but her biggest fear was facing Alim because she still loved him.

"Lord, make a way for me to handle all the difficulties when I return home, and take away all the guilt and shame that I have. I don't want to feel like this anymore; I just want to move on with my life, but I don't want to leave Savannah. I have grown to love it," Joyce prayed to God, and just as she was going to lift her head to the sky once more, a hand touched her shoulder.

"Oh, my God! What are you doing here, Alim? How did you know where to find me?" Joyce said frantically, walking backward from Alim. She was in utter shock to see him, and she dropped her journal and tablet.

"Joy, please calm down," Alim said softly as he continued to walk toward her. Joyce started to turn to run away.

"Joy, please wait! Don't run from me, please! Please don't do that to me again. I just want to talk to you," Alim called out as he ran after her. Joyce stopped running and just began to weep profusely.

"I didn't mean to startle you. I've been mad worried and concerned since you left Savannah. I didn't know what to think anymore," Alim aid.

"First of all, I just want to know how you found me because I didn't tell anyone where I was. I can't believe this is happening," Joyce screamed.

"Joy, you have been using the credit card I gave you—that's how I found you, through a private investigator I hired to track you down. That's how desperate I was to find you. Joy, I don't know what else to say or what to do, but I can't live without you, and can we at least talk about what happened? You jilted me, and I can understand why, but you could have least talked to me before running off like that," Alim said.

"What," Joyce said, dumbfounded. "No, Alim, you jilted me by being dishonest with me and had me looking and feeling like a complete fool. You thought that you were going to get away with it, but your girlfriend busted you right on our wedding day. You know, Alim, I loved you so much, probably more than I loved myself, and now what do you expect from me? You had control over every situation, and now you come down here to control this situation, but it is not going to happen!" She slowly walked along the sand in tears and disbelief over Alim's sly tactics to get her back.

"Joy, please just hear me out," Alim said as he walked closer to Joyce. "Joy, after I read the letter you left me at the church, I was torn to pieces. I realized then that I couldn't live without you. Joy, please hear me. I can't live without you," Alim said, gazing intensely at Joyce.

"I'm done with this. I don't want to hear anything! I just want to be left alone and not be bothered! You shouldn't have come here. Why do you want to taunt me like this? I just want to be left alone," Joyce begged as tears streamed down her face.

"We can put our love back together. We have something special and good together. If only you could meet me halfway, Joy. We must make this work; we have grown so close that it can't be over. Carlotta means nothing to me, and I should have realized that a long time ago, even before you came into my life, but sorry to say I realized it when you left. I just can't live without you. We have a house being built, and we can still have that storybook wedding. You just come back with me, and we can do it all over again as soon as you want or when you want," Alim pleaded.

"Lord, why is this happening to me?" Joyce said as she looked up in the sky as a brisk wind blew through her tears. Then, she spoke softly to Alim once again.

"Alim, just go home and leave me here. I have nothing else to say. The damage has been done, and tell me, how can we go back to the way it was? How can we?" Joyce asked, tears still rolling down her cheeks. She started to walk away from Alim.

"Joy, please be still and stop walking away from me, please. You make my heart hurt when you run and walk away from me like that, as if I am a stranger that is trying to attack you. Please don't do that. Remember, I am your future husband—the man that you still love. To this day, I will still say that I am still your future husband. Yes, I made a big mistake, and maybe took you and your love for granted, but not intentionally. I just want to hold you again and tell you how much I love you," Alim begged, tears falling down his face too.

Joyce was silent for a moment, not knowing how to respond to his tears.

"Joy, I know that there is going to be a baby. We might as well get it all out now. I am being honest with you, even though I should have told you everything before. I was just being stupid and immature about the entire situation, but I know that we can get through this. You said that you are a Christian woman, so you can help us both through this situation. And as I stand here on this beach in Florida, I know that only God can help us through this situation, as long as you will allow him to. Yes, I know a little about God now because I talked to my pastor about the situation while I was searching for you, and no, he didn't tell me it was going to work out; he just told me that it was in God's hands. I love you so much. You are the only woman that I am in love with—the only woman I need. I can't go on without you, I just can't," Alim holding his hands together in front of Joyce.

"Alim, you were, or are still involved with Carlotta, while leading me to believe that I was the only love of your life. I thought and trusted that you were done with that drama, but it continued, and now look where we are. We are in a drama of epic pain, guilt, and shame. This would not have been the case if only you had told me the truth that you still cared about or loved Carlotta. If you had just said those words to me, we would not be in this predicament at all. I would have gone my separate way because I cannot compete with you loving another woman and saying that you love me as well. It even sickens me to even think about," Joyce said, kicking the sand angrily.

"I know that I messed up, Joy," Alim said as he gazed into her eyes.

"I don't know, Alim. This is just too much for me to handle right now. I thought that it was just going to be us—you, Melanie, and I, until I was able to have your baby, but now that is all shot. You robbed me of that pleasure and left me with no more hopes and dreams. It's all gone now," Joyce said.

"Don't say that, Joy. We can start over and if there is something for a man to learn from this, then I have learned it. I had never been so motivated in a relationship until I met you, and I didn't think that you were going to be this good, but you're not only good—you are that sweet fragrance that any man longs for in his life," Alim said.

"How can you be having a baby with someone else?" Joyce said to Alim as she fell on her knees on the sand. Alim rushed over to console her, but his touch just compounded her grief, and she pulled away. He finally truly understood her pain because he felt it too now. He sat in silence beside her.

"Alim, to be honest with you, I still love you, and I think that I always will, but for now, you must leave me be alone and go back to Savannah. I will be coming home on Monday. I want to close this chapter of my life, so maybe it was best that you came here because I probably would have tried to avoid you in every way when I arrived home," Joyce said as she rested in Alim's arms. It felt as good to her, as though it were the first time she was in his arms.

Joyce raised herself up from the sand and out of Alim's arms before starting to walk away from him.

"Well, Alim, I'm going to go back to my hotel room. I am sorry that this has happened to us. Trust me, I have had a lost a lot of sleep over this, so don't think that I rest well at night because I don't, but I ask God to help me along this journey because it will be a struggle. Right now, I just have to focus on God and leave this behind me. I have been so torn up inside that no one, not even you, can fix me. Only God can do that," Joyce said.

"Joy, I can't make you do anything, but can you at least think about coming back to me?" Alim asked. He stood up too and watched Joyce slowly leave him.

"I still love you too, Joy, and more than you can ever know," Alim said as he put his hand over his heart. "Please come home back to me."

"So long, Alim," Joyce said as she walked away, tears still streaming down her cheeks.

"Joy, I will always love you," Alim called as he stood and watched Joyce walk farther and farther away without turning around to look back at him.

As Joyce walked, she desperately tried to stop her tears from falling. In her mind, it was a masterpiece of betrayal.

Epilogue

Where Destiny Lies

Never considered the outcome could be wrong,
The bitter sweetness of a complex song.
A beautiful relationship of rainbow's bliss,
Ending with tears of tales in a fractured twist.
It seemed that the story only applied to her,
and today it drips those lovely words,
"I will always love you," flowing from a quaint hiss,
Playing rhapsody in her heart with closure's kiss.
Where does she find comfort?
In this masterpiece of betrayal?

An unrequited love,
A marriage unknown that leads her back to being single.
The guilt buries itself,
And the innocent hides its face.
Imagination drew her,
Desire touched her, and now,
Love seeks its rightful place.
Unbeknownst and forbidden, he cleaved to her warmth,
Destiny knew not its place,
But it mingled in the arriving storm.
God over Man now becomes the choice for love in her recovery.
Pain and love are how the story goes,
While it still appeared sultry.

In whose arms do her broken heart compel to heal
In sweet compassion?
Only God's arms she sought,
Knowing that he could save her from love's feign passion.
As sure as the sun slowly sets in the east,
The best is yet to come,
As God heals the wounds from her head to her feet.
—Sharon A. Long

Sharon Anita Long

Sharon is a born-again Christian who received Christ as her Savior in February 2012. She was born in North Carolina but raised in Philadelphia, PA. In 2009, she moved back to North Carolina, where she is still residing. She is a single woman with two grown children and three grandchildren. She attended high school and business school in Philadelphia and has always loved the art of language. Sharon always had a longing for writing and expression since a young child. She is now pursuing her dreams as a writer and has a slew of poems and short stories that will soon be published. *Masterpiece of Betrayal* is her first novel, and she hopes to write many more.

Thank you for purchasing and reading my words...
Sharon Anita Long

Insight

When writing this book in 2009, I conceived all types of scenarios in my imagination. Even though this book may seem ordinary, it is not ordinary to me. I became a born-again Christian in February 2012. I am a single woman, and I have never been married, but yes, I've had my share of unsuccessful relationships, so I became saved and celibate. Even though the Bible says that sex before marriage is a sin, how many of us women have been there and done that, and even had children out of wedlock to show for our mistakes? When I finished writing this book, which was my first, I was excited about publishing it, but I got nervous and held on to it until now. After I became a Christian, I was reluctant to change any wording in the book because I didn't want the meaning or vision to be abolished by my Christian mentality that didn't exist while the book was being written. *Masterpiece of Betrayal* is a book that stirs the emotions in women and men about God and relationships if you're trying to live a faithful Christian life. Yes, it may be the same old story, but it never ends. Choose Christ today as your Lord and Savior!

Made in the USA
Columbia, SC
23 March 2023

14183232R00135